TALES FROM ETERNITY

Tales from Eternity

*The World of Fairytales
and the Spiritual Search*

Rosemary Haughton

A CONTINUUM BOOK
THE SEABURY PRESS, NEW YORK

Copyright © 1973 by George Allen & Unwin Ltd
Printed in the United States of America

LIBRARY OF CONGRESS CATALOGING IN PUBLICATION DATA

Haughton, Rosemary.
    Tales from eternity.

    (A Continuum book)
    Bibliography: p. 188
    1. Fairy tales — Moral and religious aspects.
I. Title.
GR550.H36   398.2   73-6416
ISBN 0-8164-9161-5

To
Sister Jean-Marie,
one of the 'real princesses'

Contents

INTRODUCTION   *page* 11
1 The Youngest Son   19
2 The Wise Animals   50
3 The Real Princess   72
4 Witches, Emperors and Ogres   89
5 The Quest   115
6 Happy Ever After   151
BIBLIOGRAPHY   188

Introduction

No man is an island, but each frequently feels like one. This is the Christian faith and the human predicament. It is a psychological contradiction that Christians have had to work at from the beginning, but whereas in the past they have often erred by giving too much weight to the isolation, nowadays we tend to pretend it will go away if we say it isn't true. To recognize both is the Christian spiritual effort. We need a new start in this work, one which recognizes our oneness, but also our aloneness.

An increasing tempo of effort has marked the thinking of Christians in the last twenty years or so. They found themselves forced to cope with the problem of their faith in a culture of which their forefathers never dreamt. Christianity took its forms – various as they are – and acquired its appropriate attitudes in cultures which appeared to those living in them as eternal as God himself, though they might suffer minor political alterations, generally for the worse in the view of Christians. The cultural and political changes that separate the middle ages of faith from the eighteenth century 'enlightenment' were radical ones, yet to most Christians (to Catholics first and later to Protestants also) they presented themselves less as cultural change than as a massive defection, by puffed-up sinners in important positions, from truth and religion. Their own outlook seemed to sincere Christians in each age to be the norm and, whether they were Protestant or Catholic, they regarded themselves as living by basically the same ideas as their founders and as justified in resisting any accommodation with 'the world'.

In the end, Christians were forced to realize that not only had 'the world' changed, but that they themselves could not, if they would, remain divorced from the feeling and thinking of other people. It was not just a question of finding arguments to defend the faith which might make sense to a largely secular world. It went much deeper than that. The churches themselves discovered they were part of that world, they shared its prejudices, attitudes, hopes, fears and language. They were part of history. They always had been, of course, but at last they had to recognize this, and spell out the consequences.

The result has been an upheaval of conscience comparable to

that of the Reformation in its impact on Christian life, but faster, more complicated and far more demoralizing. Some reacted by violent rejection of even the possibility of change. They feared that to adapt at all meant to sell out to the enemy. Many of the more heroic were convinced that their religious heritage was so closely shaped by a departed world that it could not be adapted, and must be set aside in order to allow the pure Gospel to be heard in an unreligious age. Others, agonized by the corruption brought about in the whole Western world – in both Church and State – by the materialist values of an economy based on competition and exploitation, felt that in such a set-up Christianity became a mere disguise for greed and the desire to preserve wealth. The churches themselves seemed so deeply implicated in the whole criminal network as to be beyond reform. The God of the churches, therefore, could only be a fake god, who must die. The real Gospel could only be one of social revolution. *Le Roi est mort. Vive le Roi!*

The revival of Old Testament studies also helped to rediscover a unique power and energy in the Hebrew religious impulse, and this cut across the traditional Christian religious thinking which, in spite of its Hebrew roots, had been shaped by the Greek culture in which it first appeared.

The greater number of Christians, unaware of the nature of the influences to which they were subjected, and unacquainted with the detailed arguments of scholars and preachers, floundered in increasing anxiety. Among the changes which struck them was a rapidly decreasing unanimity and certainty in the voices of teachers and preachers, and changes in forms of worship. These are basic supports of Christian life, and the ordinary Christian soon felt very much like the child paddling in the shallow water near the beach, who finds the outgoing tide suddenly swirling past his ankles, and at the same time feels the sand under his toes moving with it. Rocks, previously half submerged, appear high and sharp, the beautiful floating weed lies flat and dull. The landscape of his play has disappeared, though a few pools remain between the rocks.

The new Christian landscape displays several very marked features. There is a strong emphasis on community as the essential Christian thing – we are Christ's body, members of one another: it is only by our incorporation in him and in relationship to each other that we have any being at all. This has led to the rapid growth of a renewed Christian social conscience, a deep sense of the Christian obligation to serve all the brethren. Side by side with this, but sometimes at odds with it as insufficiently realistic and effective, is the realization of the Christian's obligation to be politically aware and active, since the real remedy for oppression is not soup kitchens but revolution – non-violent perhaps, but effective. And the world which is to be served is also much more deeply appreciated. Not only do Christians try to approach and understand one another across the old lines of division, they also try to understand the faiths and philosophies of people of other religions or of no religion. They are aware of the Spirit working in all creation, and realize he is not their domestic chaplain any longer.

These things vary in the ways and proportions in which they affect different groups of Christians, and different individual Christians. But in some way they affect us all, and they have altered the 'landscape' of Christian faith deeply and lastingly, at least until the tide comes in again. A strong sense of community, of the primary importance of brotherly love and service, and emphasis on the political conscience, and on the universality of God's work, are features of our Christian life which have given it a new 'climate' and also set us to tasks and problems which will keep us busy for some time. This is what our spiritual 'home' looks like in this generation, and this is where we have to live and work, whether we like it or not, whether we want to try to alter it, or whether we approve of it and want it to become even more so.

The purpose of this book is not to analyse the changes briefly sketched here, or to suggest ways of guiding and developing them. This is not, in any case, an entirely voluntary affair. We are not helpless in the tides of history, but our task is rather to understand and use them than to try to alter them. This book is trying to do something different. It is an attempt to discover what used to be called a 'spirituality' by which the individual Christian may grow into his vocation, in a set-up which is Christian in a way which is 'new' yet in many ways primitive.

There is a particular reason for adopting the approach to the Gospel suggested here at this particular moment in time. This is the fact that our rapidly increasing (and increasingly well documented) awareness of an imminent 'ecological crisis' of global dimensions is forcing mankind to rethink its values radically. It is becoming apparent that purely economic measures to halt the rush towards irreversible disaster will not do. To implement such measures soon enough and drastically enough requires either the use of law backed by ruthless sanctions, which means a police state, or a radical change in people's expectations from life, especially in the still-prosperous West. The first alternative is intolerable to most people, and the second shows that the changes required are primarily ethical and spiritual, with the essential economic and legal changes giving effective (and, if necessary, stern) form to the altered view of life.

The kind of ethical changes involved are a shift from the encouragement of consumption to the encouragement of thrift, from emphasis on newness to emphasis on conservation, from automated to 'labour-intensive' kinds of production, from regarding the big city as the norm to seeing an updated village-type community as the basic human unit. The symbol of mankind's future would cease to be the impersonal space-ship and become the self-sufficient, self-helping, human group, interacting with the land and all that it stands for. Not man in space, but man with a spade.

Until only a few years ago, such ideas were confined to a few groups of cranky people who were considered to be pathetically out of touch with reality, which was to lie with limitless achievement in technology. Now, reality has caught up with the technological dream, and the cranks are seen to have been right in principle, even if usually wrong in detail and inefficient in practice.

In this moral revolution which is required of us, Christians have an unexpectedly fitting part to play. For once, the basic Gospel ideals are seen to be ahead of our own time, though Christians themselves are still not aware of this, for the most part. Many of us are still trying to make the Gospel fit the technological Utopia which never became reality – mercifully, since the bits of it that did get off the drawing-board produced human results very far from Utopian.

How, then, do we answer the Christian vocation now? How do we take up the cross of this generation as our own?

In trying to discover an answer to such questions it seems necessary to find a way of thinking about the Christian's personal understanding which is relevant to us as we face a crisis of un-

imaginable proportions, but which links us to our forefathers and
should be equally important to our children. There is in fact a
way of doing this, and it has been set forth, generation after
generation, in the folk tales and myths. Because we are so cerebral
in our religious attitudes (or if we are not, feel we must leave the
thinking to those who are) we do not easily absorb their wisdom
as we breathe, as people once did, even if they ignored it often
enough. We need to have it unpacked for us, deliberately and
explicitly.

Fairy stories are never deliberately symbolic, yet they embody
mankind's shrewdest and most realistic insights into human nature.
We can use them to orientate ourselves in the present, and discover which way to go. They can help us to do this because they
also link us to our Christian past, link the Christian past to its
pagan prehistory, and link it also to its equally 'pagan' sub-
cultures. They throw a bridge from us to our contemporaries who
are not Christians and to our successors in the faith and in the
world. With the help of the typical figures which embody its
perennial philosophy we may rediscover the gospel values which
have become obscured and uncertain under the influence of
recent cultural changes. We may set about developing a Christian
life which, faced with unique challenges, is human, contemporary, uncompromising and hopeful. Fairy-tales can open our
minds to the human, and make us able to hear more sharply the
demand for the transformation of the human into its own completeness in Christ.

Since a great deal has been written, from various points of
view, about the meaning of fairy-tales it may be as well to make
clear how they are understood, and used, here.

One use of fairy-tales which has become familiar is as a key to
the complex workings of the human psyche. Jung's name has been
especially linked with this study of the myth structure of fairy-
tales, and its application to clinical psychology.

Others have drawn on the same kind of material in the study of
primitive religions and cultures as well as to throw light on the
psychological and cultural hang-ups of our own society. In such
studies the fairy-tales are treated as a source of myth material:
that is, the characters are seen as actors in a kind of sacred drama
which is an exposition either of the nature of cosmic events or of
the interior events of the human soul. In the 'pure' myth this is

perfectly clear, for the characters, whether divine or human, have no 'character' or personality. They simply have the characteristics that are needed to distinguish their role—they are young and beautiful, or ugly and cunning, or immensely strong, or old and wise, and so on. But in the real fairy-tale or folk tale the myth-drama is acted out by highly individual characters who vary and grow and have extra adventures according to the pleasure of the story-teller. The story-teller, however, is not simply adding arbitrary detail to an original 'pure' account. I don't think anyone knows exactly how myths began to be recounted. An explicitly religious motive in telling the story may perhaps tend to produce a seriousness that does not encourage luxuriant detail, but it seems possible that what I call 'pure' myth is simply the narrative account of what is properly and fully expressed in ritual. The ritual origin of myth is a theory supported by a number of scholars and if it is true then the puppet-like nature of many myth characters in the narrative accounts is not surprising. The 'reality' was to be found in the worshippers themselves, who took part in the ritual and were changed by it.

When a tale is told just as a tale, however, what might be called the 'verification' of the myth depends on the skill of the story-teller. Myths 'work' at an unconscious level, and there is no need at all for the hearer to understand the inner meaning of its symbols. In fact, an intellectual grasp of such exceedingly complex and ambivalent signs is often the reverse of helpful, spiritually. What the story-teller does is to tell as good a story as possible, and so the characters take on individuality, and their individuality leads to new action, and the bare branch of the myth-plot shoots and blossoms. The myth is not overlaid, it takes new form, changing and elaborating out of its inward vitality, and it is a story about people—human people. In the myths, when the characters are not themselves divine they are still the playthings of the gods, or of the destiny in which the gods also are involved. The people in fairy-tales are often pushed around by destiny, but they react to events as human beings, not as actors of preordained roles.

One result of this shift of the myth from the forefront of attention to somewhere out of sight and almost out of mind is a change in our own attitude to the curious and unnatural be-haviour of the physical world in fairy-tales. In the myth this is manipulated by gods, who change form, or become invisible, or shoot around the country in seconds, or wipe out people they don't like, but in the tales the innate power of the gods become something else. It becomes magic.

Magic is what distinguishes fairy-tales as such from other folk tales, which have similar themes but do not rely on magic to work out the plot. Overlapping is so prevalent that there is no real borderline, for the cleverness and ingenuity which often take the place of magic power in a folk tale are frequently so arbitrary and unusual as to count almost as magical; fairy-tale and folk tale are siblings, but myth is their parent.

Magic is different from the power of the gods as displayed in myths because it does not usually *belong* to the person who uses it. He may think it does, having gone to great lengths to get it, and this is often his downfall, but it is not in fact his own, he only has the ability to use it. And this is where the fairy-tales appear as something distinct from the myth, though there is no clear borderline here either. The Icelandic tales, for instance, have elements of both, thoroughly mixed, but the distinction is still valid and applicable. For fairy-tales are about people dealing with powers and destinies which they have not designed and cannot control, yet which are theirs, and in which they have something to do. And as they work out their particular destiny, reacting to one another and to events, they can be seen to operate according to a human ethic. And this ethic is very close to – I would go so far as to say identical with – the ethic of the Gospel. Although the myth-patterns underlie the tales, the myths cannot show us this ethic at work, for only the interplay of real human beings can do this, such as we have in the tales.

Fairy-tales work at two levels, which fade into each other. The people in them work out their salvation according to an ethic which becomes clear through the tales, but of which the characters themselves are only minimally aware. *We* become aware of it by the way things turn out for them, and, as we shall see, it is an eccentric, not to say disruptive, ethic when compared to those by which we normally operate. But as the characters work their way out of predicaments, or into worse ones, we may, if we are aware, perceive that they are *also* myth figures, and operate in a psychic drama which is our own. This, as I suggested, is not enough in itself to offer us much help except in the case of people whose spiritual state is so disordered as to require explicit and time-consuming analysis. Myth works below the conscious level most of the time, when it is working properly. But the combination of the two, of people who are both myth-characters and *also* people in their own right with many-sided personalities and wills of their own, really does allow us to make contact with what might be called 'folk sense'. By this I mean that sense of what matters, of what endures, and of joy at the heart of things, which somehow manages to survive the conditioning of civilization. How this works will become clear from the detailed examples I have chosen.

This is not a study of fairy-tales. They are an entrancing and extremely important subject, and much more could be drawn from even the handful of tales mentioned here. Many types and symbols are left out, or barely mentioned, because it would be easy to write a book ten times as long and still only touch the surface. What I have tried to do here is simply to reopen the fairy-tale world, not for its nostalgic charm but because it is our own world, seen in a strange but essential way. By rediscovering it we may have our eyes opened in order to realize where we are, historically and spiritually. Our sight, as Christians, needs to be cleared of all kinds of moral and spiritual dust. There is magic in the tales which can help to do this for us.

Chapter I

The Youngest Son

Feeling foolish is one of the most usual types of Christian experience in our time.

Once upon a time Christianity provided the official system of thought, life and law. In theory at least, it wasn't foolish to be Christian, though people who took their Christianity too seriously, such as the Quakers, were liable to be laughed at very vigorously. Officially, it was people whose ideas cut across the accepted Christian ones who looked silly, like Galileo recanting his ridiculous notions, or the heretics who were paraded in deliberately mirth-provoking clothes before execution. The seriously acceptable ideas and standards were the ones traditionally held by Christians, whether they were to do with religious doctrine, politics, or natural science. Everyone knew that.

But ever since the late seventeenth century this comfortable state of affairs has been changing. In those days only a minority of enlightened philosophers looked down on the primitive darkness of Christianity. But before the end of the eighteenth century established Christian churches had taken even this minority scorn to heart sufficiently to rid itself of what were to the enlightened its most obnoxious features. 'Enthusiasm', to polite Christians and their free-thinking friends, was not a complimentary term. It meant the vulgar religious emotionalism which must not be allowed to spoil the urbane ethical and intellectual system which both Catholics and Protestants had devised (in different versions) to supply their religious needs. The ones who looked foolish were eccentric individuals like the Curé d'Ars, who fasted rigorously, denounced dancing and attracted ever-increasing crowds to his confessional, and groups like the first Methodists and later the Salvation Army, who went in for emotional conversions, and appealed to the new working class who were not respectable in any case.

Even by the beginning of Victoria's reign it was becoming

fashionable in artistic and literary circles to be an atheist, or at least to subscribe to a strictly non-miraculous version of Christianity, and though the nineteenth century, in Europe and America, was a seriously and confidently pious period, there was also a steady increase in the number of people of all classes who seized on Darwinism and other advances of 'science' to prove the emptiness of the Christian claims. The ethical double-think of many well-to-do Christians made it even easier to reject what Shaw's Mr Dolittle called 'middle-class morality', which meant the version of Christian ethics which the respectable and prosperous had tailored to fit their needs and prejudices.

Altogether, by the time the 'Great War' had further weakened religious attitudes by making patriotism look sick, the reaction from nineteenth-century Christian prudery, snobbery and anti-intellectualism had given a considerable push to 'free thought'. By the thirties it was definitely unfashionable to be a Christian, though it was permissible to go to church at Christmas and to have a belief in some kind of non-interfering God. But the rejection of Christianity was no longer an upper-class or intellectual hobby—it was becoming common to feel that education naturally freed people from beliefs that were identified with the credulity of the untutored peasant. Electricity, Freud, radio, air travel, advances in medicine and in 'science' generally, seemed increasingly incompatible with a world view that involved, in the eyes of most 'educated' (or half-educated) people, an anthropomorphic God-over-the-clouds, pie-in-the-sky, and a gentle-Jesus-meek-and-mild who could never have coped with the modern world.

Gentle Jesus, in fact, looked increasingly and embarrassingly foolish, and anyone who took him seriously was on the losing side, and on the defensive. Even the famous British predilection for the under-dog could not save him. One could champion the oppressed, but those who held to a faith so clearly discredited were not so much pitiable as ridiculous. Freudian phrases provided, and still provide, ways of explaining religious feelings and beliefs in terms both satisfying to the unbeliever and discreditable to the believer, who was shown to be mentally sick in a rather degrading way.

Since then, the position has changed quite considerably. The quick and easy debunking of Christianity on scientific grounds has become less effective, at least among the better read. Psychologists have given serious attention to the religious side of man's nature. Religion is back, but it isn't Christian in any sense which most people accept. Religion is even fashionable, provided it isn't Christian. Mysticism is taken seriously, but not 'doctrine'. From being too religious, Christians are now often regarded as insufficiently, or rather naively, religious. They lack the aura of Hindu or Buddhist mysticism. And in the field of social concern Christians have to run hard to keep up; in what they once regarded as their particular territory they are treated as helpful but not really necessary. If we add to this picture the frequent and well-reported '*gaffes*' of high-up ecclesiastics, we have indeed 'the portrait of a blinking idiot'. To be persecuted is hard, but worthy of respect. To be laughed at, pitied, or politely despised, is much harder to bear without losing one's temper, one's self-respect or one's faith.

We naturally consider rather wistfully the certainties and the acknowledged heroism of our forefathers. How can we preach the Gospel, even to our own children, even convincingly to ourselves, when not only the ignorant and prejudiced but people whose judgement and moral quality we have good reason to respect regard us as irrelevant, ignorant and probably a bit warped?

This estimate is precisely the judgement of all sensible people on the 'youngest son' of the fairy-tales. In this fairy-tale category come also some who are not actually youngest, but are 'only' children whose parents are poor, for the position of 'youngest' is least important, and least is expected of the one occupying it, so that this is the psychological equivalent of a lowly social position. Whether he is the youngest of three or of seven, whether his father be a king or a woodcutter, this is the useless one, of whom no one expects much. He is often compared to his discredit with his intelligent, courageous older brothers.

This is so well known that some modern writers, using the fairy-tale form out of a desire to entertain children, keep the traditional formula without ever noticing that it cuts across all the taken-for-granted values of our culture. Victorian writers used the form to draw a Christian moral about the final triumph of virtue over sheer strength and cunning, in order to inculcate virtues of humility, patience and submission. For them it was the *good* 'youngest son' who came out on top. But the real fairy-tale is not very much concerned with this kind of moral judgement. Sometimes the 'youngest son' is not particularly pleasant; he may be cunning rather than virtuous, and lucky rather than good.

In the Armenian story of Zoulvisia, the seventh son overcomes and marries the *femme fatale* who has destroyed his elder brothers, and afterwards rescues her from deadly peril; but he escapes his brothers' fate by luck and bravado, not by courage or cleverness, and after his marriage he loses his wife because he disregards good advice and is unobservant and credulous. He is enabled to find her and help her because other people have more sense than he has and come to his aid, though why they should do so remains quite obscure. In the Serbian tale of the Prince and the Dragon the youngest of the three princes finally overcomes the dragon, and he is a brave and clever young man, but it is his shrewdness and common sense which distinguish him from his equally courageous brothers and give him the victory: when a hare dashes across his path he does not follow it into the fatal hill where it will turn to a dragon. He then persuades a prisoner of the dragon to discover his secret power by flattery, and uses the knowledge to overcome him.

Another Serbian story is about the Nine Peahens and the Golden Apple, and again the youngest of the emperor's sons discovers who is robbing his father's golden apple tree. His elder brothers try to keep awake all night and fail. The youngest, who has more sense, lies down under the tree and goes to sleep at once, and therefore wakes easily when nine peahens come to pick the fruit. The peahens are, of course, enchanted princesses, and he falls in love with one of them (the youngest, naturally), whom he persuades to leave him two apples. His brothers, jealous of his success, get an old witch to spy on him, and she succeeds in cutting off a lock of the princess's hair, at which all nine vanish. When, after much searching, the prince discovers the princess, and marries her, he ruins everything through a combination of rampant curiosity and misplaced tender-heartedness. He gives water to a thirsty dragon imprisoned in a tub in a forbidden cellar, and the refreshed dragon bursts out and carries off the princess. Yet when he sets out to find his lost wife it is this same tender-heartedness that saves him. He helps three animals in distress and is rewarded by their magic help later, when he has to accomplish difficult tasks in order to regain his wife.

This story makes particularly clear the two quite non-heroic qualities which so often characterize the 'youngest son', common

22

sense and common kindness. And with them often enough goes a certain simple-mindedness. A German tale makes this point: the youngest son of a peasant woman is laughed at by the local girls when he asks them to spin some flax for him. His elder brothers have already chosen competent future wives, but he can find none, until he is befriended by a frog. He does not even believe in the frog's offer of help, and is not at all enthusiastic about her later offer of marriage. But she is changed to a beautiful girl and all ends happily, not through any cleverness or moral worth on the part of the fortunate young man, but simply because he is the youngest.

The curious universality of fairy-tale themes has been documented and commented upon by psychologists and students of religion. The fact that in every country and time, in 'folk tales' whose authors are forgotten, in stories as recent as the eighteenth century and in a few later ones the same themes recur, makes it impossible to dismiss them as merely the product of a particular set of moral attitudes. They do not express what any particular society considers should occur, or even what does occur in normal practice. They are about much more basic facts of human nature. They are telling us what is the case about man's spiritual development, and what continues to be the case no matter how strenuously society tries to modify or suppress it.

The reactions of the king, the court, the village and the elder brothers to the vagaries of the youngest are the normal reactions of what St John calls 'the world'. This is the human world, made by man for his survival, and suspicious of anything that seems likely to undermine his precariously achieved social security. Customs and laws and mental attitudes are all part of the system. The assumption in many societies that personal effort is meritorious and deserves success is one example of an attitude of mind which is extremely important for the survival of certain kinds of society. In others, respect and obedience to the elders or to some other aristocracy are considered meritorious because this is necessary for the preservation of that kind of social structure. The rights of heredity, of personal possession, of feudal-type fealty, are among the variety of principles upon which the world depends for its strength and continuation. But they will not make men human, say the fairy-tales: there is a principle more powerful than any of these, and nothing you can do will alter it, because this is the fundamental law of man's spiritual nature. The youngest son, the

23

fool, the dreamer, the coward, the unmeritorious, socially and psychologically underprivileged—he is the one who inherits the earth.

This is the subversive message of salvation. This is the reversal of worldly values, persistently expressed through the ages in tales that could not be suppressed. They looked so harmless, they were for telling round the fire or on the ale-house bench, to children and the old and the non-influential generally. Meanwhile, power politics, kinship patterns with their laws of inheritance of possession and prestige, and the elaborate tabu systems that preserve privilege in every society, continued. And it is these that the Gospel message attacks, indirectly but devastatingly. The New Testament takes up the principles which the fairy-tales embody, but it expresses them in forceful and unforgettable sayings, and takes them to their inescapable conclusion:

Blessed are the meek, for they shall inherit the earth.

I thank thee, Father, that thou has hidden these things from the wise and understanding and revealed them to babes.

Blessed are you when men revile you and persecute you and utter all kinds of evil against you falsely on my account. Rejoice and be glad, for your reward is great in heaven.

Unless you turn and become like children, you will never enter the kingdom of heaven.

There is the unpractical and dreamy Mary, who sat at the Lord's feet and listened to his teaching as a disciple, thus flouting custom which refused instruction to women, and annoying her sister who was working hard to entertain their distinguished guest. Yet he said: 'Mary has chosen the good portion.'

Many times the Lord praises people whom most of us would regard as rogues or nuisances—the man who continues to nag at his friend to get up out of his warm bed and lend him a loaf; the widow whose persistent complaints wear down the resistance of the judge regardless of the justice of her cause; the rascally steward who, threatened with dismissal, makes sure of help afterwards by letting his master's debtors pay less than their full debt. Over and over again the people whom society despises, the weak, the dishonest, the publicans and prostitutes, the people in the lowest seats, the beggars and vagabonds from the 'highways and hedges', are preferred to the virtuous and wise.

St Paul sums it up unambiguously in his letter to the Christians of Corinth. They were a scruffy and quarrelsome lot who were inclined to pride themselves on their new distinction as enlightened believers, on the lines of the gnostic sects whose emphasis was on the saving power of secret wisdom. Paul would not allow them this luxury:

'Has not God made foolish the wisdom of the world? For since, in the wisdom of God, the world did not know God through wisdom, it pleased God through the folly of what we preach to save those who believe. For Jews demand signs and Greeks seek wisdom, but we preach Christ crucified, a stumbling block to Jews and folly to the Gentiles but to those who are called, both Jews and Greeks, Christ the power of God and the wisdom of God. For the foolishness of God is wiser than men, and the weakness of God is stronger than men. . . . Let no one deceive himself. If any one among you thinks that he is wise in this age, let him become a fool that he may become wise. For the wisdom of this world is folly with God.'

The Christian sense of values expressed here could hardly be clearer, or more totally opposed to the normal values of civilized society. And the way the Gospel agrees with the curious anti-social morality of the folk and fairy-tales is equally striking. In fact if we were not so accustomed to this kind of amoral conclusion in fairy-tales we might even be rather shocked by it. And the oddity is not due to the fact that any of the tales grew out of cultures totally different from our own, with different values and priorities. For no culture at any time has set a premium on laziness, incompetence and deceit, or encouraged people to rely on good luck or the timely intervention of magic for the accomplishment of important tasks. These tales are not moral tales, and they cut across the conscious values of society, laughing at them, or setting them gently aside. They are not even revolutionary tales, intended to promote the cause of the under-dog, for in many cases the oppressed who try to gain power or revenge are ruthlessly punished for their failure, as in the stories of the jealous but ugly daughter of a second wife, who tries to take the place of the chosen maiden, and comes to a sticky end in consequence.

The stories do not always assume, either, that the foolish or despised one has unnoticed but attractive qualities. The 'Brave Little Tailor' of the well-loved tale gains victory, prestige and a royal bride by being both astute and boastful, and exploiting other people's credulity to the limit. Jenik, the 'hero' of a cynical little Slav tale, never does anything at home except sit at the stove and dirty himself with the ashes, and his rich father is glad to get rid of him. His only good quality is the easy-going kindness which moves him to ask (at no cost to himself) for the life of three animals about to be killed. The grateful beasts obtain for him a magic which brings him fabulous wealth and finally a royal wife. But Jenik is a boring young man with no ideas and no ambition, and his wife gets tired of him and removes herself and her palace by magic, upon which everyone laughs at Jenik. By pure luck he finds his wife and her hidden palace, but far from making attempts at reconciliation he wishes both at the bottom of the sea. Having thus disposed of the problem of matrimony he returns home, no wiser or more energetic than before. Perhaps he doesn't sit in the ashes, but his good fortune has not improved him in any more important way, nor has it spoiled him. He is just the same— foolish, lazy, boring and self-indulgent. And one of Grimm's stories presents another of the tailor type, the third of three tailors, who is an improvement of Jenik only in being quick-witted. He gets his reluctant wife by cleverness rather than magic. Improbably, he and his bride remain happy and united.

The 'Little Tailor', Jenik and their like are unexpectedly recognizable to a post-war world which was assailed, in the fifties, by a collection of writers referred to (sometimes unfairly) as the 'Angry Young Men'. There are strong similarities, for instance, between Jenik and the most famous of all the gallery of 'anti-heroes', Amis's 'Lucky Jim'. Jim Dixon has ambition, which Jenik hasn't, but the things he gets come to him by undeserved good luck plus a quite amoral use of his considerable brains to exploit people's psychological weaknesses, in the manner of the 'Brave Little Tailor' and other humble but astute go-getters. Like Jenik, he loses them all, yet ends up quite contented, at least a little bit further up the social ladder and not at all ashamed of himself. He is not the type of youngest son to be sent on a mission, but he underlines one important aspect of that role, for the interesting thing about this, from the fairy-tale angle, is not the intentions of the various authors who created 'anti-heroes' during the fifties and early sixties, but the public response to them. The books varied enormously in quality, but the appeal of feckless, amoral, selfish heroes sent sales of even mediocre books into hundreds of thousands. Why did ordinary people (most of them presumably not altogether lacking in affection or some respect for the virtues) embrace this bunch of singularly un-attractive young men with such enthusiasm? Why did many of us feel a sneaking sympathy for the 'honest dishonesty' of an avowedly self-centred, ruthless go-getter like John Braine's Joe Lampton, setting aside every 'better feeling' in his scramble for social success?

There are many kinds of motive and emotional influence at work in a widespread reaction of this kind, but the fairy-tale character of the youngest son, in one of its forms, does give shape to some of them. For the aspect typified and exaggerated by Jenik and his more cunning brothers is the irrelevance of generally accepted moral standards in the distribution of luck and success of the fairy-tale kind. (What that success means in fairy-tales remains to be studied in another context.) Generally, youngest sons are despised unjustly, for they have qualities others do not appreciate, but the comic and satyrical tales of the triumphs of the wholly selfish or lazy underline the idea that the moral judgements of society are not necessarily the relevant ones. Life has its own rules. And the 'anti-heroes' came to life at a time when the virtues proper to youngest sons of the more heroic type had been de-valued, *because they had become attached to a 'class'*, and that 'class' had demonstrably made a huge mess of half the world. Gentleness, sensitivity, compassion, truthfulness—these are often the virtues of the despised youngest son of many tales, and with them he overturns an order based on power, birth and money. But what if the situation is turned upside down? What if a generation emerges, newly educated by the State, to find that these virtues are being deployed by their 'natural' owners, the upper class, to keep the rest down? What if sensibility and altruism and integrity have been used as a last-ditch defence against the common herd—a defence maddeningly impossible to penetrate?

This is what happened after the last war. The virtues of the

27

'good' youngest son had actually been appropriated by his elder brothers, to prove their fitness to remain on top. A whole mystique of 'officer-class' war virtues (courage with sensibility, patience with inflexible honesty, etc.) had been developed in war novels and films to support it. The new, working-class, educated young with no war record were sick of it all. So a new kind of youngest son was created, or rather a very old kind acquired a new relevance. Cocky, irreverent, ignorant by 'cultured' standards but astute and totally self-absorbed, he stepped out of the fairy-tales and into the novels and films. But his significance there remained, in one aspect at least, the fairy-tale one. He was the assertion of human nature's refusal to be completely organized according to any human system, however lofty its ideals appear to be—to itself. The elder brothers, however high-minded, do not rule in men's hearts. Defiantly, the worthless, nose-thumbing anti-hero will demolish their claims to be the only reality. One of the curious aspects of the situation was the way the authors of the books were so often of the same type. Colin Wilson, whose book *The Outsider* caused a furore among the critics and brought him quick fame for its Nietzschean exaltation of the new, self-valuing supermen, was a 'Little Tailor' type of youngest son to perfection, gaining wealth and position by a mixture of luck, rudeness and enormous, calculating conceit.

The emergence of a type of hero so entirely without virtues or even charm as to deserve the prefix of 'anti', yet by his very perverseness standing as a symbol of man's refusal to be bamboozled by the Establishment's moral claims, is only one of the varied manifestations of the youngest son. This cultural oddity was the result of the particular psychological circumstances of a disillusioned generation, while at other times the virtues they rejected as phoney – the ready compassion, the selfless friendship, the single-minded dedication of the romantic hero – were equally valid as a protest against an Establishment openly keeping itself going by graft and treachery. This helps to account for the vast range of characteristics displayed by youngest sons, who yet have the same basic role. But it is worth noting that the 'anti-hero', though a fairy-tale type, was the creation of novelists who did not enter into the fairy-tale ethic. They displayed it unknowingly, but the conclusions they drew were generally not those of the fairy-tales. The cynical apathy or self-seeking of the anti-hero was often a protest without hope, a humorous comment without ethical weight. And it is interesting that two of the most famous creators of anti-heroes, John Braine and Kingsley Amis, have since moved steadily to the right, disowning tacitly the fairy-tale significance of their protest, and making an Establishment virtue of the right to do well (modestly) at other people's expense if necessary. The creators of these subversive youngest sons of the Jenik and 'Little Tailor' type, have, as it were, institutionalized the morals of their own 'anti-heroes', and by so doing have become elder brothers of a more traditional type. The real fairy-tale type of anti-hero still survives, however, in more authentic forms, such as the pushed around, coat-turning, but recognizably *good* 'youngest son' of the film *Little Big Man*.

That is one type, and I have dwelt on it because it is one especially familiar to us, but it exemplifies only one (though important) aspect of the role. We must put the anti-hero in his place among all the others. For there is clearly a big range of qualities and behaviour among youngest sons. Some are courageous, some cowardly; some are quick-witted, some stupid; some are cheerful and sensible, others are dreamy, credulous and soft-hearted. What they have in common is the fact that, whether or not they actually are foolish, they are expected to be. They are despised and put last, they lack, or are supposed to lack, the heroic qualities that are needed for accomplishing difficult tasks. They are left behind when others go adventuring, they are even persecuted if they show signs of succeeding, because in a sense they have no right to succeed.

One story is especially 'typical' and helps to sum up the theme. Grimm's tale of the Golden Mermaid begins with the usual three sons, whose royal father is being robbed each year of the golden apples on a magic tree. The two elder sons are sent to look for the thief, the youngest is forbidden to go because 'he had always been looked upon as the stupid one of the family'. When his persistent pleading finally wins consent to his departure, he is given 'the most wretched horse in the stables' because he is too foolish to ask for a better one and leaves 'amid the jeers and laughter of the whole court and town'.

When he meets a hungry-looking wolf, instead of trying to kill it he offers his horse to the animal in the usual soft-hearted way of younger sons. The wolf, in gratitude, carries him on his back and

29

advises him on his quest. The prince twice bungles the difficult tasks set him by various tyrannical emperors, in spite of good advice and magical help from the wolf, but the wolf continues to help him and he finally wins a beautiful mermaid. When, after many adventures, he sets out for home with his mermaid his jealous elder brothers ambush him and kill him. He is later restored to life by the wolf's magic and the faithfulness of the mermaid and returns to his father, who welcomes and makes much of him, repenting of his misjudgement. The elder brothers are banished. Once more, the foolish, despised and incompetent are blessed and the skilled and far-sighted are 'put down from their seats'. Here, the 'incompetent' aspect of the youngest son is fitted into the full context of his role as hero.

In considering the case of the youngest son – the fool of the family – the verdict of the fairy-tales goes against most of the goals and virtues which our society admires, and the gospels, on appeal, confirm the judgement. This coincidence of judgement against the wisdom and morality of the world can be upsetting to Christians who find themselves reasonably adjusted to society and have managed to accommodate their faith to the demands of a world which does not make this too difficult.

It is equally disturbing to the type of modern Christian who has learned to identify the increasing technical mastery of nature with God's command to subdue the earth and to the one whose respect for the great traditions of Eastern mysticism leads him to hope for self-mastery, and an ultimate insight into reality, by this road. Secular Christianity and the various Christian adaptations of Eastern religious insights both come up against the Gospel-and-fairy-tale send-up of all success values, even the rarer and more admirable successes in self-command, wisdom and inner knowledge. Yet these ways have severally been acclaimed as the way ahead for modern Christianity, and it is perfectly true that each – the way of active service and technical mastery, and the way of mysticism – has come in to redress a lost balance. For generations Christians had regarded science and any kind of political and social change with suspicion amounting to phobia, so that the enthusiasm for progressive movements, the involvement in schemes for relief and reform at all levels, and the attempt to recognize God's hand in the movements of scientific and technological expansion, were a necessary amendment of life. Likewise, the rediscovered wisdom of the inner world, as the Eastern religions cultivated it, was needed to bring Christians back by a detour to their own heritage of mysticism, neglected and despised for a time because Christians were so busy trying to be better humanists than the humanists.

Yet both, when we begin to assume that here lies the answer, come under the condemnation of the Gospel. 'The wisdom of this world' is just as worldly when it is esoteric and mystical as when it is scientific and practical, for its worldliness does not consist in its concern with material achievement but in its centring on the power of human effort and know-how, of whatever kind, to provide the answer to life and the way of salvation. It is this arrogance which we have to repent, as the facts of the earth's condition now show us.

This is why the undermining of Christian self-confidence described earlier is not a disaster. It is God's greatest gift to his people. There has always been an emphasis on individual humility among Christians, but this personal sense of dislocation and helplessness, cultivated quite consciously by the set-up of traditional religious life and of some of the smaller sects, was usually lived within a wider Christian world which was certain of its possession of truth and confident in its ability to guide the destinies of men. The Church, of whatever kind, was right and correct. Now it is the Church that gropes and hesitates, and struggles to re-define, and to hold on to truth without distorting it.

It is perhaps because the Christian set-up as a whole has lost its self-confidence (though sometimes it will not admit the loss) that humility is not a popular virtue among Christians at the moment. Quite apart from the fact that it has often been distorted and misunderstood (the squirming ghost of Uriah Heep˙ still haunts the Christian consciousness) humility seems too much like surrender when there is no secure framework of living and thinking within which the individual can safely acknowledge his own inadequacies.

The high diver leaves the safety of the diving board because he can see the deep water below and knows its buoyancy will co-operate with his skill. The actress about to stage a faint is sure that someone will catch her on cue. To take a lower place without assurance that one's descent makes sense in terms of the set-up in which one operates is not humility but muddle-headedness. Queen Victoria, secure in her royalty, never looked behind her before she sat down. She never doubted someone would put a chair for her and did not even think about it. The Empress Eugenie, beautiful parvenue with no such heritage of royal privilege, took a quick but careful look. She could not risk ending up on the floor.

Humility implies confidence, not in oneself but in the continuity and reality of the human spiritual principles. If the religious systems once visibly supported the individual, and do so no longer, how is it possible to achieve the confident lowliness of the youngest son?

The fairy-tales offer a very clear and sensitive definition of the Christian virtue of humility. The youngest son does not seek humiliation or consciously lower himself, he simply *is* lowly, yet he sets out on his quest confidently. He does not know how things will turn out, nor has he necessarily the skills needed to cope with the adventures and tasks which he actually foresees. He relies on advice of the right kind, but principally he just goes on, from one thing to the next, until the quest is accomplished. There is a sense of inevitability; this is how things are, this is what I have to do; the outcome is not in my control but I must go on.

The youngest son makes mistakes. He is given instructions and forgets them, or is distracted by beautiful fairies or more attractive adventures, or sometimes he is simply clumsy and inefficient. So he fails in some part of his task and it has to be done again, usually with added tasks and extra dangers in consequence. But he does not give up. The elder sons, who set out on the quest because they are sure they have the knowledge and skill and prestige needed to accomplish it, fail and turn back. The youngest son, who has little skill or foresight, and makes serious mistakes, does not turn back. The difference is one of basic attitude. The reliance of the elder sons is on their obvious importance in the scheme of things, on their own courage and skill. They expect to get what they want because they always do. They are the eternal James Bond, but he is a fictional elder brother who can be carefully provided with tasks he *can* accomplish. The fairy-tales would give him short shrift.

For when the elder sons meet failure, their confidence is destroyed and they give up. The youngest son does not expect anything, he simply goes because he has to, often reluctantly, and he pursues his adventure as best he can, working at it but not at all surprised if he makes a mess of it, since he never supposed he was immune to mistakes and failures. His perseverance is not the result of defiance or any inner personal conviction of final triumph, rather it springs from a knowledge that he is part of a movement, of the story unfolding, which must unfold. He is not passive, he can make or mar the story and much depends on him, but what is unfolding is greater than himself, and greater than he can understand or foresee. Therefore he can only take a step at a time, as events unfold, seizing opportunities and keeping an eye open for pitfalls. He does not expect to see the way ahead very far, but he does try to get advice that will help him to deal with the dangers he expects, whatever they turn out to be.

It is strange to turn from the fairy-tales to the Gospels and encounter this same attitude in Christ himself. He, who is in theological terms the 'only begotten' is, in the terms of the fairy-tales, the youngest son. The prophets, meditating on the meaning of Israel's downfall, saw in God's people the despised one who is, just because of this, the one chosen to accomplish what the mighty cannot do:

He was despised, and we esteemed him not. Surely he has borne our griefs and carried our sorrows. . . . Therefore I will divide him a portion with the great and he shall divide the spoil with the strong; because he poured out his soul to death, and was numbered with the transgressors.

(Isaiah 53)

This is a familiar and repeated theme, so that when Luke composes a song to express Mary's sense of her Son's calling, he sums up this traditional awareness of the inversion of normal values which must be embodied in Israel's Messiah. When the Lord 'shows strength with his arm' he does not do it through the obvious people, the powerful and wise and skilful, but rather

he has scattered the proud in the imagination of their hearts.
He has put down the mighty from their thrones, and exalted those of low degree.

(Luke 1)

Cinderella is called from the ashes, the youngest son is sent out on a fantastic mission—ill equipped, without a clear plan of campaign or any distinct notion of the outcome. 'The foxes have holes and the birds of the air have nests, but the Son of Man has nowhere to lay his head.' The characteristic fairy-tale combination is evident, a single-minded determination to carry out a mission with a certain fatalism about how it will turn out. The incident in the synagogue at Nazareth, told in Luke 4, shows both a clear sense of mission and a certain indifference to the reaction of those who hear about it. Jesus' words to those who are, at first, favourably impressed and admiring, are provocative and tactless. He angers those who might have been his friends, yet the impression the little scene gives is not one of deliberate provocation but of someone whose sense of mission takes small account of possible reactions because it is so certain. The quest has to go on, not because the one sent is impressive, courageous and wise (though he is all these things) but because he is sent. The same take-it-or-leave-it attitude works the opposite way when he summons his first followers, after casually displaying the power which he seems to regard as a natural and inevitable concomitant of his mission: 'Do not be afraid: henceforth you will be catching men' (Luke 5). There are no explanations, no attempts to convince, but an unassailable confidence which is yet entirely un-self-centred.

This confidence in the mission, and in the one who sends, is the root of real humility. Jesus prays for guidance, but not in uncertainty. It is this confidence which makes him able to accept adulation or mockery with equal patience. He is not indifferent to the way people feel about him. He can be loving, tender, sad, angry or bitterly cold, according to the kind of person he is dealing with, but the changes of mood are not evidence of changeableness. They spring from an inner core of certainty. When Jesus describes himself as 'meek and humble of heart', this is the meekness and humility of utter confidence in a power greater than one's own, and this central strength of humility creates a detachment which is the very reverse of indifferent stoicism. Jesus can speak with patient reasonableness to the soldiers who slap him at his trial before Caiaphas, reply with an almost philosophic calm to Pilate's panicky bad temper, or keep silent in the face of injustice and lying accusations, because he is doing what he has to do, and so long as he is true to his mission he is strong with the power of humility.

It is possible to be strong because one is assured of personal excellence, or of powerful protection, or because one is contemptuous of one's opponents, or because one is practised in self-discipline and control. But the strength that springs from the humility of confidence in mission is the only kind that can be combined with an open sensitivity to others, with tenderness and hope. Even the famous cry from the cross, 'My God, my God, why hast thou forsaken me?', is not a cry of despair as it has sometimes been made out to be, but a quotation from a psalm of appeal and hope. It indicates the depth of unwavering assurance of mission which allows such a typically Jewish outcry at being left in ignorance and darkness in spite of faithful service. The Jewish religious tradition bound all of life so intimately to God's will and purpose that it was possible to cry out and protest, to argue with the Lord and accuse him of injustice or indifference. His presence and rule were at the heart of all knowledge and feeling, and whereas the modern reaction to appalling experiences may well be to abandon belief, the Jewish reaction was to fight back at God.

Jesus' humanity was wholly Jewish, and the basis of Jewish life was God's choice of Israel, a small, barbarous nation without notable artistic achievement, without (except very briefly) political power or influence, given to internal strife and marked by a streak of obstinate chauvinism. So Israel, the 'youngest son' of mankind, was summed up in Jesus, who came from an obscure little town with a slightly shady reputation ('Can any good thing come out of Nazareth?'), who had no recognized higher education, and was followed by a group of enthusiastic but unlettered young men mostly from the labouring classes. As striking as his quality of inner conviction of mission was his lack of what would normally be regarded as proper equipment for such a mission.

It was this that shocked his more distinguished hearers, and caused many to laught at his claims and others to persecute him as a rabble-rouser and a dangerous distraction from the proper concerns of the nation. Like the youngest princess in the story of the girl who pretended to be a boy, and like many others whom nobody expects to succeed in a difficult mission, he set aside the obvious and impressive accompaniments of an important undertaking. In the account of the temptation in Matthew 4, Jesus refuses to make use for his own satisfaction of the power that belongs to his mission. The power that has been entrusted to him, like those keys, nuts, purses, phials, and so on with which the youngest son is often equipped by some helpful magician or fairy, must be used only for purposes essential to the mission. It must not be used to satisfy personal need ('Command these stones to become loaves of bread'), or to impress others ('If you are the Son of God, throw yourself down'), or even to gain immediately, by one's own power, the dominion that may be freely bestowed at the end of the mission, as part of its accomplishment ('All the kingdoms of this world and the glory of them . . . all these will I give you'). But these identical gifts can be, and must be, used when the mission demands it. Dickens's gay and flippant little fairy-tale of the Magic Fishbone is true to the tradition when the hard-working little princess refuses to use the magic fishbone to help herself and her family through various predicaments. As her fairy godmother commanded, she only makes use of it when all normal ways of dealing with a difficult situation have failed.

It may be that, in the time to come, this will be one of the most important lessons that the youngest son has to teach us, for the great sin of our culture, the one that has brought us to the edge of destruction, is pride, the conviction that we know best what is to be done with our gifts and powers, and when. Ironically, computer calculations seem to indicate that the 'youngest sons' among the nations may be those who come out best, because they have not had the power to misuse their resources for their own comfort and aggrandizement. They are no more virtuous or far-seeing than other nations, they are merely powerless, and therefore able to survive and go on. Jesus, the despised peasant, without financial backing or organized supporters, knew this upside-down political truth from inside, and it looks as if his remark that the meek shall inherit the earth is going to turn out to be literally true in a very uncomfortable way. (Uncomfortable for the proud, that is.)

It is one thing to be powerless, however, and quite another to be incompetent. The tendency of the youngest son to make a mess of his mission does not seem at first sight one that should be found in Jesus, the Son of Man. Yet, from any common sense point of view, and even from his own point of view, he made some bad mistakes. He chose as his friend and follower a man who finally betrayed him, he misjudged the mood of his audiences quite often, he antagonized people who were well disposed at first. But youngest sons are not upset by their own mistakes, because they have not undertaken their mission with any assurance of inerrancy. Like the Duke of Wellington (no youngest son, however!) when a project goes wrong they 'tie a knot and go on'. And the ordeals through which they pass, sometimes as a result of mistakes, turn out to be a necessary part of their mission.

Christ, the youngest son among saviours, has the confident humility that can cope with ridicule or flattery. He uses the gifts that are given him for his mission only for the purposes of that mission, and he is not daunted when his words or actions happen to antagonize people, or when he is misunderstood or persecuted. His rejection of 'worldly' values and ways extends even to activities that would appear to be in keeping with his role. Even prayer and religious activities are unspectacular. He shocks people by leading a normal social life instead of being markedly ascetic and aloof, not because he despises asceticism – his praise of the Baptist is warm and enthusiastic – but because for him it would not be an integral part of his mission, but merely a way of self-advertisement, like throwing oneself off the pinnacle of the temple. He does not make a cult of his spiritual experience, and often hides himself when he wants to pray, as if to avoid remark. Apart from these night-long 'prayers of God' his religious observances are just the same as anyone else's. If people are shocked by his lack of obviously 'spiritual' behaviour, and even find in this lack a proof that he is not what he claims, that cannot be helped. Even in order to help the doubter he will not put on a show, either of piety or spiritual power or of human eloquence. He will do only what is absolutely required for his mission, but this he will do wholeheartedly.

He can even seem brusque and unfeeling with people who ask him for favours or advice which don't appear to him to be required by his mission. The Syro-Phoenician woman has to convince him that her daughter really does fit into his appointed task, even if only marginally, before he will use his power and heal. He has no time for people who want to get on the bandwagon of his popular success, and daunts well-meaning would-be disciples who do not seem to him to be sufficiently single-minded. 'Any man who, having set his hand to the plough, looks back, is not fit for the kingdom of God.'

The youngest son is God's fool, and his final foolishness lies in the fact that he does not really know how his mission is going to be accomplished. He sets out with scanty equipment and inadequate skill, and copes with each new difficulty as it comes up, but up to the very end things can go disastrously wrong, and the hero may find himself betrayed and thrown into a dungeon just when it seemed that the prize was within his grasp. After the triumphant entry to Jerusalem it might have been expected that Jesus would quickly be enthroned in the hearts of his people, yet that moment of glory was followed quickly by betrayal, humiliation, torture and death. The victory comes out of all this, not be any effort or achievement of Jesus himself but because that is how, in fact, these things work. Salvation happens that way. Yet until the last he does not fully know this: 'If this cup may not pass from me . . .'. But it might have passed, he almost still hopes it may.

The youngest son is victorious and rewarded, not by his own efforts or foresight but by the inner logic of the fairy-tale which is the pattern of human spiritual events. 'He that is faithful shall inherit all things.' And faithfulness is just about all that is required. Courage, insight and patience grow from it but are useless without it, and it also breeds that openness to the needs and feelings of others which is characteristic of the youngest son. Because of his knowledge that his power and mission are not his, but belong to him that sent him, he can afford to notice and feel for pain and need in people who have no apparent connection with his mission. This does not contradict his refusal to be concerned about irrelevant demands. The point is that *his* estimate of what is relevant is seldom identical with that of people who look at it from the point of view of worldly success.

The youngest son bandages the trapped lion, frees the imprisoned dove, rescues the ill-treated apprentice, and afterwards reaps the reward of a compassion which, at the time, sprang simply from being the kind of person who does help the helpless, for this is the kind of person who is chosen for the great adventure. The willingness of Jesus to be apparently side-tracked into lavishing attention and care on anyone whose plight could be brought to his notice became notorious, for he decided for himself which demands were those of his kingdom and acted accordingly. His disciples frequently tried to prevent this by keeping people in need away from him. It did not seem to them that all this love and power poured out on the very poor and helpless could possibly advance his real mission, and in this they were like many now who cannot see any point in keeping alive those who are of no obvious use to society. But the disciples, like the elder sons who brush aside all that seems distracting, had mistaken the nature of the mission. Jesus, who refused to work wonders in order to impress people, however useful their support would have been, and was suspicious of demands that seemed to be of that kind, knew that these 'little ones' did indeed belong to the developing pattern of the story of salvation: 'Of such is the Kingdom of Heaven.' And he was the kind of person who does listen to the little voices of misery, which is why he was 'indeed the Son of God'. Our refusal to hear them is our rejection of God's fatherhood.

Jesus, who came from a depressed little town in a despised, unsophisticated district, is clearly identifiable with the youngest son, and seeing the pattern of the tales in his life we can rediscover our own mission. Each Christian is the youngest son, ill equipped, ignorant, liable to make hair-raising mistakes and to suffer for them, but upheld by the knowledge that he is sent. But in order to discover in this light our own renewed spirituality, we have to learn to recognize the image of the youngest son in the whole people of God. With all its tremendous power and vision, the great mistake of past spirituality has been to situate the mission of the individual Christian, himself following Christ in humility, simplicity and faithful love, within a Church which (in practice and even in theory) was anything but humble in its assessment of itself. It was complex and self-aware, confident in its own re-sources to the point, sometimes, of arrogance. And arrogance, leading to blindness of heart, is the besetting sin of the elder sons, now as ever.

It seems natural enough that a body of people to whom has been entrusted the task of preaching the word of power should be given by its founder every kind of impressive gift and every possible guarantee of the authenticity of its mission. Personal humility seems perfectly compatible with an attitude of worshipful awe towards the Body of Christ on earth, and an unswerving conviction of its rightness in all respects. Whether the Christian body be regarded as a Universal Church or as a comparatively small group of the elect, it carries in this view the prestige of its founder, which appears to exclude the possibility of failure or obscurity.

Yet if the founder of Christianity is truly Lord and God he also 'humbled himself to death, even the death of the cross'. The power of his Spirit, at work in his people, is a power that shapes human nature towards its own inner glory and reality, but it does this in the only way in which it can be done, the way of the youngest son.

Human nature is like this. If it is to grow, and outgrow the things that stifle and distort it, it has to grow in this way, and no other. The lesson of the folk tales is firmly stated, it is verified in the earthly life of Jesus, but it is also verified in the actual history of his people, the Jews, and of the churches that have tried to carry out his mission. The spirituality of the fairy-tales is not an extra for the saintly but a matter of historical fact which can be verified, never more certainly than in our own time and moment.

The criterion by which we may judge the success or otherwise of attempts at human living is a simple one: it is the ability of people to live together in peace and love. The elder sons fail altogether to achieve this and do not even want to, they only want to be successful and secure themselves. This ability to live together contentedly is, after all, the increasingly explicit aim of all those concerned with social philosophy or planning, with welfare legislation, town planning and political engineering. Yet all of these in the past have become entangled in the elder sons' reliance on pursuit of prestige and power for town, city or nation, and their achievements, or projected achievements, appealed to emotions of envy, or pride. And at this point in history we are being forced to recognize much more clearly than formerly the disastrous human consequences of this approach. The sprawling industrial slums that brought wealth to the 'advanced' nations and condemned their millions to misery, hatred and sickness; the blighted landscapes round coal mines, factories and steel mills, which commemorate a pursuit of gain and prestige that ignored every other aim; the agricultural folly by which greed created a desert out of fertile land in the United States and is threatening to do so in Britain; the exploitation of 'backward' peoples for the profit of their conquerors; the building of huge blocks of flats that destroy community life and stand as a (steadily emptying) memorial to the arrogant stupidity of planners; the poisoned air, earth and water which remind us what happens in the pursuit of technical achievement without regard for the quality of life: all these are the results of imitating the elder sons. And the political philosophy of the elder sons, evident even if unformulated in this kind of approach to human society, finds a clearer expression in the creeds, whether of 'left' or 'right', that treat people as means to achieve an end. The end may be excellent in theory, but it is arbitrarily defined and all must be sacrificed that is not obviously relevant to the achievement in view.

These lessons are being learnt at last by governments, scientists and by ordinary people. They are being learnt reluctantly, perhaps too late. But if we can recognize past mistakes as the results of being 'elder sons', we can also see that this was virtually inevitable if no other standard was offered. We can see the same mistakes being made in the history of people explicitly dedicated to the mission which is that of the youngest son, with the right kind of advice provided and the right approach demonstrated. The people of God, old and new, have chosen the way of the elder sons, and they have suffered the same humanly destructive results. But at those times and in those places in which the mission and attitude of the youngest son were recovered they have been successful in that rarest and most fragile of achievements, a true human community.

The Jewish prophets, trying with no great success to bring the people back to the Lord when prosperity and success had weakened their faith, recalled over and over again the time when Israel wandered in the desert, after Moses had led the people out of Egypt. This period of danger and hardship, with no settled home and no certain future, had been the honeymoon time in the stormy union of Israel with Yahweh. The prophets look forward to a time when Israel will repent of her unfaithfulness, her 'harlotry' with foreign gods and her greed for luxuries and power, and will return to the Lord. Then he will open his arms to her with forgiving love:

And there she shall answer as in the days of her youth, at the time when she came out of the land of Egypt. And in that day, says the Lord, you will call me 'my husband' and no longer will you call me 'my Baal'.

(Hosea 2)

The time of weakness and poverty was the time of true love, when the people depended on God and knew it. In those days a

41

fragment of an obscure tribe, rescued from bondage in Egypt, was forged into a people with a sense of mission, a powerful faith and a confidence in their future which relied solely on the Lord's promise. The youngest son – foolish, unpractical, despised, and unimpressive – is the chosen one, who carries out the mission. But, like many youngest sons, Israel fell away, betrayed its trust and behaved with the arrogant blindness of the elder sons. In the end, the fate of the elder sons overtook Israel and the people suffered humiliation and crushing defeat. It was only in exile in a strange foreign place that the survivors returned to their proper role and remembered the words of the prophets. They rediscovered the faith of the few who had not been misled into regarding power and prosperity as proofs of divine election. It was in Babylon that Israel recovered her identity, and learned, this time at greater spiritual depth, the nature of God's calling.

It was during this time that the synagogue grew up, from the weekly gatherings of the exiles to remember the Law and the prophets, to pray for guidance, and to forge the community into one united and faithful people. That sense of mission, and the mutual devotion that goes with it, has not been entirely destroyed to this day. It survives as the Jewish sense of family, in the close community feeling of Jewish groups in many countries, and in the expanding achievement which is the modern state of Israel. Yet, with increased prosperity and military success, the role of the youngest son is partly forgotten, and with it the spirit of the brotherly love and sacrifice that drew young people from all over the world to offer their help in the kibbutzim. They hoped to find, and often did find, the rare experience of true community which survives only when people recognize the irrelevance of 'worldly' power and prestige in creating a truly human life, and work together in a hope that depends solely on the confidence of mission.

The history of the Christian churches shows equally clearly that when God's people loses its grasp of the role of the youngest son it also loses its own nature. It ceases to be a true human community, which is subject to quarrels, betrayals and failures but preserves in spite of them its sense of oneness, mutual obligation and hope. It becomes, instead, a grouping of individuals, anxious, wary, and greedy for the proofs of its reality provided by worldly achievement.

This loss of vision accompanies increase in security and worldly prestige with dreary predictability. It is not increase in numbers as such that brings this loss, for in times of persecution even huge numbers remain single-minded, but increase in numbers tends to bring increase in political influence and in social acceptability. The hero is tempted from his mission by promises of comfort and influence—the temptations that Christ, the youngest son, rejected as a total contradiction of his mission. And in the history of Christianity there have always been those in the churches who realized the danger, and called others to turn away from the broad road that appeared to lead straight to the kingdom of heaven by a splendid and effortless short cut. They knew it led only to a human desert. Perhaps only now, when we have been given convincing samples of the literal and spiritual desert (nuclear, industrial or urban) to which it leads, can we begin to see that they were not dreamy idealists without practical sense but, instead, the only really practical people around, because they had grasped intuitively and vigorously the fact that it is not possible to achieve human life that way.

For the one thing that marks out the varied and often bizarre attempts to recreate the Gospel ideal in a human community has been sheer spiritual joy. Sooner or later, all of them in their turn lost their impetus and looked for easier ways, until perhaps someone else came along to stir things up once more with an inconvenient and obstinate adherence to the original mission. But while they lived by the values of the Gospel, which are the values of the fairy tales, in humility, openness, detachment from wordly ambition, poverty and hope, they also lived in love and in joy, often in spite of acute hardships, with or without persecution from outside. They were happy human beings, living together in a real human community.

St Benedict's first collection of uncouth shepherds mixed with sons of the nobility, all living a rigorous common life far from the city, was marked by this happiness that can only be compared to the bliss of young lovers, to whom worldly values are irrelevant to the point of seeming insane. The followers of Francis of Assisi were so happy they seemed quite mad to ordinary people, accustomed to anxiety and a defensive attitude to life. The little colony of John Brown's Separatists, living in Amsterdam to escape the persecution of King James and his Established Church, were poor to the degree that some gave up and went home, but in spite of their many quarrels, their exaggerations and mistakes, they were happy, and they loved each other. The early followers of Wesley, rediscovering religion as a personal experience rather than a set of ethical norms for the respectable and well-to-do, gathered in their little groups, helped each other and loved each other and knew happiness. For the time, the weaknesses that later became evident could not spoil that spirit. The excessive individualism, the over-emphasis on past sexual sin in conversion histories, were likely to occur in a movement which got at least some of its impetus from reaction to opposite tendencies. They were unimportant compared with the sense of hope that came to these people who had discovered what it meant to be alive. In our time, the Sisters who work with Mother Teresa in the slums of Calcutta, rescuing and nursing people dying of hunger, carrying on a task essentially futile (since those they help are near to death anyway) from the point of view of the elder sons, in conditions of squalor and hopeless misery, have brought to the world's television screens evidence of the joy, unity and hope of the Gospel. A chance of the news-hunger of the nations brought these particular women to the attention of millions, but they are not unique. All over the world, Christians of all denominations, and many non-Christian groups and sects, continue to prove that the Gospel promises are accurate to the letter even when they themselves do not acknowledge Christ. When people live the values enshrined for all men and all times in the humorous, shrewd and truthful words of the folk tales, as they are spelled out by Jesus, they do find, and bear witness to the fact, that the way of the youngest son is the way to human goodness and happiness. They discover this despite all contrary indoctrination in the overwhelmingly accepted values of our society (and of any other successful civilization one can think of).

'But you cannot run a country like that!' is the cry. No one has ever tried to 'run' a country, or a church, like that, and no one ever can because Christ's kingdom is not of this world. Bits and pieces of the Gospel have been lifted out and incorporated into legal codes such as that of the Puritan theocracy of early New England, with disastrous results. The Gospel is not amenable to translation into legal and customary terms, and the attempt to do so not only leads to hypocrisy and cruelty, by forcing people to display a virtue their hearts have not developed, it also misses the point entirely. For the values of the youngest son cut across the customs and standards of any possible human society, and challenge their usefulness, if the full human glory we call salvation is in view.

They are essentially subversive. No society, nation or church, or even family, can be 'run' like that, because 'running' a society is something that belongs to a world untransformed, half-blind and knowing only in part. Laws and customs and the various social 'drives' – ambition, conformism, chauvinism and so on – are the mortar that holds together the fabric of human groups in a condition in which people are basically strangers to each other and therefore unable to trust and give and love freely. 'Perfect love casts out fear', but fear, though often of a mild kind, pervades human life in this world.

It is the fear that inevitably grows from ignorance and isolation. Fear of people with superior powers, fear of groups with different ways, fear of being despised, fear of losing status, fear of personal hurt from uncomfortable personalities or uncontrollable situations, fear of one's own weaknesses or one's own unknown potentialities for evil, fear of the gods, the dark world, the 'other'; all these fears arise from our isolation from each other, and make necessary the varyingly successful systems of coercion, persuasion and 'brain-washing' by which societies manage to live in comparative content. And yet in this situation even the half-conquest of fear, the half-victory of love, makes life often lovely, and hopeful, because it shows that fear is not essential, but accidental. But the attempt to cast out fear altogether, or rule life by love alone, is always suspect to the well-run society, and always unsuccessful in the long run. It is suspect because it calls in question the need for the structures of society, which therefore feels threatened. It is unsuccessful because it is based on the belief that human beings are capable of living in love and without fear. They *are* capable of it, but only in the fully human kingdom of Christ. This is indeed present in the world, but so far only in a fettered and secret way. The rebels, whether they are Elizabethan Separatists, early Franciscans, back-to-the-land Distributists, or Hippies, are right about the fundamental truth that the kingdom of this world *is* evil, *is* corrupt, *is* doomed. They know that the human reality is elsewhere, in the kingdom whose nature is shadowed through the ages by the myths and folk tales, and spelled out ruthlessly in the Gospels. Yet they are mistaken, as Christ was not mistaken, about the immediate possibilities.

The Gospel of Jesus is subversive, it undermines the necessary structures of society, yet without these the Gospel could not be preached, for Christians could not live. They, too, are human. This is the basic paradox of being a Christian, which has become much more apparent in our own time. It is not a new one, but we are able – even forced – to see it more starkly. So a modern playwright, Robert Bolt, drives home to modern audiences the dilemma which was real to Sir Thomas More, but is even more rigorously present to us: the dilemma of the recognition that God's law of love and freedom is greater and more real than man's laws, yet without man's laws Christians, with all men, are lost. In the play, More has refused to employ Rich, whom he distrusts, but refuses to take any further action against him. Margaret, his daughter, protests.

MARGARET: Father, that man's bad.

MORE: There's no law against that.

ROPER (*Margart's fervent and puritanical fiancé*):
There is! God's law!

MORE: Then God can arrest him.

ROPER: Sophistication upon sophistication!

MORE: No, sheer simplicity. The law, Roper, the law. I know what's legal, not what's right. And I'll stick to what's legal.

ROPER: Then you set man's law above God's!

MORE: No, far below: but let me draw your attention to a fact—I'm not God. The currents and eddies of right and wrong, which you find such plain sailing, I can't navigate, I'm no voyager. But in the thickets of the law, Oh! there I'm a forester. I doubt if there's a man alive who could follow me there, thank God. . . .

ALICE (*about Rich*): While you talk, he's gone!

MORE: And go he should if it was the Devil himself, until he broke the law!

ROPER: So now you give the Devil benefit of law!

MORE: Yes. What would you do? Cut a great road through the law to get after the Devil?

ROPER: I'd cut down every law in England to do that!

MORE: Oh? And when the last law was down, and the Devil turned round on you, where would you hide, Roper, the laws all being flat? This country's planted thick with laws from coast to coast – man's laws, not God's, and if you cut them down – and you're just the man to do it – d'you really think you could stand upright in the winds that would blow then? Yes, I'd give the Devil benefit of law, for my own safety's sake.

ROPER: I have long suspected this; this is the golden calf; the law's your God.

MORE: Oh, Roper, you're a fool. God's my god.... But I find him rather too . . . subtle . . . I don't know where he is or what he wants.

Yet More's life and death are testimony to the fact that in the last resort man's laws are not enough. The ultimate human reality lies beyond them. More, in fact, was the sort of man who *could*, if he was forced to, stand upright in the wind of the Spirit, but for that very reason he knew the strength of it, and knew that the power to walk in that wind comes only from the same source as the wind. He knew the value of the protection that man has devised for his own weakness, yet he knew when to stand up in the open country beyond that protection. And that is the perennial task of the Christian: to recognize and use the shifts and stratagems of this world (as the unjust steward did) but at the same time to know with certainty that ultimately the ways of this world are no good to man. The call of the youngest son is a call to those who are foolish because they are uninterested in the things the world values, and who are despised because they recognize (even though, like More, reluctantly) an ethic the world knows to be inadequate to cope with the situation. When it came to the crunch, Cromwell was the man who could cope with the political realities of the royal divorce. More saw them but knew that, beyond a certain point, they were *un*real, because anti-human.

The mission of the Church, as the youngest son, requires it to be a constant witness against the final importance of all that this world counts important. Yet, as a church, a body of people, it must run itself as the things of this world are run. Therefore, paradoxically, its existence is most fully justified when it is, in worldly terms, unsuccessful, just as the youngest son is unsuccessful. He carries out his mission, not by his own cleverness or courage, but by his conformity to the human values that are foolishness to the world and yet are bound to prevail because they belong to the real human life, the life of God's kingdom. The final glory of the youngest son comes at the end, when the whole situation has been transformed. Meanwhile, he blunders along, making mistakes, or profiting by strokes of unmerited good luck, or, like Thomas More, using his wits to get out of a sticky corner, but never being remarkable for heroism or transcendent wisdom.

There is another and more obviously creditable side to the mission, which I shall examine in the chapter on the quest, but in this period of Christian history, we who are called (for entirely obscure reasons, of course) to be followers of Christ need to learn, as a body as well as individually, to accept the role of the youngest son as our own. We, who are not much use, are useful in this way provided we accept our role, and are foolish if necessary, and mistaken because as human beings we cannot help it. The foolishness of the youngest son is often his own fault, but this is also part of the witness the world needs, which is so certain of its rightness, if only it could discover a few more of the answers. As the elder sons discover, knowing the answer so easily leads, in the long run, to shame and bitterness, even to banishment or death.

The youngest son does not know the answers. Even when the Church in the person of its leaders forgets its role, there must be enough individual Christians who remember and who understand what all mystics have always understood. They go on all the same, even when, like More, they do not know where God is or what he wants. This is summed up by the late Thomas Merton, the greatest of contemporary contemplatives, who shows us the contrast between Christians who seek salvation as the elder sons do and the one who sets out on the perilous quest in the faintly ridiculous and quite insignificant way of the youngest son. Here is the eldest son:

'A man who is not stripped and poor and naked within his own soul will unconsciously tend to do the work he has to do for his own sake rather than for the glory of God. He will be virtuous, not because he loves God's will, but because he wants to admire his own virtues. But every moment of the day will bring him some frustration that will make him bitter and impatient and in his impatience he will be discovered.

He has planned to do spectacular things. He cannot conceive himself without a halo. And when the events of his daily life keep reminding him of his own insignificance and mediocrity he is ashamed, and his pride refuses to swallow a truth at which no sane man should be surprised.'

This might be a description of the way in which the established churches have so often failed to be the sign of their master. And here is the true way, obvious, ordinary, basic and utterly mad and irrelevant, according to the values of this world—the way of the youngest son:

'Be content that you are not a saint, even though you realize that the only thing worth living for is sanctity. Then you will be satisfied to let God lead you to sanctity by paths that you cannot understand. You will travel in darkness in which you will no longer be concerned with yourself and no longer compare yourself with other men. . . . To find love I must enter into the sanctuary where it is hidden: which is the essence of God. And to enter into his sanctity I must become holy as he is holy, perfect as he is perfect. None of this can be achieved by any effort of my own, by any striving of my own, by any competition with other men. It means leaving all the ways that men can follow or understand.'

49

Chapter 2

The Wise Animals

The murmur of anxiety about man's misuse of his environment has in the last few years changed to a yell of near panic. Twenty or thirty years ago a small number of zealous people patronized health food shops, refused to put chemical fertilizers on their farms or gardens, and murmured potent words—compost, ecology, soil conservation, natural food. But since they were popularly supposed also to wear homespun, sandals and beads, and to perform esoteric rituals with dung and cow's horns at the new moon (some actually did), sensible people dismissed them as cranks. When, six years ago, Rachel Carson wrote *Silent Spring*, a grim warning of future results of the destruction of wild life by chemical sprays and fertilizers, the touch of reality merely caused an uneasy shudder to run through the sleeping Western world deep in its technological dreams. It shuddered, but did not wake.

Now it has at last awoken, but like a man awakened by smoke in a burning house: it is too soon to tell whether he has awakened in time to escape the flames, let alone put them out. But at least it is no longer possible for anyone who reads newspapers to avoid knowing that man has come near to destroying himself, not by nuclear or germ warfare, but simply through a culpable ignorance of his own relationship to the other forms of life on earth. We have made the humiliating discovery that the lord of creation is totally dependent on the well-being of his vassals, and that to rule the earth means to serve it.

Jesus demonstrated this natural law of all life at the last supper, when he washed his disciples' feet, but we have been too conceited to apply the lesson. Most Christians have signally failed to give it anything but lip-service, even in relation to human beings, and only a handful of eccentric saints have even noticed that it applied to the non-human creation. 'He that is first among you, let him be the servant of all': this has to be the slogan of the new ecologists, which means all of us, if we are to survive.

The abuse of actual servants has led to a distrust of the very idea of service, but it is not in itself degrading, as Jesus demonstrated. And being a servant does not mean only working for others when they demand it. A good servant is observant, he watches and studies his master and learns to anticipate his needs and respond to unspoken wishes. He has a responsive awareness of the habits and feelings of the one he serves. This is how we need to live in relation to the rest of creation. We need to acquire an intelligent but also an intuitive responsiveness, one which is respectful but never servile, to the fantastically complex and powerful interplay of natural forces. When God brought the animals to Adam he expected him to name them, that is, appreciate and identify their particular qualities, not to re-invent them, which is what Adam's unruly descendants have been trying to do ever since.

The fairy-tales have always made it clear that man needs to respect the lower creation. The would-be hero who ignores the needs or advice of animals invariably lands in trouble, whereas the real hero or heroine has compassion on the trapped bird, or listens to the advice of the faithful old horse. The quest is eternal life, and while the present turmoil over possible ecological disaster is certainly not consciously concerned with that it is equally certain that the changed attitude to his environment, animate and inanimate, which is required if man is to survive physically on earth is also a condition of his entrance into the kingdom of God. Pride and ignorance – the ignorance that springs from an arrogant and illusory self-sufficiency – effectively prevent us from being aware of the kingdom which lies about as well as within us.

In the stories and myths of many lands and times, animals play an important part, not indeed as representing the animal world as such (the fact that they have speech shows that they are not 'really' animals), but rather the non-rational and non-conscious aspects of human life, part of which links human beings to their animal heritage. Recent studies of animal aggression, especially the work of Konrad Lorenz, and of territorial behaviour have sometimes been used to bolster *a priori* behaviourist positions, but however interpreted they show how closely our human reactions are related to those of our non-human brethren in creation; and by this link we discover our present and essential bond with the rest of creation.

The animals of the myths and tales are always talking animals, for they are there to influence the actions of the fully human characters, who must make human rational decisions, with full responsibility for the results. The wise animals speak with the voice of the human unconscious, warning against actions which are, in the end, destructive or futile because they take account only of the narrow world available to the conscious reason when it pays no attention to other equally 'real' realities of human life. It is just because the fairy-tale animals are not 'proper' animals at all, but rather express a humanness which we ignore at our peril, that they are necessary for us at a time when failure to listen to this aspect of our humanness has led us to despise and misuse the world of nature to which we also belong. For the openness to experience, the humility and the sense of respect which is necessary in order to appreciate the value of the wise animals of the tales is exactly what we need if we are to live at peace with and within nature, instead of ignoring it and arousing its powers of revenge.

Attention to the wise animals, and obedience to them, has nothing in common with any kind of nature worship or the attempt to be something called 'natural'. These are doomed to failure because the full human 'nature' is precisely what we have not got; we have only the fragmented and half-grown affair which causes all the trouble. Real animals can be (and can't really help being) 'natural'. We can not. The wise animals of the tales do not ask that the human self be surrendered to them—the people in the tales who do this are the witches who have given up their human conscious reason altogether and allowed the unconscious powers to take its place, instead of simply informing it. The wise animals, in fact, often die, or disappear, when they have provided the necessary guidance. They may even ask the hero to kill them, their work being over, because he has made their wisdom his own. When they are treated in the right way they provide help when human characters in the stories have failed to help, or when they even threaten the hero's life.

Two African tales show ways in which the wise animals come to the rescue when the hero or heroine can get no help from humans. The Xhosa story of the Magic Horns tells of a boy called Magoda whose mother died when he was young, and who was overworked by the other women of the village in return for a meagre allowance of food. He finally grew tired of being ordered about all the time by women and decided to leave home, taking with him his sole possession, an ox which his father had given him. The escape was successfully accomplished, and when the boy and the ox encountered a herd of cattle led by a fierce bull, Magoda's ox told the boy to get off his back so that he could go and kill the bull. After he had successfully fought and killed the bull the ox said to Magoda: 'I have proved my strength.' But what really had to be proved was Magoda's *own* ability to be a man and not be ruled by others, for the ox was, in a sense, his manhood which he dared not claim. Later, when he was hungry, Magoda discovered that the ox's horns had the power to provide him with food, but soon afterwards the ox met another herd which, he told Magoda, was destined to kill him. Magoda begged him not to fight the herd, for he would lose his only friend, but the ox would not listen and after a fierce fight was indeed killed. Magoda took the two horns from the dead ox and found they still had their magic power. In other words, they were now his own horns, symbols of his power to provide for himself, without further need to prove himself by attacking others. Magoda's manhood was now part of himself and not, as when he was afraid to claim it, liable to run around destroying things. Eventually he used his magic horns (which provided clothing as well!) to present himself in respectable guise to the father of an attractive girl, whom he married and with whom he lived happily ever after.

The other story comes from the Swahili of East Africa, and tells of the adventures of a girl whose selfish and cruel elder brother claimed all their father's inheritance and finally cut off her hand in a jealous rage when her one remaining possession, a pumpkin seed discovered in the thatch, yielded fruit and enabled her to prosper a little. She ran away in despair, but was befriended by a prince who found her in the bush, took her home to his parents and married her. But the wicked brother heard of her good fortune and in her husband's absence accused her to the king and queen of witchcraft and murder. They reluctantly believed him and banished the woman and her baby from the city telling their son on his return that she and the baby had died.

The woman and child were driven into the forest, taking nothing but a cooking pot. A snake appeared and begged the woman to hide him from his enemy. Overcoming her fear, the woman allowed the snake to hide in her cooking pot, and when the enemy snake appeared she told it that the other snake had already passed by and gone deep into the forest. When the enemy had gone, the rescued snake came out of the pot and was told the woman's sad story, upon which he offered to help her as she had helped him. He led her to his own home, after restoring her lost hand, and rescuing her baby when he fell into a lake on the way. In the kingdom of snakes the woman and her child were welcomed with gratitude and kindly looked after. When she decided to go back to the world of men the snakes gave her magic gifts, a ring and a casket, which would provide food and a house when asked. With these the woman returned to her husband's country, where she caused a magnificent house to rise not far from her husband's palace. The bereaved husband was distracted from his grief for his wife and son by the strangely sudden appearance of the house, and went to see it for himself. The woman saw him coming and prepared for him and all the court a magic banquet. He was overjoyed to recognize her and his son, and heard the whole story of her adventures while they feasted.

Here, once more, the wise animal helps the heroine to discover her own dignity. He restores her right hand which the unjust power of her brother had cut off, and so gives back her power to help herself fully. When, with the snake's help, she has regained her confidence in herself, she goes back to her particular job, but this time she herself has something to give; she is not simply dependent on others, whether on her unkind and selfish brother or her kind and compassionate husband. She has discovered in herself the ability to give and be generous, and she begs her husband to spare the life even of her wicked brother, for she has no need to fear him any more. But all this comes about because, in her destitution and fear, she is able to listen to and help the snake, whom she might at other times have ignored, or run away from.

The snake is a common symbol of the dark unknown side of human nature, which we usually fear, and it is also quite often a sign of wisdom: to be 'as wise as serpents' is Christ's advice to his followers, and this is held to be good advice in folk tales across the globe. Real serpents are not especially intelligent; the 'wise' serpent is the dark, easily ignored or even feared wisdom in human beings themselves, and humans can only profit by it when they have ceased to rely on worldly power and the workings of their own reason alone. Perhaps the snake is its symbol because snakes are usually felt to be repulsive and dangerous, and are avoided. The woman in the story could not have proved her innocence by argument, for the wicked brother's arguments were logically credible and forceful; she was driven out, powerless. She was re-established by the growth of the inner power in herself, represented by the snake which emerged and was accepted by her, against her natural inclination, in her hour of desperate need. But when she had helped and been helped by the snake she decided of her own free will to take up her real task once more. As the story says, 'she felt braver now, with her right hand grown again and the ring and casket in her possession'. The gifts were 'her possession', but freely given to her. She did not, like Eve, covet a gift in order to make herself great. This is the crucial difference, which makes the advice of the serpent either a means of spiritual growth or a surrender to the power of evil. For these human unconscious powers become evil in human nature when they are surrendered to, out of fear or avarice or pride, instead of being accepted and used as a basis for better and more humane decisions. These decisions are taken by the conscious will, based on a rational, common sense assessment of the situation, made wiser by the kind of knowledge signified by the wise animals.

This tendency to see in animals of various kinds a source of sensible guidance and advice is not confined to cultures whose mythology vitally links the spirits of humans and animals, such as that of the American Indians, and some African tribes. The folk tales of medieval Europe, in a culture that had a very utilitarian and often brutal attitude to animals, show the same array of creatures who know better than the cocksure hero, who ignores their advice at his peril. The myth-convention of the talking animal is not only universal but so common that we take it for granted, and it scarcely occurs to us, when introducing a new generation to old stories, that this idiosyncrasy might require explanation; to children whose own cats are obstinately taciturn the chattiness of a bossy puss-in-boots seems to come as no surprise at all. But the fact that the animals speak is not a mere convenience. Language is essentially and exclusively a human ability. Humans are talking animals, but animals that talk are not humans in disguise, and the animal helpers are not merely dressed-up humans. A different type of tale, the 'beast-fable', simply uses animals as symbols of certain human types, and from Aesop to George Orwell this device has been recognized. (Beatrix Potter's stories are partly beast-fables, but they blend into the fairy-tale form.) The true wise animals are closely related to man, but even when they have a better grasp of the situation than the human characters in the story they are not superior to them; they are there to serve, and then to step aside. Their work, or the treasure or power they have helped to win, becomes part of the hero's own life achievement, as in the story of Magoda.

This role of the wise animals appears at first to be a purely individual one. The animal guide helps the hero or heroine to wisdom, or to success in the quest on which he or she has been sent. In terms of our experience, they help us to realize the need to understand and respect the part of ourselves which is below our conscious awareness, as well as to respect, in the light of their wisdom, the other members of the family of God. But there is something else that emerges from some of the tales of wise animals, which is certainly needed by the individual who is called to a difficult quest, and which he needs because his quest is not, and cannot be, his private affair.

The hero often undertakes the quest for the sake of his father the king, who, in his turn, bears the burden of the whole kingdom's welfare and future. The hero, however unsuitable and inefficient, bears a responsibility to the whole people, who are his people, and this is a people whose present existence is the fruit of its past. If the hero is called to a quest which is essential to the future of his people, it is also essential to his own future, and theirs and his grow out of their common past.

> Not the intense moment
> Isolated, with no before and after
> But a lifetime burning in every moment
> And not the lifetime of one man only
> But of old stories that cannot be deciphered.
> (T. S. Eliot, *Four Quartets*)

The quest cannot succeed unless the work of the past (good or bad) is accepted and understood and carried forward into the future, and this is why the animal helpers sometimes speak not only with the instinctive wisdom that our culture has despised, but also with the voice of traditional common wisdom from the past. In several tales, the adviser is the horse who belonged to the hero's father, whose guidance is essential if the king's heirs are to succeed in their mission. These tales are paralleled by others in which the necessary advice comes from an old servant, a nurse or a dwarf met on the way, but when the wise survivor of former times is an animal this links the idea to the more usual type of animal guide who appears to descend out of nowhere just for the sake of the hero. Both have a type of knowledge which is evidently more than normal human knowledge; it is akin to the 'second sight' with which some people are endowed, or the 'fey-ness' with which some countrywomen from the Highlands are gifted— not unexpectedly.

One very long, almost epic-size tale from eastern Europe is the story of the Fairy of the Dawn. It is closely paralleled by the Grimm story of the Water of Life, in which the adviser is a dwarf, not an animal, but the story of the Fairy of the Dawn is longer and more exotic. The structure of the tale is familiar. The old and anxious emperor has three sons, one of whom must, if the emperor is to be satisfied of his fitness to rule in his place, bring back water from the palace of the Fairy of the Dawn. Petru, the youngest son (of course), is the one who really takes the thing seriously, having been the only one with enough humility and disinterested affection to brave his father's anger in order to find out what is worrying him. The youngest son is naturally the person who is likely to realize the need for other guidance and help than his own wits and courage can provide. When he, like his two brothers, meets a fearsome dragon guarding a bridge near the outset of the journey he does not, as they did, turn tail and run, but tries to get by, and when this proves impossible returns home unperturbed to get a better horse. But his aged nurse, Birscha, tells him that he must take his father's old horse which (as the emperor tells him angrily when he inquires) has been dead many years.

But Birscha weaves spells over a blackened scrap of the dead horse's reins and the horse is brought back to life. The horse's advice takes the young man unscathed through one hair-raising adventure after another, and on his triumphant return protects him finally from his brothers who, jealous of his success where they have failed, and anxious to rule, plot to kill him. In this tale the old nurse and the horse which has returned from earlier days both offer guidance from the past. This is not simply the past of an older *individual*, but the past wisdom of the community. The nurse has the white witch's skill to offer, which belongs to the traditional lore of the people, and the horse was the servant of the old emperor; but an emperor represents his people, defends them in war, and, in this story, is concerned that his successor shall be fit to rule them.

In the tale of the girl who pretended to be a boy, the youngest princess rejects the beautiful white horses in the stable and chooses her father's ancient war-horse, shabby and neglected, but with power and wisdom to offer if only he is well treated. These representatives of old days – the nurse and the two horses – are able to help because the hero or heroine realizes and admits a need of their help, whereas their elder brothers or sisters do not. Likewise, the youngest prince and the youngest princess set out on their respective missions out of compassion for their father's anxiety and out of obedience to his wishes, whereas Petru's elder brothers set out only because they know that the quest is the way to power. Stories like these make the links between the theme of the youngest son and that of the wise animals very clear. The wisdom of the 'animals' is available and helpful for good ends only, and only to the one who brings to his mission humility and love. Without these the very same quest leads to destruction.

Two very different types of story may illustrate this common theme. One short slapstick German tale describes how an ill-used boy (the youngest) leaves home on the advice of a little old woman he meets, who is clearly a 'wise' woman. She then tells him to steal a certain beautiful swan. (The ethics of fairy-tales are often, in such ways as these as well as in larger issues, startlingly anti-social.) The swan attracts much attention, but anyone who tries to pull out one of the shining feathers gets stuck to it. This gift finally produces a long and angry procession of people all un-willingly attached to one another, for one had tried to take a feather and the rest to rescue the first or subsequent victims—who had acquired the swan's adhesive properties. The moral is clearly that whoever interferes with the swan, without the right to do so, bestowed by the 'fairy' power (that is, without the sense of humble obedience to mission) is likely to make a fool of himself, if not worse. The story ends fittingly, for the procession attached to the swan is so ludicrous that a princess, who has never smiled, suddenly bursts into laughter on meeting it. The king rewards the boy, who releases his victims, but immediately catches the princess by the same method and marries her! The swan, having served its purpose of giving good fortune, flies off and disappears, as the animal guides often do. But the old wise woman is rewarded with gifts; tribute, at least of respect, must be paid to ancestors and their wisdom.

Much more psychologically elaborate and detailed is the Swahili story of the Gazelle. This is one of the many tales of riches bestowed through the chance acquisition of an animal with magic powers, which vanish in the end through excess of greed or lack of gratitude. The tale of the old cottager who catches a magic fish is probably the most familiar. Inevitably, in the end his vaulting ambition o'erleaps itself and lands him back in the hovel where he began. But the story of the gazelle is sadder, even bitter. This is one of the few fairy-tales in which a real psychological development takes place, for usually the characters are established in their types from the beginning, virtuous, lazy, benevolent, tyrannical, selfish, and so on. The lucky fisherman who caught the magic fish was a greedy old rascal from the start (or in some versions it is his wife who is the greedy one) and native greed lacked only the opportunity to stretch itself, so they got their obvious deserts in the end. But the story of the gazelle is a story of goodness corrupted by wealth.

A man who kept alive by scratching in dust-heaps for food found a tiny coin, and instead of spending it on a decent meal as he intended, he bought with it a gazelle which was offered for sale. He shared with the gazelle the few grains of corn which were all he could find to eat, and the grateful gazelle made his fortune for him when it dug up a diamond and took it to the sultan. It asked for the hand of the sultan's daughter in marriage for its master, saying he was a sultan. When it had won her father's consent it returned to its master, who wept for joy and embraced the gazelle he had thought lost. The gazelle led its master to the sultan, but on the way it beat him and left him lying in the road. It then told the assembled court that its master had been waylaid by robbers, beaten and left naked. The Sultan, of course, wanted to help his unfortunate future son-in-law and provided beautiful clothes, which the gazelle took to its master. The man put on the clothes and promised to obey the gazelle which had arranged such good fortune for him. The sultan greeted the man and the wedding took place. Then the gazelle went off, and with cunning and courage succeeded in winning a great palace for its master to live in, by killing the seven-headed serpent which owned it. The adventures of the grateful gazelle are described with great skill, for it is both delicate and courageous, a sensitive little creature which slew the monstrous serpent and then fainted from the strain. The house was also inhabited by an old woman who was forced to serve the serpent. She loved and admired the gazelle as her deliverer, but it told her to cherish its master instead. As it turned out, everyone admired the gazelle rather than its master.

Meanwhile the man, now rich and important, had become hard-hearted. When his gazelle became ill he was quite indifferent. The old woman told him of the gazelle's sickness, but he merely ordered her to make a coarse gruel for it and would not go himself to see the sick animal. His wife was shocked and reproached him, but he merely abused her. He was plainly jealous because everyone loved the gentle, brave and courteous gazelle, and when further messages told of the increasing seriousness of the illness he only scolded the old woman who brought the news, saying he hoped it would die and cease to be a nuisance to him. The man's wife tried to make him ashamed of his callousness, but he would not listen. At last she herself went to the gazelle, and she and the old woman did their best to nurse it. But it was too late, and it died in sorrow and bitterness. Everyone mourned, but the man told his servants to throw the body into the well. Then his wife sent a letter to her father, who came and buried the body with weeping and general mourning. And in the night the sultan's daughter dreamt she was at home once more, while the man dreamt he was back scratching in the dust-heap. And in the morning they both found that their dreams were truth.

This story runs very close to the heart of the Gospel ethic and there is an obvious similarity in moral attitudes between this tale and the parable of the servant whose master forgave him a large debt but who refused to forgive the small debt owed him by another servant. The types of relationships concerned are quite different, but both stories emphasize that the expected reaction to generosity should be a reciprocal generosity, either to the giver or by help and service given to someone else who needs them. Generous help in time of need should make the one who is helped more able to respond to the need he may see in others. But if what is given is received as a due, grasped as a rightful possession to be guarded, this distorts the proper development and the result – not as a punishment arbitrarily imposed but simply as cause and effect – is the loss of what had first been given.

In daily life this does not often mean that the grasping and hard-hearted lose their material wealth: what they most certainly do lose is the proper human result of being treated generously, which is a growth in spiritual 'wealth'. The ungrateful and grasping not only do not grow, they actually lose whatever generous impulses they may formerly have had, just like the man who ceased to love the gazelle when he began to value himself by his new possessions. He feared to lose the sense of possession if he acknowledged his debt to the gazelle.

The debt of the poor man to the gazelle which he bought for the price of a coin picked up by chance in the dust, is the image of our debt as Christians. We pick up our faith, perhaps as children because we happen to have Christian parents. Older converts may be attracted by the glint of something shining in the words or life of a friend, or chance acquaintance, or in a book or on a poster. We pick up the little coin and use it, still scarcely aware of the meaning of what we do, to get knowledge of this thing called Christianity. But – and this is why the wise animals are so important to us – we shall never come to a full knowledge of what faith in Christ can be unless we are willing to admit from the start that we cannot fully grasp with our intellect the reality of what we have found, and that we therefore need guidance. We cannot even expect to understand completely the guidance given, or the reasons for it. Karl Barth, in a sermon on 'The Beginning of Wisdom' emphasizes the basic importance of this recognition of ignorance.

'Wisdom has this characteristic: nobody has it stored away; nobody is *already* wise, not in his mind, and even less in his heart. We may only *become* wise. All may, and all should, gain wisdom, and yet all may and all should gain it only as people who ask for it with empty hands outstretched. The fear of the

Lord is needed to make this beginning in the art of living. He who does not fear the Lord betrays himself by his insistence that he needs no counsel but his own counsel. If only others will let him alone to go his own way! Thus does a man think and talk who does not fear the Lord. He who fears him stretches out his hands, asking for discernment and understanding, for wisdom, and for the art of living which he does not yet possess. He is ready to receive, to accept the gift.'

This gift of wise guidance is given, but it is given in the hidden places of ourselves, in ways we do not easily recognize. We have to have the drastic humility symbolized by the despised and foolish youngest son, or the ill-treated apprentice boy, or the poor man in the dust. Then we can obey the command to search for the kingdom, not out of a desire to be fulfilled or to possess insight or peace of mind, or even to achieve the vision of the One, but simply because God tells us to. On that search we shall accept the guidance of the Spirit which is God's spirit, and is our spirit, and is the spirit at work in all creation.

We shall recognize that we are part of creation; we are called out from it, but we must not in scorn reject the parts of ourselves that we share with other animals and even plants, or try to cut the threads that weave us, body and soul, into the intricate and subtle fabric of living things. If we try to detach ourselves from all this we destroy ourselves, spiritually and physically; that is the lesson of modern ecology and psychology, and of tales so old that their origins are often untraceable.

The animal guides represent this truth. It is not a moral law if we think of that as a rule that God imposes because he likes it that way, but it is truly a moral law (perhaps *the* moral law) if we think of it as what it really is, a description of how human nature functions and will 'go wrong' if it is misused.

The law of our nature which tells us to listen to the non-rational guidance of the 'wise animals' in ourselves, and warns us of disaster if we fail to do so in humility, comes to us with a new force and a new sense of immediacy in our own time, because we have a much more precise understanding of the ways in which the various forms of life relate to each other, and of the ways in which groups of animals, including humans, react to changing pressures, both within the group and between groups.

The results of overcrowding, of deprivation of contact with natural things, and of ignorant attempts to manipulate our environment, human and non-human, are being forcibly presented to us every day. But the remedies proposed, though often reasonable and right, are inevitably worked out on one plane only, which is that of rational decision based on all available information. This is right and proper up to a point. The fairy-tale hero must never surrender responsibility for decisions, for the quest is his and the wise animals are there to serve him, not to subdue him. But from the point of view of the Christian's calling, the efforts to understand and decide about human life purely by means of collecting scientific data, however reliable, are incomplete. It is not enough to examine the animal guide and establish his credentials, it is necessary to *listen* to him, and from the purely 'scientific' point of view the wise animal, the non-human world, has no voice. It is not human, it is dumb, though obviously important and to be reckoned with. The animal – the non-rational, ancient and powerful subconscious of human beings – only has a voice for one whose ears have been opened by faith, which, in this context, means the unconditional acceptance of the quest on which God sends us, not for the sake of our own safety or that of the race, or even to make a better world for our children, but purely out of love. Love breeds humility and obedience: not a frightened and childish surrender to an unknown power but a mature and yet childlike confidence that the one we love is worth fighting for. He is worth the long uncertain quest and knows what it is all about.

This is the Christian vocation, which cuts across the attempts of even the most enlightened human society and its experts and rulers. Perhaps this is what Christians are for, in a time of questioning and anxiety and near-despair about the future of the planet.

If we draw together the indications given us by various kinds of tales in which wise animals show the way, they bring us by one of the paths to the very edge of the Christian chasm. They bring us to the edge only, for faith in Christ is not a matter of the age-old wisdom of folklore or of its contemporary confirmation by inexorable physical fact. These show us where we have to make the leap that only faith can make, and that is not an unimportant service, since the way is easily missed. They take us there and show us the need to make such a leap. There are two ways in which they lead us, one which relates us to the world around us and the other which relates us to the world within. The two are not really separate, for it is by the growth of the inner vision and knowledge that we come to understand the world we live in. Also observation of the outer world illumines our spiritual search.

The wise animals are heard by the humble, those who are ignorant and know it but do not give up. Blessed are the poor in spirit, for theirs is the kingdom which is the transformation of the whole man into the perfection of his fulfilled nature. They do not look for reward or a sense of achievement, they simply love. They learn to discern the breath of the Spirit in themselves, in others, in the movements of life in every form.

The wise animals tie us to the past, the good human past that lives in us and by which we must live if we are to be human and capable of redemption. They demand from us an obedience and a gratitude that leaves no room for possessiveness, yet receives the riches of the kingdom with joy. The wedding guests are gathered in from the gutters and the doss-houses, after the busy and efficient have refused the king's invitation, for they have lost touch with the realities of creation. The down-and-outs accept their good fortune with open-hearted gratitude but they do not take it for granted, or feel that the love and respect they have received entitle them to behave with arrogance; therefore they wear the wedding garments provided—a robe of ancient and symbolic shape, no doubt. The one who is excluded is the one who grabs, who thinks he has a right to take what is given without thanks, and without accepting the dignity and responsibility that go with it. The wise animals lead to mission, not possession as of right.

The animals teach us to trust ourselves; what we are to trust is not the self-confident, self-directed part of ourselves, the 'plain man' who knows what is what and how to get on, but the whole of ourselves. And the greater part of this whole we can only become acquainted with after many years, and only then by the patient surrender of pride in a willingness to live with the shabby and unpredictable in ourselves, without trying to pretend it isn't there. It can destroy us if we ignore it, but if we acknowledge it it becomes our guide. It is itself changed, no longer hidden but a known part of ourselves.

The Gospels are full of this double emphasis on the need to know one's sins yet not give up because of them. The fault of some of the Pharisees whom Christ condemned lay in assuming that they must not admit to sin, must claim and prove their virtue most strenuously because to be a sinner was to be a non-starter in the quest for God's kingdom. Jesus was equally emphatic that it was smug self-sufficiency that disqualified. Obvious sinfulness and inadequacy might even be an advantage, because it would make it easier to realize one's need for help and so to accept love, and the wisdom that is learned by loving attention.

Above all, the wise animals demonstrate for us the Gospel teaching about the way lordship and service go together. We, God's people, are to rule the earth because we are clever enough to do that, but cleverness alone, as the tales point out with relish, leads most often to failure and humiliation, if not worse. The Christian notion of the role of those who 'sit on twelve thrones' and judge the people is of a kind of service that requires a limitless devotion, a sensitivity, an awareness and a selflessness that are not possible unless the motive for that service be something stronger than any normal human motive.

The nearest thing we can discover to this degree of self-forgetting, among accepted categories of human motive, is the devotion of the lover in the Romance tradition. (This will be turning up in a later chapter, since the spring of the Romantic quest enters one of the main streams of fairy-tale tradition.) The Romantic quest is a potent image of the Christian spiritual quest, since whatever power, or wisdom, or happiness is to be gained is sought solely for the sake of the beloved, and it is for her sake only that the arduous service is undertaken. But the Christian service is a much more down-to-earth affair than that, and the ground-level humour of many tales is a useful reminder of the fact that human beings are not only called to great things but are also slightly ridiculous in the heroic role. This reminder is needed if we are to be good servants of creation, because there is a constant temptation to feel that we are really as clever and capable of managing things as our obvious superiority to less intelligent creatures would lead us to suppose. The recurring symbol of the talking animal helpers reminds us that human beings are animals and must never forget it, and this is not only a physical fact but a spiritual one. It affects the deep places of the psyche where all kinds of odd things go on which we prefer not to think about. But humans are also more than animal, and the wise creatures of the tales are endowed with human speech, and often with more than human powers. They show us that the transformation to which we are called can only come about if the depths are opened up and the frightening powers that lie under the surface of human life are converted by love into the wholeness of eternal life.

This is why animals help only those who show them humility and love. The true quest hero serves those who serve him, and does not despise the animals, dwarves, crones or ancients who offer help, however ugly they may be. He looks with the eyes of love, which reveal to him his kinship with his guides, whereas the arrogant elder brother sees only the brutish face, the great teeth, the twisted dwarf's body, the feeble and useless little bird or hare.

The animal helpers are there to help us to rediscover our Christian quest at a time of especial peril for humanity, not only in the sense of peril to human physical existence but in the more horrifying sense of peril to the humanness of life. Always at risk, it is assailed more fiercely now than ever before. There are comparatively few who recognize the extent of the danger, even fewer who realize that it is a spiritual as well as a physical one, and few indeed who also know what kind of danger it is. Among these few, Christians ought to be found. They frequently are not because we have so cleverly made our religion a protection against the inner vision instead of a way to quicken and sharpen it. But it is clear that the Christian above all should be engaged in the quest for the way through the region of danger, because he knows there *is* a way through.

We have all been busy tidying up the Churches, and this is necessary because our Christian houses have been cluttered and draped with furniture, gadgets and decorations that were once useful and beautiful, but whose use is forgotten and whose beauty is cracked and dusty. We had become curators of an inefficiently recorded museum, and it was difficult to find the truly beautiful and lastingly valuable items among all the accumulated bequests of spiritual great-aunts and ecclesiastical grandfathers. We have begun a great spring-clean and reorganization in order to be able to recognize what is worth keeping and give it due appreciation. But we are in danger of being so absorbed in our own skill in re-presenting the treasures of Christianity that we forget actually to look at them and see what they are. For the Gospel vocation is first of all a call to repentance and conversion, and afterwards to the undertaking of the quest to which so many parables refer.

This quest involves us inevitably in varied and strenuous activities but the animal helpers keep on turning up to remind us that it must be an inward one, if the outward efforts to transform human society are not to end in a sterile utopianism. Secular society has done things Christians have failed to do, and one of the great worries for Christians has been the doubt of the value of an inwardness which can seem to be an escape from responsibility for the struggle for human welfare. But this is a false antithesis. The Christian vocation is a strenuous one, but its wrestling is not with flesh and blood, or at least not primarily. The principalities and powers against which the hero is sent out are in the high places of the spirit. St Paul probably conceived of the powers of darkness as beings working against man, though he was vividly aware of their presence in human beings. But the argument about whether we are dealing with something within human nature or beyond it is fairly futile at this stage of our understanding of ourselves, because we just do not know what are the 'boundaries' of the human spirit, if there are any. We should, therefore, avoid the two extremes of thinking of the search and the struggle as concerned either purely with a private 'interior' life, or purely with 'social' forces 'exterior' to the individual's consciousness. The truth lies somewhere between the two, for the Gospel shows us ourselves as both less private than the first of these and more personally responsible than the second. The inward search is the condition of the outward one. The outward struggle for the kingdom drives us to realize more urgently the need to discover and draw strength from the depth of the spirit, where the kingdom already is. And that need makes us aware of the enemy within, who also needs to be converted if we are to be fully available for the work of the kingdom.

Thomas Merton's short book *Seeds of Contemplation* sold, and still sells, in large numbers because it said in terms our time can take hold of the same things that mystics had been saying through the centuries, and which his readers recognized as true. His words rang bells in the depths of their own souls. He summed up

'one of the greatest paradoxes of the mystical life . . . that a man cannot enter into the deepest centre of himself and pass through that centre into God, unless he is able to pass entirely out of himself and empty himself and give himself to other people in the purity of a selfless love.'

The unheroic, unself-confident obedience of the youngest son, who binds himself to the quest purely out of love, is the condition of hearing the voice of the animal helper, who shows the way into the depths of the spirit, and then leaves us, for he can only go a certain distance with us. The inward journey is essential, but it depends on the outward direction, as Thomas Merton says, and this is the constant teaching not only of mystics of all religions but of those more detached inquirers who have poked around, respectfully but curiously, into the deeper places of man's spirit, to try to discover what makes us tick.

The psychologist P. W. Martin attempts to get people to set out on the quest, but he knows, from the evidence of many people's experiences, what Thomas Merton and all the mystics have known, that the 'inner' and the 'outer' search are not separable, for they are part of one process of transformation. The following passage expresses very well the true outward aspect of the total discovery:

'The fully effective means of realization [of the discovery of the self in the depths of the psyche] is the return, the creative contact carried over into the outer world. This is in no way to commend the tendency to "cry out from the housetops" which comes upon some people the moment the forces of the deep unconscious are encountered, before anything about them is fully understood. Still less is it to advocate the false return, substituting action in the outer world for the inward transforming experience. But where the withdrawal is carried through to the return, according to a man's own unique pattern of growth, then there is a realization properly so called. The Self, formerly little more than a theoretical concept, becomes a being operating in its own right. The experiment in depth ceases to be an experiment and becomes life.'

In order to become a whole life, the search has to be wholly in the spirit, so that outward behaviour reflects the inner quest and discovery, and the inner struggle is encouraged by the encounter with the spirit in creation.

The ideas stirred up by the animal helpers who trot, creep or fly through the fairy world all tend to send us back to the beginning—the beginning of ourselves. Ourselves begin in the earth, in the living cells that proliferate and diversify so strangely through the world. Ourselves, socially and individually, begin with the sub-human world of life. Ourselves, entering into this world, may find the way open to something transcending whatever we had managed to envisage of the perfection of the human. But we have to enter it first.

We have to open eyes and ears, to make the little immediate commitment that lets us attend to each thing and each person as if it were the only one, for that is what God does to the sparrows, the wild flowers, the poor. We have to listen to the interior value of each experience, making a kind of miniature act of faith in each event, so that we gradually learn to detect and reject what is destructive and to respond to and cherish whatever has in it the seeds of new life. Soon we begin to realize this, not as a series of episodes, but as the way of life, of contemplation and so of joy. For as Tolkien perceives in his analysis of fairy tales, the place at which the tales touch most importantly on the human reality giving us a taste of the 'good news', is when they reveal to us 'a piercing glimpse of joy, and heart's desire, that for a moment passes outside the frame, rends indeed the very veils of the story and lets a gleam come through . . . a sudden glimpse of the underlying reality of truth'. This breath-catching truth is the joy of the Gospels, as we reread well-worn passages in the light of this new awareness. We discover in them not moral precepts, nor commands, nor even reassurances, but a whole new essence of life, which transforms it in a way that we had not dreamt of.

The fairy-tales have preserved for us, once we learn to attend to them seriously, not the key to life but the key to the attitude of mind and heart that can feel, hear, taste, fear and delight in the revelation of life which only Christ can offer us. The heart that is child-like because it is serious, whole and hopeful can listen to the wisdom to which the animal helpers give a voice. For this is the voice of the basic human need for life, which is the life of God; and it is in response to this need, when it is recognized as the 'one thing necessary', that Christ tenders the invitation to utter self-abandonment, to trust beyond reason, to the forgetting of self-interest and the loss of the protective devices of our timidity. It is an invitation to set out on the journey of the youngest son, which he alone can take because he alone hears, and on this journey he must follow advice that tears open the depths of himself and sets him free.

It is, perhaps, only a coincidence, but a very good one, that the passage in St Luke's Gospel which precedes Luke's version of the 'beatitudes' shows Jesus healing diseases, especially those of people who were 'troubled with unclean spirits':

> And all the crowd sought to touch him, for power came forth from him and he healed them all.

This power is not his private possession, he made it perfectly clear that it was available to those who gave themselves to the kingdom as his disciples. This is the power of the Spirit which is freely available to anyone who is willing to set out, however ill-equipped and however tentatively, on the quest for God's kingdom. On the other hand, not everyone is likely to realize the glory and urgency of that search; the beatitudes, and the passage that follows, give a description of the kind of people who *are* likely to set out on this journey, and the kind of attitudes they ought to have as they travel. As we read, we can realize that here is the pungent essence of the more diffuse and elusive teaching of the fairy-tales. Here, we can feel the joy at first hand, but only when we have already learnt to hear, as Jesus tells us to hear, and as the king's youngest son heard the strange advice of his father's horse returned from the dead.

> And he lifted up his eyes on his disciples and said:
> Blessed are you poor, for yours is the kingdom of God.
> Blessed are you that hunger now, for you shall be satisfied.
> Blessed are you that weep now, for you shall laugh.
> Blessed are you when men hate you, and when they exclude you and revile you, and cast out your name as evil, on account of the Son of Man.
> Rejoice in that day and leap for joy, for behold, your reward is great in heaven; for so their fathers did to the prophets.
> But woe to you that are rich, for you have received your consolation.
> Woe to you that are full now, for you shall hunger.
> Woe to you that laugh now, for you shall mourn and weep.

Woe to you when all men speak well of you, for so their fathers did to the false prophets.
But I say to you that hear, love your enemies, do good to those that hate you, bless those who curse you, pray for those who abuse you. To him who strikes you on the cheek, offer the other also; and from him who takes away your cloak do not withhold your coat as well.
Give to everyone who begs from you; and of him who takes away your goods do not ask them again.
And as you wish that man would do to you, do so to them. . . . Judge not, and you will not be judged; condemn not, and you will not be condemned; forgive, and you will be forgiven; give, and it will be given to you; good measure, pressed down, shaken together and running over, will be put into your lap. For the measure you give will be the measure you get back.

(Luke 6)

But after all the advice comes the description of how obedience to this guidance is expected to affect those who hear. And the little parable shows very exactly how it works, how these commands that cut across all the wisdom of this world serve to build human beings from the depths of themselves, not merely changing the surface but erecting a structure that can endure to eternal life. This is something we need to reflect on with particular urgency as we try to build a world for survival.

For it is only by digging deep that we can raise the temple of God on earth. We have to dig below the level where we can see results and account for them to ourselves as obviously handsome and useful. And the temple we build is each man, and also the whole people. The digging goes down into each one's personality, but at the same time into the strata of the common human past which are the layers of our personal foundation also.

'Everyone who comes to me and hears my words and does them, I will show you what he is like: he is like a man building a house, who dug deep, and laid the foundation upon rock; and when a flood arose, the stream broke against that house, and could not break it, because it had been well built.'

We have a world to build, and it has to be built on principles never tried before on such a scale. It had better be well built.

Chapter 3

The Real Princess

Much time and energy has been expended by Christian apologists over the last two or three generations in trying to convince the young, and especially the masculine young, that Jesus was a real he-man. He went for long tramps, he could lose his temper and be extremely rude on occasion, and he actually spat on the ground quite openly! But, as the title of a recent article in a Christian review proclaimed defiantly, it was really wasted labour, because there is no doubt about it that, on the only evidence available, 'Jesus *was* a sissy'.

There is no getting round it, he was a sissy according to all the accepted criteria. He cried in public; he cuddled babies; he thought flowers were beautiful; he gave gentle answers to insulting remarks; he confessed to being hungry, thirsty, tired; he minded when people were ungrateful—in fact he minded a great many things, and admitted it far too often to preserve any claim to the correct masculine image as defined by the Establishment culture of the West. No amount of rudeness or physical toughness can contradict the evidence of a sensitive, tender and highly emotional type of personality.

This fact points to an aspect of Christian spirituality which is fundamental to any attempt to rediscover and release the full power of the Spirit in our time. No progress can be made in holiness, by either the individual or the churches, unless both men and women are willing to release the captive princess, the 'feminine' side of human nature. She has been carefully walled up like Rapunzel in her secluded tower, lest she cast doubt on the absolute value of the system by which our civilization survives. This is geared to the pursuit of power and material wealth, in cash or territory. It is encouraged by the intensive study of those subjects which formed the Mock Turtle's 'regular course': Ambition, Distraction, Uglification and Derision. (The Mock Turtle's school also offered French, Music and Washing Extra;

its priorities seem to have been remarkably similar to ours, so it is
to be noticed that the Mock Turtle failed to attend the Classical
Studies of Laughing and Grief. These were taught by 'an old
crab', who undoubtedly belongs in the previous chapter, since
the lack of these two skills is a normal mark of the 'elder sons'
who run our society. But that is by the way.)

The theme is summed up neatly in the Servian story of the
Prince and the Dragon, in which the youngest prince, employed
as a shepherd by an emperor, wrestles with the local dragon in
defence of his sheep, and finally overcomes him only when the
emperor's daughter kisses him:

'The princess . . . ran up and kissed him on the forehead. Then
the prince swung the dragon straight up into the clouds, and
when he touched the earth again he broke into a thousand
pieces.'

The princess's kiss releases the power that is needed to shatter the
rule of the dragon.

In this story the princess is scarcely more than a symbol. She
has nothing to do but be there at the crucial moment, and of
course marry the prince afterwards when he has rid her father of
the dragon. Her need for a rescuer springs from the distress of her
father and her people. Princesses in fairy tales often have more
personal adventures and torments, and a number of tales are in
fact entirely concerned with the rescue of unfortunate princesses.
On the other hand they often do the rescuing themselves, making
use of magical gifts on occasion, or perhaps merely of the feminine
virtues of endurance, constancy and adaptability. In either
capacity, the princess is the comforter, in the old sense of giving
strength as well as the newer sense of giving consolation and a
sense of well-being.

An unusual story from the Sudan tells of a prince called Samba,
who is driven away from his own country because his extreme
cowardice has turned everyone against him. In another country
his splendid looks and good nature win him the hand of the
princess, who cannot believe that anyone so large and impressive
could fail to be a great warrior. She finds out her mistake when
she discovers her husband hiding in the grain store to avoid leading a troop to repel desert robbers. When her exhortations to

courage prove useless she disguises herself in his clothes and helmet and rides to battle in his place. This happens twice, and the city rings with the news of 'Samba's' courage. But during the second sortie the princess is wounded in the leg, and when the enemy attacks again she is not well enough to go and begs her husband to take his proper place. He is appalled, and refuses, but she persuades him to saddle the horse and tells him to ride it to a rendezvous where she will meet him and change places.

Once he is in the saddle the princess whips the horse sharply and it dashes off, straight into the troop who are setting off to battle. Poor Samba is carried along with the rest. But once in the fight he goes quite wild, whether from panic or anger, and lays about him with a will. When he returns victorious to the congratulations of his father-in-law, Samba gives all the credit to his wife, for he is loving and honest in spite of his cowardice. The story ends there, and we never know whether Samba's reference to his wife as the real heroine is regarded as literally true, or as a compliment to the princess's power to inspire deeds of valour. It would be intriguing to speculate on the future of that marriage, but fairy-tales do not allow that kind of thing.

This story, it is true, contains no element of magic, but the princess's power, used to shield and finally to 'convert' her husband is of the kind which the tales generally attribute to their heroines, whether it works magically or not. It is motivated by love, and it is characterized by resourcefulness and a special kind of wisdom. Unlike the youngest son, who also sets out on his quest out of loyalty and love, the rescuing fairy-tale princess (or some other kind of heroine with the same role) generally comes in to deal with particular dangers, and she does not rely on good advice, or go ahead into the unknown in simple goodness of heart without resources. The princess knows she can get on with the job because she can rely on an acquired wisdom, magical or otherwise. Far from going ahead in blind faith, relying on some animal guide, or on luck or simply because it has to be done, the princess lays her plans carefully and generally has a few extra tricks up her sleeve in case anything goes wrong.

In the Portuguese story about the prince who wanted to see the world the hero is no quester but a good-natured prodigal who plagues his father to give him money to travel, and loses it all to the first smooth-spoken fellow traveller who persuades him to play cards. Not only that, but his final lost game commits him to six years' servitude to the winner. After three years he has to travel to the home of his master (a king in disguise) and on the way gives his last bit of food to a hungry baby, in true 'youngest son' tradition. In gratitude for his kindness, the baby's mother tells him to watch by a pool where three doves come to bathe, and to grab the last by its robe of feathers. Of course the dove is a princess in disguise, and in order to get back her feathered robe she gives the prince a ring, a collar, and one of her feathers, and promises to help him at need. She reveals that she is the daughter of the king who purposely made the young man gamble in order to be revenged on his father for some offence which we never discover. (One of the attractive things about fairy-tales is the number of loose ends which continue to hang loose, something no novelist would tolerate. But life is full of loose ends. An important lesson which is quite explictly stated in some fairy-tales is not to ask questions out of mere curiosity, when it is not necessary to know the answers in order to do what has to be done.)

The dove-princess helps the prince by her magic to carry out impossible tasks laid on him by the king. When he is successful, the king plans to kill him another way, by disguising himself as a wild colt which he tells the youth to break in for him. The queen is the colt's saddle, two of her daughters the stirrups, and the bridle is the dove-princess herself. She tells the prince what is in store, and on her advice he takes a stout club with him and soundly beats the 'colt' as soon as he is mounted. When he returns to the palace he finds the entire royal family, except the youngest princess, nursing extensive bruises and aches, and he and the princess escape while the invalids are too preoccupied with their ailments to notice. At this point the prince nearly spoils everything by choosing the fattest horse in the stables, instead of the leanest as instructed by the princess, so that when the king finally discovers their flight and groaningly drags himself to the stables he finds the lean horse, the swift and magical one, still there.

This kind of near-disastrous incompetence is typical of youngest sons, and the princess's ability to counterbalance it by her wisdom and swift use of magical powers is a necessary complement to the prince's simplicity and openness. For when the king on his swift magic horse overtakes the fugitives, he finds only a cell, a nun and a hermit. The 'hermit' says (truthfully) that he has seen nobody pass that way, and the king returns home disconsolate. But his wife, who is a witch, tells him that the cell and its occupants were really the horse, and the prince and princess. He sets out once more, only to be once more deceived by the sight of a plot of ground on which grows a rose-tree, with a gardener in attendance, who has seen nobody go by. The third time the queen goes herself, and is not taken in when she comes to a pool, an eel and a turtle. She tries to get them into her power by telling her husband to put some of the water of the pool in a bottle, but the turtle twice knocks it out of his hands, and the queen admits defeat. Her parting shot is to lay a curse on the princess that the prince shall forget her, which he does as soon as he gets home and sees his family again. However, the princess is not defeated. With the help of her two sisters (all three in their dove shape) she gets herself into the palace where the prince is contemplating marriage with another. The three doves show him the princess's three magic gifts, the ring, the collar and the feather, whereupon he remembers the past, and all ends with a wedding.

A similar tale retold by Andrew Lang is the story of the Grateful Prince, from Esthonia. Here again the prince is advised by, and finally escapes with, a beautiful girl, but there is an interesting difference. The girl is not a princess, but a peasant's baby adopted secretly by the prince's father in place of his son. This was done in order to deceive a strange old man who helped him when lost, and claimed 'the first thing you meet on your return home'. Of course the first thing he meets is the nurse carrying his new-born son. The baby girl is taken from her family and substituted for the prince, becoming thereby a sort of proxy princess. But when the prince grows up and learns about this he is ashamed of the trick and determines to rescue the girl. So in this case the prince goes to save the princess. It is the thought of her that moves him to adventure and he takes service with the old man who had obliged his father to give him the baby. But he is no match for the old man's magic, and it is the proxy-princess who helps him to accomplish his impossible tasks and finally to escape, with the usual series of disguises to elude the pursuit. This prince, an altogether more admirable character than the easy-going incompetent of the previous tale, does not forget his rescuer but in spite of her protests insists on marrying her and making her his queen, since his father is now dead. So she becomes royal in dignity as she has been in role throughout.

This story shows a mixture of the princess as rescued and as rescuer. The prince's quest is on her behalf, but without her wit and magic powers he would have failed in it. In this way it links the type of tale where the princess runs the whole show and the kind where she is mainly the occasion and motive for the hero's adventures. The best-known tale of this latter type is probably the myth of Perseus and Andromeda, in which Andromeda is purely the victim, and all the achievement belongs to the hero who kills the sea-monster; in this story the wit and power which often belong to the princess are attributed to the goddess Athene.

But one of the traceable differences between myth and folk tales (at least for practical purposes, since the distinction is not clear-cut, as I said earlier) is that the human beings in myths tend to be characterless types. The real decisions are made by the gods, whereas the people in folk and fairy-tales, though they have clearly defined and recurrent roles, are individuals, often with a complete set of ordinary human characteristics, even with personal weaknesses apparently inconsistent with their usual role. An example of this inconsistency is the princess in the Magyar tale about 'the Boy who could keep a Secret'. She keeps the unfortunate hero alive when he is walled up in a tower by bribing the masons to leave a hole, and passing food through it; yet it was her own fault that he was walled up in the first place, since this was her father's way of punishing the boy when he refused to tell the princess his secret, and finally slapped her face when she would not stop pestering him about it.

This kind of extremely 'feminine' princess is only a very distant cousin of the pre-Raphaelite type – serious, mysterious and distressed – who provided the image of the fairy-tale princess on which most of us were brought up. Once we can make the effort to get behind this elegant archetype and look at the individuals who occur in each tale we find a great variety of character within a remarkably consistent role. As we have seen, the youngest sons follow a scarcely varied pattern of action and reaction, yet they are widely different in personality, varying from the selfish buffoon who succeeds by sheer luck to the courageous and compassionate knight who fully deserves the bride he finally gets. The princesses are an equally oddly assorted bunch. It includes the

Wagnerian heroine, the pert opportunist, the helpless victim, the ultra-feminine doormat, and even a curious child-magician in one of the Icelandic series of tales about the prince Sigurd. This one, Helga, is found by the prince playing on the shore, and he plays with her. Later she protects him by magic from her father who is an ogre, and helps him to escape with the ogre's magic horse; he kills the ogre with his own magic, and finally marries his child-helper.

The connecting link between these various princesses or quasi-princesses is simply their relationship to the hero, who is often the youngest son. The princess has a role parallel to that of the wise animals, to such an extent that they are interchangeable in some cases, but the princess, unlike the animal guide, does not fade out but remains a permanent part of the hero's life. The princess, in fact, is not so much the apparently accidental (though invaluable) helper as the reason for the hero's quest, or its reward, or both. But she does not act merely as a lever to the action.

Even when her role is passive, the fairy-tale princess releases powers in the hero which would otherwise remain unused, and it is this aspect of her role which makes the most obvious contribution to our understanding of Christian spirituality. It is here that we can see how the 'feminine' qualities which are so obvious in the personality of Christ, and of those of his male followers who have been noticeably 'Christ-like', are not accidental. They are not a matter of cultural conditioning, or a spiritually neutral personal characteristic like a long nose or a cheerful temper. The feminine qualities of the princess—a strong sense of purpose, an opportunist approach to circumstances, a conviction of responsibility for the welfare of another, and a certain ruthlessness in carrying out a task once undertaken—are necessary in order to release the power of the spirit in the Christian disciple. The Christian is the youngest son, he is sent on a mission not of his own devising, and for which he can claim no fitness or prerogative of rank or talent. But in order to bring the mission to a successful conclusion he needs to turn to the princess—who is part of himself.

This means, in practice, that he who has no wisdom of his own can call on the wisdom of the spirit, which then *is* his, in the sense that it belongs to his mission and is freely available to him for that end, and for that end alone. When he 'forgets' the princess who has helped him he is immediately in danger of losing all he has gained, because he is then open to the persuasion of the false princess, who wants him in order to make herself great, and has no interest in his mission.

In the next chapter we shall meet one kind of false princess, the witch, more intimately, but the existence of the false princess is implicit in every 'real' princess, and the difference between the two is the same as that between the youngest son and his elder brothers: the true princess helps the hero out of love for him, just as the youngest son acts out of affection for his father, or from an adventurous temperament or even by chance. He never acts out of self-interest or pride, as his brothers do, and as the false princess does, who wants the hero for herself, to use or possess. One kind of false princess is very familiar to us, for she turns up on the television screen in various disguises, several times a day. She has magic powers of various kinds; she can make shirts whiter, or food more appetizing, her children healthier, or men more desirous, whenever she wishes. She does these things, however not in order to help anyone, but in order to attach others to her service.

Each fairy-tale princess is different, and in so far as each princess has a rounded personality she has elements in her character that belong to roles other than her own. The confusing and fascinating story of 'The Girl who pretended to be a Boy' seems to show that the underlying psychological wisdom of the human race, expressed in folk and fairy-tales, is aware of the danger of labelling the classical fairy-tale roles as 'masculine' and 'feminine' in the sense that they are proper to real people of one sex or the other. That story, already referred to in the previous chapter, shows a princess adopting the role of youngest son and going on a mission disguised as a boy. In the course of it she captures another princess as bride for her master, the emperor, and is helped by her in traditional fashion. Yet details in the story are clearly designed to emphasize her femininity, for she gains her father's permission to set out on her mission by 'petting and coaxing' him, she 'trembles all over' at her encounter with the huge wolf in her path, she longs to get down and pick flowers on her way; an excellent cook, she delights the other pages with her cookery and attracts the attention of her master the emperor when she takes over the imperial kitchens in an emergency. Yet in the end her genuine role as hero and youngest son in validated by a magical change of sex, and 'she' marries the rescued princess Iliane.

This curious tale is a warning against the traditional Christian habit of classifying virtues according to sex, a habit which should have been unnecessary when, as I suggested at the beginning of the chapter, the personality of Christ so clearly shows 'feminine' characteristics alongside the 'masculine' ones. The complementary roles of the youngest son and the princess are combined in Christ himself, and in the Christian vocation. There are incidents in the Gospel accounts of the public career of Jesus which remind one forcibly of the resourceful, quick-witted princess, as well as the victim–princess who inspires and motivates her rescuer. The temptation account in Luke, for instance, shows Jesus giving replies that exemplify the role of the youngest son, yet the method – the swift and neat replies to tricky questions – reminds one of the princess who knows the answers to the wizard's trick questions, and primes the hero with them in good time. Several of the miracle stories show the same kind of quick wit combined with 'magical' power. One of these is the story of the cure of the paralytic in Luke 5, in which the wise reply confounds the malignant critics while at the same time the gesture of healing utterly disarms further opposition. The motive is the motive of the youngest son, single-minded and indifferent to public opinion, but the technique is that of the resourceful princess.

For the role-name of the princess is surely Sophia, the divine wisdom, and the frequent use of the Old Testament description of wisdom to illuminate the role of the Christ seems 'natural' and unforced because this 'real princess' is an integral part of the nature of the Son of God. Her description in the seventh chapter of the Book of Wisdom might be a description of the typical fairy-tale princess of the helping type. The language is the language of theology, but here is clearly the archetypal sister of the wise princess of the tales:

'For within her is a spirit intelligent, holy, unique, manifold, subtle, active, incisive, unsullied, lucid, invulnerable, benevolent, sharp, irresistible, beneficent, loving to man, steadfast, dependable, unperturbed. . . .'

In some ways the 'princess' role is more difficult for modern

Christians to envisage than that of the youngest son, for although it is humiliating to be the fool of the family there is at least no temptation to smugness. The perfect assurance of the real princess who is never at a loss seems inconsistent with Christian humility. But it is just here that we need to understand the princess in the Christian vocation, for the competence of the real princess is a *magical* one, in other words it is a power and wisdom which have been given to her or taught to her, and which work in a certain way, and no other. Magic is a tricky thing. It can be misused, but misuse brings its own punishment which is apt to be hideous. The princess Sophia knows this, and she works her magic in the proper way, for the rescue of the prince or the accomplishment of his mission. She can rely on its efficacy for the right purposes, but just because she knows her magic so thoroughly she does not use it for selfish or trivial ends. Dickens's little princess Alicia is one of the true line, for she absolutely refuses to make use of the magic fishbone until she is sure the appointed time has come. She will not call on its magic help when the queen faints, or one of the many little princes cuts his hand, or the baby falls under the grate and gets a swollen face and a black eye, for on all these occasions her own resourcefulness and hard work are sufficient to cope with the situation. She only uses the fishbone when the trouble is beyond her, for, says she, 'When we have done our very best, Papa, and that is not enough, then I think the right time must have come for asking help of others.' This secret she had 'found out for herself', being a proper princess.

The princess Sophia, the divine wisdom which is freely given to the one who asks for it, does provide a resource beyond what people can be expected to develop by their own gifts and abilities, but its proper use depends on the way in which natural human gifts and resources are used. I cannot resist citing the example of one not at all well-known Christian saint who actually was a princess, one whose magnificences outshone that of all but a few extra spectacular fairy-tale ones, and who resembled some of them in other ways. Her name was Melania, and she was the sole heiress to the colossal fortune of the distinguished and vastly ancient family of the Valerii. Her estates, scattered all round the Mediterranean, amounted to overlordship of a moderate sized nation, and her place on the Coelian hill was the size of a small town, with its own temples, theatres, public baths and streets. Her family were Christians, and Melania was an enthusiast.

Her father married her at thirteen to a boy of seventeen. She wanted them both to remain virgin, but he felt they ought to ensure the succession first. So she had a daughter, then a baby boy who died immediately, and the couple took this as a sign that they should renounce sex, which they did, though their love for each other was deep and sincere. Melania was the planner, and her plan was to get rid of her fantastic fortune and live in poverty for Christ. She had not the faintest idea what poverty meant, and her attempts to rid herself of riches involved her in complicated lawsuits lasting decades. She wanted to free her slaves, or at least the ones in Rome, but they refused to leave. 'They dared to disobey us!' cried the outraged Melania, who had not stopped to wonder what would happen to thousands of men without property if they were thrown out of work. (Her husband's brother took them over in the end.) Melania did her best to carry out what she felt was the mission entrusted to her, which was both personal and social, for she wanted to be poor in order to follow Christ better, but also her scorn for wealth was a tremendous prophetic gesture in the face of a society which valued power and possessions above everything. The attempts of a teenage multimillionairess to cope with the practical problems of disposing of her huge fortune were often clumsy, and those who suggested she might have made better use of her wealth than to discard it may have been right.

This princess was not as totally in command of the situation as the fairy-tale ones, but she was trying to do the same thing: to use her gifts and possessions in the service of the quest to which the prince was dedicated. And when her practical efforts were still showing only partial success the 'magic' came into play, in a very drastic fashion. The Visigoths invaded Italy and sacked Rome. The Valerian palace was burnt down, but Melania and her husband escaped to Sicily, then Africa. Here Melania went on getting rid of her remaining property, causing a lot of trouble in the process, for she was still doing it *herself*, but finally she was really poor, and her influence and prestige vanished with the wealth that created them. Melania found she disliked this very much! But from then on she and her husband lived according to the wisdom that is proper to real princesses, whose springs are deeper than ordinary good sense and ordinary goodwill. Unlike the fairy-tale princesses, Melania continued to be tactless and impulsive and to make mistakes, but the true wisdom was hers. She found many friends who loved her for herself, not her money. She lived in Palestine, founded convents and monasteries with her husband's help, discovered other people who were on the same quest. After her husband's death she lived as a nun, and although she had nothing to give except a great love and zeal, she drew people to her. When she was dying huge numbers of people came from all around to file past and see her for the last time. The bishop who was at her side said: 'You go gladly to the Lord, but we, we weep, for all the good you have done to our souls.' But Melania, who knew the source of her wisdom, said quietly: 'As God willed, so it has befallen.' God's will had been assisted by some vigorous pushing on her own part, but she knew that, at the last, it was the 'magic' of a wisdom not her own that had brought her to the end of her quest in peace.

This combination of ordinary but well-cultivated qualities with an inner assurance that relies on a wisdom not one's own is the hallmark of the true princess who is an essential part of the Christian character, both in the individual and in the whole community. But if initiative, sense, patience, devotion to duty and 'magic' wisdom are all aspects of the princess in the Christian character, there is another aspect of it which is less comfortable. Hans Andersen's 'real princess' proved her claims to royalty by suffering insomnia through the presence in her bed of one pea under twenty mattresses and twelve feather beds (a degree of sensitivity which must have made her an inconvenient, though distinguished, bedfellow). But the idea that to be 'royal' means to be delicate and easily hurt by things other people scarcely notice is not just a snobbish medieval superstition, provided we put it in the proper fairy-tale context. We can then realize that the vocation of the real princess requires her to be aware of, and hurt by, symptoms of evil in a way that people who lack the doubtful pleasure of the royal vocation need not be. Christians are required to be hypersensitive to evil if they are to do the 'royal' job properly, but this sensitivity is not attained by hard work, nor is it automatically bestowed in baptism. It is the result of a constantly maintained openness to life, backed by the confidence of faith that life is about God. For the right kind of sensitivity is not squeamishness, it does not mean a rejection of the evidences of evil and a withdrawal from contact with them. It is the trained sensitivity of the one who has learnt to see the world as the place where the Spirit is at work and is therefore opposed by evil. It is like the sensitivity of the good nurse or mother, who is immediately aware of something wrong, even when it is not obvious, because she is 'tuned in' to the patient or child.

But to be very sensitive to what is wrong is not a recipe for popularity, and Christians have never been popular when they were doing the job properly, nor has the Church been popular on those (comparatively rare) occasions when it has stood up to public opinion on some moral issue. (The churches seem to take moral stands against public opinion most often on positions which were favoured by earlier public opinion. This is not sensitivity but fear of confronting new situations.) Hans Andersen's real princess turned up at the palace in pouring rain, with the water running off her soaked clothes, and no visible means of support. This is a very likely fate for real princesses. People who insist on saying that something is rotten in the state of Denmark, when the population is busy celebrating its freedom from old-fashioned guilt-feelings or bourgeois prejudice about the value of human life and freedom, are apt to be shown the door, if not the firing-squad.

The long history of the Church is starred with martyrs who died, sometimes at the hands of other Christians, because they were real princesses and could not rest content when they felt a lump that no one else noticed under the mattresses of public apathy. It is not easy to be a martyr, and the virtue of courage is its most obvious requirement. But a willingness to suffer is not enough, for men have died in very bad causes and for quite wrong motives. Before courage is required there must be other qualities of the real princess. One is a sense of the greatness of the vocation which is not hers as a possession but as an honour which she cannot deserve and, growing from that, another is a sensitivity to the spiritual realities which are her realm. There are many stories of persecuted princesses, driven from home or forced to work as under-servants by jealous step-mothers, and often it is the princess's truthfulness or constancy that cause people to hate her. The youngest son is equally often ill-treated, but that is usually because he is regarded as stupid or inadequate or because someone wants to claim credit for his achievements. His sufferings are unmerited, but they arise from his character and situation rather than from any positive act of his own. With exceptions (there is quite a lot of overlapping, when the youngest son and the princess seem to have exchanged roles for a while), persecuted princesses are more likely to bring their sufferings on themselves by some deliberate act which is demanded by their calling. Beginning with Stephen, the first martyr, who refused to stop pointing out what was wrong with first-century Judaism, many names occur. Not all these people were deliberately killed, but they all suffered because they recognized evil when others did not. Elizabeth of Thuringia actually was a princess; she died, banished and persecuted, because she knew how the poor suffered under their overlords, and would not accept that situation as normal. Thomas More and John Bunyan spring to mind and, nearer our own time, Dietrich Bonhoeffer and Franz Jägerstetter, Protestant and Catholic, who both saw through the Nazi myth and died in consequence. At the time of writing, penal camps in Siberia are the reward of over-perceptive Russian writers who, out of love for the country, protested at what spoiled it. The Christian motive is explicit in the case of Solzhenitsyn. In the United States, Daniel and Philip Berrigan, among others, are in prison for the un-American activity of destroying draft files in protest at their country's involvement in an unjust war involving indiscriminate destruction and murder.

The real princess still toughens the Christian will as she makes tender the Christian conscience. She cannot act except as a princess should, like the nameless princess in Grimm's tale of 'the Many-furred Creature' who runs away from her father's court rather than make a marriage arranged by her father for political reasons. She blackens her face and disguises herself in a curious robe of many furs, and when she is caught by the soldiers of a neighbouring country she is put to work in the kitchen. The happy ending comes, as it so often does in tales of this type, because she reveals her beauty to the king of the country, arriving incognito at his ball, then slipping away to her disguise and the kitchen. He finally penetrates her disguise and tears off her cloak, as the churches have so often belatedly paid homage to their own once-despised princesses. But even while she is a servant she is still always a true princess, courteous and capable, patient and courageous.

These qualities of the true princess have come to be taken completely for granted in children's stories, and after three-quarters of a century Frances Hodgson Burnett's *A Little Princess* is still loved by children who buy it in paperback. It is not a fairy story, but tells how Sara, a child so rich that people nickname her 'the princess', is put to school in London; but she loses her father and all her wealth and is made to work as a drudge in the school where she was once the show pupil. Sleeping in the attic, insulted and bullied by mistress and servants alike, cold, shabby, hungry and humiliated, she keeps up her courage by pretending to herself that she is really a princess. Because she is a princess she must not show distress, she must still consider others, speak gently and truthfully, and never ask for sympathy or give way to her feelings of despair. 'If I am a princess in rags and tatters, I can be a princess inside', Sara tells herself. She confides to the rat whom she has tamed with crumbs, 'It has been hard to be a princess today, Melchisidech . . . it's been harder than usual . . . when Lavinia laughed at my muddy skirts as I passed her in hall, I thought of something to say all in a flash—and I only just stopped myself in time. You can't sneer back at people like that—if you are a princess.' Later, her fortunes are suddenly restored in proper fairy-tale fashion and the headmistress sneers at her: 'I suppose that you feel now that you are a princess again.' Sara, though she is embarrassed at having one of her private 'pretends' exposed, answers: 'I tried not to be anything else, even when I was coldest and hungriest—I *tried* not to be.'

The story, which though not a fairy-tale so obviously follows a fairy-tale pattern, makes a curious link between the fairy-tale character and the real life ones, a few of whom were mentioned above. It also shows very well why the princess, with all her admirable qualities, is not a sufficient guide to the rediscovery of the Christian reality. 'Princess' Sara is brave, kind, resourceful and patient, but what keeps her going through everything is an indomitable pride. It is admirable, this obstinate refusal to give in and become the broken, degraded creature which she is expected to be when the props of wealth are removed, but it is the way of this world, not of the kingdom. It is necessary, because the human spirit under attack must defend itself as it can, and if the stage of spiritual development is not sufficient to allow a truly spiritual response then some other way must be found. Sara draws on the resources she has, and they are very like those of the typical fairy-tale princess. But the important thing about the typical fairy-tale characters is that they are no use on their own: it is the interaction of the various roles that creates the full pattern leading to the happy ending. And so in the full Christian personality, both individual and communal, there has to be this interaction. The wisdom and wit of the princess must fill out the simple obedience of the youngest son, and the selfless service of the wise animal is needed where the hero's own abilities fail him. But also the self-assurance of the princess must not overrule the lucid fatalism of the youngest son, who will go where he has been sent when there seems to be no good reason to do so. If the author of *A Little Princess* had made her heroine humble as well as brave, not courteous out of a sense of *noblesse oblige* but from perfect charity, she would have carried little conviction as a picture of a real child, for children can very seldom have achieved such a degree of spiritual maturity. (A few have, but they probably wouldn't make good stories.)

But exactly this kind of spiritual stature is the perfection which Christians must seek. If we look back to famous people in Christian history we see that they did approach this kind of balance, though there must naturally be a greater development on one side than the other. It is noticeable that great Christian women have very often been the predominantly 'energetic princess' type, like Valeria Melania (and Hilda of Whitby, Joan of Arc, Teresa of Avila, Octavia Hill, Gladys Aylward), but they had the 'youngest son' side without which they would have been, probably, intolerably bossy and self-sufficient.

Other women have had the role of 'victim princess' and these were mainly mystics, such as Margaret Mary Alacoque and Catherine of Siena, but they had a good share of the other kind of princess as well, for they were not passive Andromedas but lived with a blazing assurance of the divine wisdom at the heart of even the most terrible sufferings, and their 'wise animals' played a big part in their lives. But great Christian men have been 'princesses' too, and both as victims and helpers they have inspired thousands. The founders of religious movements have to call on the princess in themselves as they face problem after problem and danger after danger. Paul himself, 'tying knots and going on' after each fresh setback, describing himself and his flock as the pot-scrapings of the Empire, never daunted by persecution, is an obvious princess. Yet if he had not trusted his gut-reactions rather than his reason on some occasions, thus obeying the wise animals, and if he had not had, in the last resort, the tremendous and passionate humility of the youngest son before God's work in himself, he would have been an unbearable autocrat. St Bernard, St Benedict, George Fox, John Wesley, all ran the risk of spoiling not only their work but themselves if they failed to balance initiative by humility and inspiration by common sense. Their modern successors, like Mother Teresa of Calcutta or Dorothy Day or Anton Wallich Clifford, have the same problem.

We have to come back in the end to the only one in whom we can discover complete spiritual maturity—Jesus himself. In him we see the princess who needs to be rescued, giving strength to her rescuer in his adventures on her behalf. Jesus let people know his needs, for affection and acceptance and loyalty as well as for water, and he evoked in people a response that another with the same need might not have received, because Jesus had in himself what he asked of others. They never felt in danger of being swamped by his need. So people gave to him naturally and easily (the Samaritan woman, Martha and Mary, the twelve, the crowds on 'Palm Sunday'), and got more than they gave, because he was also the rescuing princess, who guides the bewildered hero to safety. When he healed and comforted, or pulled a man out of a tangle of motives into the freedom of clear understanding (as he did for the scribe who asked for the 'greatest' commandment) he drew on the 'magic' wisdom which belonged to his mission, and whose nature he thoroughly understood.

Though at first sight the princess role seems to have nothing in common with that of the youngest son, neither can do without the other in the life of the spirit. Jesus is indeed 'the youngest son' whose loving obedience, and indifference to worldly standards, saves his father's kingdom, but without the divine wisdom, the princess Sophia, to enlighten and guide and improvise on events he could not reach the full stature of Messiah. It is the youngest son who dies on the cross, obedient to his mssion however futile it seems, but it is the well-taught, far-seeing and opportunist princess who takes up ancient ritual, and the immemorial gesture of shared life in shared meal. From it she creates a rite where the past opens into the future and draws all men unto her in the simplicity of bread and wine eaten and drunk. Therefore the risen, fulfilled, humanity is a wedding.

Chapter 4

Witches, Emperors and Ogres

When the Greeks of the Dorian age (which Robert Graves describes as 'barbarous') wished to justify the suppression of women to the status of possessions of the male they told useful stories about how Zeus punished Hera for plotting to overthrow him and regain her former power as the Great Goddess. Hera, deprived of the ancient power of the dark mother goddesses, took to the traditional weapons of the oppressed, intrigue and disguise. She used her powers in a magical way to carry out all kinds of small revenges on Zeus and to gain her own ends. She became, in fact, a witch in the traditional fairy-tale sense. So, at least, Graves suggests, and if (as I am informed by those whose business it is to know this kind of thing) early mother goddesses are rather *passé*, anthropologically speaking, this does not do away with the tales. Whatever their origin, the stories are persistent and perennial. Queen-witches, like Snow White's step-mother, occur in many tales, and they are the supplanted, or threatened, wielders of power.

Witches of this kind are made, not born. They are only one type of evil as the tales show it, but a very familiar and influential one. The Pelasgian pre-Hellenic creation myth, for instance, begins with the Goddess of All Things, Euronyme, dancing upon the waves. She was beautiful and creative, but later she ceased to be beautiful and bountiful, and in the Orphic version was called Night. She had dark wings, and laid a silver egg in the womb of Darkness. From this egg was born the four-headed, double-sexed, Eros, or Phares, who brought the universe into being. Night remained in a cave, whence she still ruled the universe, but secretly, until finally her power was taken over by Uranus, son of Earth.

The landless Jews who formed little colonies all over medieval Europe kept together for emotional as well as physical security, because the ways of the host peoples were strange and often repulsive to them, and because they already had a very strong sense of nationhood and of national destiny through their faith. But their oddness and secretiveness were easily interpreted as a mystery of evil, when other people wanted (as human beings always do) a way of getting rid of responsibility for evil in themselves by transposing it onto someone else. All kinds of minorities, as well as eccentric individuals, have been made the repositories of communal guilt, and the Jews are only the most flagrant example in our culture of the scapegoat technique, or at least they were until the black population in white cultures took over that role. But the suffering inflicted on innocent people because of this kind of guilt-dumping is not the most unpleasant aspect of the matter horrible as it is. What is more sinister is that people cast in the role of incarnate evil begin to accept that role and gradually to fit it. The displaced queen seeks revenge by malicious and ruthless manipulation of other people, first in order to defy her oppressor, but after a while simply for the sheer satisfaction of destruction.

> Thou call'dst me dog before thou hadst a cause,
> But since I am a dog, beware my phangs,

says Shylock, when Antonio pleads with him. Centuries of racial oppression, years of personal humiliation, have not simply made Shylock a victim of Christian unkindness, but have changed him into a witch, who will use any means to obtain, and luxuriously enjoy, the power to hurt. The victim of evil becomes evil, and even if we are moved with pity for the wretched man, and anger at the arrogance of his Christian tormenters, there is no doubt that he is evil. And this evil has the very character of witchcraft, for it is, in a way, beyond his control. The evil has possessed him, yet he enjoys using the evil power. Shylock, asked the reason for his adamant refusal to accept the money instead of 'his bond' (the pound of Antonio's self-righteous flesh), admits there is no reason:

> So can I give no reason, nor I will not,
> More than a lodg'd hate, and a certaine loathing
> I beare Anthonio, that I follow thus
> A loosing suite against him.

It is not a coincidence that so many fairy-tale witches are also step-mothers, for the second wife is a second-best, at least symbolically, and in the tales she is clearly the unloved. Humiliation turns to bitterness, bitterness breeds the desire for revenge, and the desire brings the power. The victim of her revenge is not, however, the one who caused her suffering, but usually the child of the former wife, the living reminder of her humiliation. In the tale of 'The Child who came from an Egg' , the successor to the princess's own mother is so beside herself with jealousy that she beats the child on sight. This step-mother is not a witch, and her helplessness drives her to do physical harm for lack of any better means of revenge. But magical methods of wreaking harm are also curiously limited, as in the well-worn story of *Snow White and the Seven Dwarfs*. Her step-mother's magic is twice defeated by the prompt action of the little dwarfs with whom she is living, who loosen the stay-lace, and remove the poisoned comb. The old queen's final, successful attempt only leads in the end to her complete overthrow when the besotted prince lifts up the glass coffin in which the 'dead' Snow White lies, and the piece of poisoned apple is jerked from her mouth. Fittingly, the wicked old queen dies, choked by her own rage, at the wedding.

In the Irish tale of Nidir and Etain, it is on the 'other woman' herself that the first wife's vengeance falls, and Nidir's wife Fuamrach turns the lovely Etain into a butterfly and buffets her with storms. In the end the spell is broken and the lovers are reunited in the land of Faerie, while jealous Fuamrach simply is not mentioned again.

The malicious revenge of the oppressed, or the one who feels defrauded, is a familiar theme of psychiatry, as well as of myth and fairy-tale. It is a factor in national and international politics, and has had a lot to do with the shaping of history, whether we consider the story of individuals with an obsessive grudge like Adolf Hitler, or the more complex revenge of a whole group. One such group consisted of the embittered artisans in medieval Germany, who did so much to unseat the feudal power of the princes and transfer the real power from the castles to the towns and cities. The weavers and other artisans who, with odd wandering preachers, formed fanatical anarchist and heretical sects, were the first genuine 'proletariat', being landless wage-earners. They achieved nothing permanent for themselves, but they helped to undermine the established power and make way for the merchants whose power was that of money and political know-how. The weavers and their kind wielded a power of the witch-type. It frightened people very much but it could not create, it could only destroy.

This form of evil, a kind of possession of malice which invades and takes over the whole mind of humiliated individuals and groups, is one of the most sinister and yet most understandable kinds of human sin. We cannot help pitying Shylock even while we are revolted at his inhuman passion for revenge. And even while we are most revolted we are also most wrung with pity for the thing he has made himself, for we can easily understand his feelings.

It is because this kind of consuming malice is so very understandable and so easy to succumb to that Jesus faced it head on and defeated it in the only possible way: by giving it no foothold at all. The most difficult of all Christian moral precepts to accept, let alone to put into practice, is the one about submitting to evil rather than retaliating. It has also been more consistently misinterpreted, in action if not in theory, than any other. The command is stated fully and absolutely unequivocally by St Luke (6: 27–38):

Love your enemies, do good to those who hate you, bless those who curse you, pray for those who treat you badly. To the man who slaps you on one cheek, present the other cheek too; to the man who takes your cloak from you, do not refuse your tunic. Give to everyone who asks you, and do not ask for your property back from the man who robs you. Treat others as you would like them to treat you. If you love those who love you, what thanks can you expect? Even sinners love those who love them. And if you do good to those who do good to you, what thanks can you expect? For even sinners do that much. And if you lend to those from whom you hope to receive, what thanks can you expect? Even sinners lend to sinners to get back the same amount. Instead, love your enemies and do good, and lend without any hope of return. You will have a great reward, and you will be sons of the Most High, for he himself is kind to the ungrateful and wicked.

This extremely dense passage contains a great range of doctrine

on the nature of evil of a familiar and domesticated variety, as well
as an extraordinarily demanding political ethic for the Christian.
Here, on one side, we have the expected 'natural' way to behave—
inviting one's friends to a meal; sending wedding invitations to
people who are likely to give a big present; doing a good turn to a
good friend; returning the lawn-mower with a box of chocolates;
the non-aggression pacts, the trade agreements, the coalitions and
treaties. All very friendly and necessary, they keep the social and
political wheels turning. And this is not exactly condemned, it is,
simply and starkly, 'what sinners do', though there is nothing
particularly sinful about doing it. It has to be done. Why, then, the
other side, the dreadful humiliation of accepting slights and even
persecution, and the distasteful drudgery of being helpful and
courteous to people one dislikes or the pain of submitting to
unjust power?

These things are so hard that attempts to obey the letter of
Christ's law while evading the real command have been common in
'Christian' societies. The awfulness of Uriah Heep and his near-
relations squirming their way to heaven in the Victorian 'tracts',
has brought this kind of long-suffering into disrepute. 'Christian
duty' became a slogan for all that was most repressive and even
cruel in the 'training' of servants and children to be submissive,
and as a way of keeping the poor (just) alive but also at more than
arm's length. The beauty of Christian submission has long been a
wonderful moral weapon in the hands of authority in Church and
State as well as of landowners, industrialists, and husbands, when
these gentlemen require subordinates with a slave mentality to
ensure that they themselves continue to live in the manner to
which they are accustomed, or better.

It is not surprising that common honesty makes people reject
the whole idea of Christian humility as a huge 'con' game on one
side and a repulsive form of masochism on the other. Why should
Jesus ask his followers to behave in such an unpleasant, as well
as uncomfortable, way? The answer is demonstrated by the
witches of the fairy-tales, and their spiritual relatives the magicians
and emperors. All these gentry are willing to be kind and helpful,
but only if they stand to gain by it, or to lose by not co-operating;
or perhaps as a gesture to a proved equal. There is nothing wrong
with that. But a slight, or the fear of losing something desired,
or the possible frustration of their plans, shows up the other side,

and they demonstrate what Jesus meant when he said that normal and harmless reciprocal giving is what 'sinners do'. These 'sinners' may descend to depths of malice, distort and eventually destroy themselves rather than give without return, or submit to even slight neglect or accidental discourtesy.

In two well-known tales we can see these two reactions. The witch in 'Rapunzel' is outraged when her poor neighbour creeps into her garden to pick some of the salad for which his wife craves. She finally allows him to pick some, on condition she gets something she wants even more, which is the baby daughter soon to be born. Children who listen to the old tale very properly hate the witch, but a pathetic longing for someone to call one's own is evident here, and typical of the wrong kind of 'love' is the way the possessive foster-mother imprisons her 'daughter' in a high tower and allows her to see no one but herself. She is prepared to care for and cherish the girl and provide her with every comfort, but only if she may keep all this human sweetness and prettiness for herself. She is quite ruthless in disposing of the prince who threatens to take away her human possession.

Othello has the same attitude:

> I had rather be a toad,
> And live upon the vapour of a dungeon,
> Than keep a corner in a thing I love
> For others' uses.

And it is perhaps not a coincidence that the alternative to this exclusive possession is expressed as that typical witch's 'familiar', the toad. This toad lives in a dungeon, on 'vapours', and the whole atmosphere is that of the witch's cave where she brews noxious drinks in order to revenge herself on those who threaten her power. Othello's alternative is not really an alternative, it is what actually happens to people who let themselves feel like this about other human beings. The obsession with keeping the beloved is enough in itself to turn a person into the malevolent toad which attends on, and is really 'part' of, the witch, and an agent of her destructive power. Because Othello will not 'keep a corner in a thing I love for others' uses', even in the most innocent friendship, he becomes possessed by the witch spirit, and finally destroys what he loves, and himself. Othello is the typical witch-type, because his panicky possessiveness grows out of the humiliation of his colour. He has been despised and therefore constantly expects to be despised even when he is not. He wants revenge where no injury exists or was intended. He never could 'turn the other cheek' to insult, and so the insult he would not stomach grows and grows until it fills the whole of his world. Iago makes it grow, but the seed was there already. As Iago himself says:

'Hell and night must bring this monstrous birth to the world's light.'

But hell and night always do so, and always in the end bring about their proper result, which is destruction. The witch is always defeated and usually destroyed in the process. The wicked fairy of the *Sleeping Beauty* acts out of malice when she feels slighted by the scatter-witted king. She will not believe the slight was unintentional, because her kind of evil is so self-conscious in its own actions that to do harm without deliberate purpose is to her unthinkable. Her revenge is out of all proportion to the imagined insult. In the end, the curse of death is turned to a curse of sleep. The power of evil which for so long strangled ordinary life in choking thorns finally wears out, and the prince conquers the thorn hedge and wins the princess. This is a very accurate image of the effect of possessiveness, which squeezes the joy out of daily life by its watchful suspiciousness. It wants a return for every gesture of love. It exacts gratitude as a money-lender exacts interest, and finally the interest is so huge that the pledged love is irredeemable. Affections are poisoned, and die.

Only someone or something from outside can break the spell. This someone is clearly present in the Gospel passage. The one who interferes, who cuts through the thorn hedge and wakes the sleeper to life is the one who can break the power of fear and jealousy by drawing their princess–victim beyond that power at his call. It is as if she must squeeze, with terrible pain and struggle, through the tiny aperture which is the only way out of her prison. That little opening was, until then, closely guarded and barred. It needs a very compelling reason to make the self-imprisoned regard the way in as a way out, and risk destruction in order to find freedom. But the narrow way of accepted humiliation is the only way to that freedom, and once the journey is undertaken the intolerable pressure is suddenly released and the prisoner is free. In fact she discovers that the struggle itself has freed her, for the prison was a magic one and once the spell is broken (by a kiss, naturally) there is no prison, and no need to struggle out of it.

Jesus commanded his disciples to give without looking for return and to accept humiliation and unjust power with generous love. He did these things himself, so it is by contrast with his life that we see how distorted the distortions are. The patience of Jesus is never smug, his refusal to answer insult with insult leaves the way open for real contact. The stoic silence of the tortured Nordic hero sets him above and beyond his persecutors, and is meant to demonstrate superiority. It infuriates and hardens hatred and malice. The silence of Jesus is open to speech when words can reach the other person. It is a way to keep communication open, not to close it. In the same way, his giving makes a return of giving easy. He may give gifts of healing and love that no one else could possibly bestow, but his giving is never condescending. It makes the recipients feel *themselves* more generous and more able to love.

Reading about the generosity of Jesus, both in giving and in his behaviour under insult and persecution, it seems 'natural' for him to behave that way. There is nothing forced about his attitude, as if he were behaving in a way demanded by his vocation but rather against the grain. He is as we expect him to be. This is not only because he is Jesus and that is the way we have learnt that he is, but also because it seems a good and right way to be. In some of his greatest followers we find the same quality of magnanimity and patience; occasionally it is rather more forced, the effort is apparent and painful, but at its best it has the same kind of utter 'rightness' that it has in Jesus. Joan of Arc asking for a cross, and getting one from an English soldier; Thomas More joking with the executioner and praying for the King—these incidents have that quality of 'naturalness' which is the special mark of Christian generosity-in-humility. It is the opposite of, and the only antidote to, the false humility of the witches.

The witch is the embodiment of the attempt to keep whole by 'pushing away' with implacable hatred anything that appears to threaten that wholeness. Yet it can be, and often is, combined with apparent weakness and pathetic dependence, as in the Scottish tale of Finlay the Hunter, which is derived from older

Norse sources as well. In this tale the witch comes to Finlay's door in the guise of a poor, frail old woman seeking food and shelter. In other versions she comes as a draggled bird, or a weather-beaten cat, but in all of them kind treatment makes her grow larger and larger until she appears at last as the vengeful Hag. This is why 'appeasement' of minorities who have been oppressed and are showing the stirring of new power usually leads to a bloody mess. It is by then too late, for the oppressed have been converted to witches, and concessions only give them a sense of power, to be used for revenge. The French Revolution is only one example of situations where concessions came too late; the witch was already in control. There are signs of this in some aspects of Black Power, too. Those who bring a witch to life by oppression reap the consequences.

The malice of the witch is essentially underground and devious. She works from 'underneath', since her malice derives from being (at least in her own eyes) despised and put upon. The magician and the emperor are also intent on gaining or keeping power, but they embody a different version of evil, for they work from strength. They are convinced of their right to power, and anything that appears to attack it is seen not as an unjust oppression, as in the case of the witch, but as an unlawful rebellion against the rights and prerogatives of the powerful. The magician or wizard may occasionally be simply a male counterpart to the witch, but he usually shares with the emperor (who is often a magician as well) one thing that is missing from the witch role. The witch is, by the fact of being a witch, warped and evil. When she appears in a tale she appears as already evil, but the magician and the emperor, and occasionally an enchantress who is probably a left-over goddess, have a power which can perfectly well be beneficent if it is rightly used. Unlike the witch, their role in the tales shows the corruption of power, rather than the corruption of weakness. (The 'wise-woman' or 'white witch' is not really a witch at all; she is beneficent and could not be anything else.)

This is an important concept in a culture such as ours, in which the gaining and keeping of power, in the form of money or prestige as well as direct power of command, is the basic proof of human worth. But in its Christian interpretation the role of the magician or the emperor is different from that of the youngest son, though both have to do with the need to obey a higher command than one's own will. The emperor and the magician are *meant* to have power. The youngest son is essentially powerless, and the success of his mission depends on his knowing this, and taking courage from the nature of the mission itself rather than from his own worth. The emperor or magician is essentially a person who has power, and is meant to use it, but to use it in the service of some overriding purpose which is the same as the younger son's quest. Their wickedness lies in using this power for their own ends.

It is interesting that the really wicked ruler usually has a title such as 'emperor', or some equivalent which shows that his power is greater than that of ordinary kings, chieftains, dukes, or other vaguely noble characters. The mere king, since he is not 'top' ruler, is often foolish, even to the point of gross injustice and cruelty, but he is seldom wholly corrupt, and is forgiven his bad behaviour at the end of the story. But the overlord, according to the oldest tales whose wisdom anticipates Lord Acton, is extremely liable to be 'absolutely corrupted'.

A story from Java tells of 'the most powerful king in Java, King Pulagra', the equivalent therefore of a western 'emperor'. He wants the princess for his wife, and demands that if she be betrothed already her betrothal be broken off. And if she is married, he says she must be divorced. Her father tries to force her to agree, though he knows King Pulagra to be a fierce, brutal old man. He is afraid for himself if she does not agree. She runs away, and her father tells King Pulagra's chief warrior to find her and carry her off to his master by force. After many hair-breadth escapes the princess finds the prince she really wants, and they hide in the jungle, founding there a new settlement with the help of a friendly chieftain. But King Pulagra hears about it, and of the failure of his warrior to catch the bride, and he sets out with a great army and lays waste the new settlement, spoiling all the crops. At this, the gods intervene on behalf of the peaceable farmers. King Pulagra is routed and his army 'swept away like dead leaves', and the faithful couple are united with the blessing of heaven.

Such high-handed methods as King Pulagra's are routine among overlords, in history as in tales. In tales he goes too far and finally destroys himself, as historical tyrants often do also. In the story of the girl who pretended to be a boy, which was mentioned in earlier chapters, the emperor who commands the service of the disguised princess is, like King Pulagra, convinced that whatever he wants he must have. His only moral standard is that of fulfilling his own desires. He sets his servant the task of winning for him the beautiful Iliane, which involves fearful adventures, but when she is brought to him the unfortunate girl–boy has to undertake fresh tasks set by Iliane herself in her attempts to postpone such a distasteful marriage. But the emperor's whole will is concentrated on winning Iliane, and he will use or abuse any other being in order to get her. The obedience and loyalty of the disguised princess draw no gratitude from him, but only more and harder tasks. When the final task is accomplished, the emperor tells his vassal (who has now become the boy she pretended to be) that he will appoint him as his successor, unless he has a son of his own to follow him, in which case the son will require his counsel! It is his succession the emperor cares about, not what is due to his loyal servant. But Iliane, more vengeful than the abused heroine/hero, decides on revenge. In this she is carrying out the proper role of the princess, which is to overcome usurped power and save the person and mission of the youngest son. She does this by magic, the power which is properly used not in order to preserve or aggrandize the user, but for good, in this case for the inevitable destruction of power used for its own ends. She invites the emperor to bathe with her in the milk of her herd of mares, and when both are in the bath she summons her magic horse, who blows from one nostril a cool breeze on herself and from the other a scorching wind that 'shrivelled up the emperor where he stood, leaving only a little heap of ashes'.

After all this, Iliane marries the girl-turned-boy, for 'people who long to be rich [and not only in money but in prestige and in sensual satisfaction or power] are a prey to temptations; they get trapped into all sorts of foolish and dangerous ambitions which eventually plunge them into ruin and destruction'. This is not the fairy-tale teller speaking, but the letter of Paul to Timothy (1 Timothy 6: 9). Whether Paul actually wrote it is not important. It certainly expresses a basic conviction of the young Church, and one based on experience, as other parts of this passage show. And there is another curious passage here, which echoes the fairy-tale doctrine that the *right* use of power, including magic power, is rewarded. 'True religion', the Christian teacher emphasizes, must be the only guide, and this evidently means a proper understanding of how power is to be used. (The question under discussion is the behaviour of slaves, among other things.) The alternative, according to the down-to-earth Christian perception of what actually happens, is 'jealousy, contention, abuse and wicked mistrust of one another. [It leads to] unending disputes by people who are neither rational nor informed and imagine that "religion" is a way of making a profit'. Religion, of course, does bring large 'profits', but only to those who are content with what they have. 'We brought nothing into the world and we can take nothing out of it' (1 Timothy 6: 4–7).

This passage is a really shattering swipe at the very foundation of a culture built on the sacredness of competition and the 'virtue' of ambition, but it is only repeating in pithier and less ambiguous language the more vividly expressed verdict of the fairy-tales. In the surviving letters and records of the earliest church as well as in the teaching of Jesus as presented by the evangelists, the Christian Gospel hammers at one unpalatable lesson: lose all to gain all, die, carry the cross, happy are the poor, woe to the rich.

The greedy wizard in the Breton tale of the Stones of Plouhinek wants to gather a treasure from under the great standing stones while they (being magical) have gone to drink at the river. He knows that to get the money someone must be sacrificed, and he tricks a young man called Bernez into going to seek the treasure with him. The youth lacks the protection of the spells he himself can use to hold back the stones from crushing him, and the wizard is quite without compunction in preparing a horrible death for a perfectly innocent boy, because to him his own desire for colossal wealth is the only relevant moral consideration. Before we accept this as merely fairy-tale behaviour let us recall the cases – much more frequently exposed nowadays – of firms that subject workers to conditions known to produce disease and even death. The grape-pickers of California, sick and dying of poisonous pesticide sprays, are only one example, and it took years of bitter struggle to stop this; in some places it still goes on. Nor are workers the only victims. Unsafe cars, poisonous food additives, are still sold whenever the makers can do so undetected.

But in the Breton story one stone has previously had a cross carved on it by Bernez, and it not only refuses to destroy a Christian but, being 'baptized' and therefore impervious to evil magic, it is unaffected by the wizard's spells. It turns on him and crushes him to powder. 'It was the stone rejected by the builders that has become the corner-stone. Anyone who falls on that stone will be dashed to pieces; anyone it falls on will be crushed.' The verdict of the fairy-tale is the verdict of the Gospel. This passage comes as the punch line at the end of the parable of the tenants of the vineyard who wanted it for themselves, and therefore, in the absence of the owner, beat and wounded the messengers who came to collect the rent, and finally killed the owner's son who was sent to them. The owner decides to 'make an end' of the tenants and give the vineyard to others (Luke 20: 9–18). This parable primarily refers to the false leaders of Israel, who wanted to run God's people for their profit and to satisfy their own craving for power. They therefore rejected the prophets and finally killed the son, the Christ. But it also applies to all those who grab at power. Whether the power be in the form of wealth, sexual domination, emotional blackmail, intrigue, a political career, the verdict is plain: the values the power-seeker rejects will prove to be the one thing needed for life. The rejection will rebound on the power-seeker. The ecological troubles which have resulted from misuse of industrial power have already begun to do this.

But the young man in the tale of the stones also wanted money. Why was he not punished? The reason is that Bernez the carver wants money simply because his sweetheart's father would not allow her to marry a poor man, and for all his hard work he could not earn enough. He wants the money for the sake of his love, not in order to be rich or powerful. When the wizard tells him about the riches he can win, his first thought is to divide the wealth among 'all the people in the world' to make them 'wealthy and happy', and he wants to do this in the name of his love, Rozennik. This may be a simple-minded idea, but there is no trace of self-seeking in it. There is nothing inherently wicked about wanting prosperity, and even modern industry is not a born villain. Power *can* be used for good.

In the event Bernez picks up enough treasure to fill his pockets, and he wins his bride by proving he is now a man of substance. Bernez is, in fact, one of the 'poor in spirit' even when he is no longer impoverished. And this same distinction is the reason why, although 'it is easier for a camel to pass through the eye of a needle than for a rich man to enter the kingdom of God', it is still not 'impossible with God' for such a phenomenon to occur. But it is phenomenal, all the same.

There was no doubt whatever in the minds of the earliest Christian teachers, as in the minds of all Jesus' real followers ever since, that wealth and power are the enemies of the Gospel, and that only exceptionally, and with great difficulty, can a person who has wealth and influence avoid corruption and be 'poor in spirit'. The warnings are fierce, the demand absolute: 'Anyone who wants to save his life will lose it. . . . What, then, will a man gain if he wins the whole world and ruins his life?' (Matthew 16: 25–6). 'Do not store up for yourselves treasure on earth.' 'You cannot be the slave both of God and money.' There is danger even in properly used power: 'Do not rejoice that the spirits submit to you; rejoice rather that your names are written in heaven' (Luke 10: 20). Knowledge can be used for personal power, and is likewise condemned: 'Alas for you lawyers who have taken away the key of knowledge! You have not gone in yourselves, and have prevented others going in who wanted to' (Luke 12: 52), for to keep knowledge for oneself means to refuse to deepen it. New knowledge shows up any inadequacies of the old and weakens the self-esteem and prestige of the learned. But the hoarding of knowledge, like the hoarding of any other wealth, is futile: 'But God said to him, "Fool, this very night the demand will be made for your soul; and this hoard of yours, whose will it be then?"'

Perhaps most insidious of all is the desire to exercise power of an apparently spiritual nature, to which the third letter of John refers in a passage with a very familiar ring to it:

'I have written a note for the members of the church, but Diotrephes, who seems to enjoy being in charge of it, refuses to accept us. So if I come, I shall tell everyone how he has behaved, and about the wicked accusations he has been circulating about us. As if that were not enough, he not only refuses to welcome our brothers, but prevents the other people who would have liked to from doing it, and expels them from the church.'

Western nations have believed (sometimes quite sincerely) that they had a mission to alter the lives of 'backward' nations and make them more 'civilized'. Their growing oppressiveness, suspicion and touchiness are drearily familiar in the history of British, French, American, Spanish (etc. etc.) foreign domination. The friars with the cross and the Inquisition, the G.I.s with schools, medicines, and bombs, are all in the same tradition.

For the wicked (that is, self-seeking) magician is always at enmity with the princess whose wisdom is not directed to her own profit, and who uses magic in the service of the great quest. (As we saw in the last chapter, she easily ends up in prison or worse when the wicked are in power.) John, of all New Testament writers, is most clearly the princess-type, wise, observant, patient and yet forceful. Like the rescuing princess, he is clear-sighted about human motives yet certain of the final triumph of goodness. His quiet but unambiguous condemnation of the power-seeker, as in the passage quoted, has behind it an essentially simple apprehension of true values, but one which is very difficult to put into words. He returns again and again for support to the fleshly fact of Jesus whom 'we have seen with our own eyes, that we have watched, and touched with our hands', who is, also 'the Word, who is Life'. It is this closeness to the actuality of Jesus that makes him sensitive to what is false in a human situation and also able to recognize the enemies of life, the sensual body, the lustful eye, the pride of possessions, which are the means employed by the false magicians and emperors to appeal to their victims and gain power.

This elusive and yet basically important distinction between the use and abuse of human power and human relationship is expressed with great sensitivity and sureness of touch in the words of Charles Williams, whose poet–knight, Taliessin, lives· in and comments on the people and symbols of Arthur's court. Here is another bridge between that fairy-tale world and ours, a disturbing comment on the ease with which what seems a useful and necessary device to ensure the smooth working of man's world can be turned to evil, and become a destroyer. The following poem from *Taliessin through Logres* is concerned with the minting of the first coins in Arthur's kingdom. They are stamped with dragons on one side, and the King's head on the other, and the steward, Kay, welcomes such a convenient way of making trade easier and quicker. But the poet realizes the peril involved when it becomes easier for people to treat *with* other people without

treating them *as* people. Coins are impersonal, money can make
it easier to oppress and abuse people, for selfish ends. So can words.
The lustful and greedy emperor, the rapacious, ruthless wizard,
are given their chance and their great scope so easily:

> They laid the coins before the Council.
> Kay, the King's steward, wise in economics, said:
> 'Good, these cover the years and the miles
> and talk one style's dialects in London and Omsk.
> Traffic can hold now and treasure be held,
> streams are bridged and mountains of ridged space
> tunnelled; gold dances deftly across frontiers.
> The poor have choice of purchase, the rich of rents,
> and events move now in a smoother control
> than the swords of lords or the orisons of nuns.
> Money is the medium of exchange.'

> Taliessin's look darkened; his hand shook
> while he touched the dragons; he said: 'We had a good thought.
> Sir, if you made verse you would doubt symbols.
> I am afraid of the little loosed dragons.
> When the means are autonomous they are deadly; when words
> escape from verse they hurry to rape souls;
> when sensation slips from intellect, expect the tyrant;
> the brood of carriers levels the good they carry.
> We have taught our images to be free; are we glad?
> Are we glad to have brought convenient heresy to Logres?'

The convenient heresy is that whatever can be ours by might,
money or diplomacy is rightly ours, and we can do what we like
with it. The witch and the emperor both operate by this rule,
but there is an implicit awareness that they might have done
otherwise. Witches are created by oppression, at some point
however distant. They might otherwise have been good queens
or goddesses, though by the time they appear in the tales they
are past redemption or they would not be witches. Wicked
emperors and magicians might just as well have been beneficent.
But the convenient heresy is just as convenient when it is believed
by creatures who are incapable of operating by any other rule,

since it defines their nature, as we shall discover in turning to the third type of evil in the fairy-tales.

The fate of the cruel and ruthless emperor or wizard rouses little pity. By the time he is punished he has proved himself too thoroughly evil to leave much scope for compassion. The witch, though entirely evil, is sometimes as much pathetic as wicked. The revenge of the under-dog is naturally much more understandable, though the 'classic' witch becomes so monstrous in her way of wreaking vengeance that her ultimate fate is acceptable. There is one kind of evil agent in the fairy-tales, however, who often seems more ludicrous than wicked, and his pathetic stupidity rouses a kind of chivalrous pity when the inevitable disaster overtakes him. This is the giant, with whom may be classed some kinds of dragon, especially the very large ones, and an occasional giant-type witch or ogress. (There are other dragons who are really witches in disguise, or have a witch or wizard's role, though they are dragons in form, just as there are 'witches' who are too stupid and gullible to fit into the more usual witch-type. There is the usual overlapping and shading off of fairy-tale roles here, between witches and wizards, and magicians or wizards and emperors.)

The giant, or the ogre (his fiercer aspect) is a ferocious dim-wit. He is destined to be defeated by the cunning of the youngest son, and to be deprived of his castle, his riches and his head. One of the best-known ogres is the one who owns the castle on which Puss-in-Boots casts an acquisitive eye. Perrault's Puss, the favourite and elegant wise animal of the nursery, is equipped with no magical power but he has all his wits about him and is a shrewd judge of character, a gift which proves sufficiently powerful for him to get everyone else in the tale exactly where he wants them. The ogre has magical gifts – ogres often have – but is far too conceited and confident of his power to see through Puss's rather transparent trick. So when Puss expresses doubt of his power to change his shape he proceeds to make good his claim by turning himself into a lion, and then into a mouse, whereupon Puss catches and eats him. His fine castle is handed over to the good-natured and biddable youngest son, who marries the princess as a matter of course. The ogre's fate seems very unjust, since he did no harm whatever to either the cat or his master, but this is a 'made up' fairy tale that takes the traditional roles for granted. Everyone knows ogres are there to be killed off.

However, some traditional tales throw more light on the nature of ogres and giants, like the one from Persia about Amin and Ghul. Amin is the usual clever opportunist, and Ghul is the huge, brutal creature who is no match for him. The Ghuls are described as 'demons', but their vast size and crude reactions put Ghuls firmly in the giant class. This particular Ghul is tricked in traditional fashion, among other methods by being challenged to crush a stone and get the liquid out. Amin cracks an egg while the Ghul tries in vain to crack the stone, just as in a parallel tale the Brave Little Tailor squeezes a large round cream cheese until the whey runs out, while the giant fails to get a drop out of a large round stone.

But the Ghul is not just gullible, he is also nasty, and Amin's tactics are partly self-defence, since the giant will not let him go and could easily kill him. In the night the Ghul, worried and angry at Amin's boasted power, plans to kill his bothersome prisoner, but Amin has left his bed and put a sack of rice in his place and the Ghul's huge tree-club falls on that. When the Ghul discovers Amin quite unhurt in the morning he is frightened, and in the end Amin frightens him away altogether. Amin remains in possession of his cave and all the treasure the Ghul had gained by robbing travellers.

Ogres and giants may be so stupid as to be outwitted by any sharp lad on the make, but any sympathy they arouse is accidental and misplaced, for these great creatures are the embodiment of the sort of mindless greed which doesn't even try to rationalize its own brutal desires. It is the final delusion of great power, symbolized by the enormous size of the giants and ogres, that it is invincible and absolute, a part of the unalterable and proper nature of things. The witch, feeling despised, wants to regain power or to get revenge. The evil magician and the emperor want to increase their power, or gain various objects with it, and are ruthless in trying to get what they want. But the giant has power, and takes it as a matter of course. He robs, murders and destroys, not in order to get any special prize, but because that is, or has become, his nature.

The tales of the adventures of Thor, for instance, are among the most lavish of the embroideries on the myths of the Norsemen, and there are many about his battles with the frost giants. Unlike the war to the death with the World Monster who threatens the very life of the world, these are not the great cosmic struggles we usually associate with myth. They are varied, often funny, stories, as reported by Snorri in the *Prose Edda*. The giants are a characterless lot, distinguished as a group merely by their hugeness, and their blind malice and greed. They are out to steal the treasures of the gods, and also to harm mankind. A tenth-century poem by Thorbjorn Disarskald gives a long list of Thor's unpleasant opponents, and how he overcame them. It shows the giants as by nature destructive and very powerful. Whether or not they attack, they need to be destroyed if human life is to prosper. Of the same kind are the monster Grendel and his even more terrible mother in *Beowulf*. They raid the wonderful new Hall at Heorot and tear the bravest warriors limb from limb. The poem tells how the king's minstrel sang in the Hall of the creation of the world, of light and order and beauty on earth, and the breathing of life into every species. It was this song that maddened the listening monster and drove him to fearful rage. It is Grendel's nature to grab and destroy, to hate beauty and flee the light.

A more recent relation of Grendel's is Captain Hook. He is made less terrifying because his creator did not really believe in him, but he is still recognizably of the race of ogres, even if on the wrong side of the blanket. Though he is strong on good form his nature is totally pirate. He lives to plunder and murder, without needing further reason except the added incentive of a desire for revenge on the insufferable cockiness of Peter. His ogre-ish proportions are not physical, but psychological; all his evil qualities are larger than life. The happiness and peace of the Lost Boys' ménage under Wendy's care infuriate him even more, and encourage what Barrie whimsically calls his 'fell genius'. Peter Pan is in many ways a revolting book, but Barrie's effective use of fairy-tale structure underlines yet again the fundamental truth of the ancient symbols. They work even when they are sentimentalized and weighted with coy adult innuendo at the expense of the children at whom the book is ostensibly directed.

Not all ogres are as horrible as Grendel or as vindictive as Hook, and some giants seem too stupid to do much harm at all, but these huge creatures are all 'against' man. In some stories the point of them has been lost and they have become merely funny, but the ridiculous quality which makes then 'fair game' stems from the fact that though they have a human kind of shape they are somehow 'monstrosities', useless and greedy parasites on the human race. The tricked and beheaded giant is not an object of real compassion. He is merely revolting.

It ought to be odd that our generation should find giants and ogres more funny than frightening, but then the neighbours of ogres in the tales do become accustomed to their presence, and to keeping them quiet with bribes of human sacrifice. 'Fee, fi, fo, fum! I smell the blood of an Englishman!' says the most famous ogre of all, and the pantomime-watchers giggle a little nervously; only the very youngest are afraid. But if an Englishman is a decent, unsuspicious, reasonably selfish and comfortably optimistic chap, then he is certainly the type the ogre feeds on. He is probably also the father (and mother, aunt, uncle and grandparents) of all the audience of innocents who enjoy the delicious horrors of Jack-and-the-Beanstalk's tame ogre. For there have never been so many ogres and giants (not to mention dragons and monsters) around as there are nowadays.

Their nature is well drawn in the description of the peculiarly nasty ogress who features in that curious mixture of vision, political subversion and social criticism which we call the 'Book of Revelation'. She is closely related to the fairy-tale ogres, monsters and boorish giants. She 'glittered with gold and jewels and pearls', which were the treasures she had accumulated by seducing 'all the kings of the earth', and 'she was drunk with the blood of the Saints'. The author was referring to the great, corrupt city of Rome as the 'famous prostitute' but he might just as well be referring to General Motors, the Supreme Soviet, I.C.I., the Bunny Clubs, the Home Office, the Pentagon or, to be thoroughly traditional, the old-style Vatican. All of these 'ogres' may include in their population many good and even heroic people, as well as many gullible or indifferent ones, and probably very, very few who are downright evil. Yet the body as a whole is clearly anti-human.

The inhuman, mindless and amoral greed for power of huge organizations is one of the most frightening aspects of modern life (for although these giants are not a new race there has been a population explosion among the giants, too). It is frightening not because human wickedness on a large scale is a modern phenomenon but because of the gradual corruption of our thinking which allows us to accept their self-proposed goals as of absolute value. This acceptance naturally makes it easier for their members to feel free of all guilt. We have reached a point where, for instance, it has required all the pressure of local indignation, parliamentary eloquence and painfully aroused (and still muted) public indignation to persuade the British Government that there just might be a case for not destroying some of England's most lovely villages and countryside in order to build yet another huge airport in the interests of more trade, more tourism, more prestige —in fact, more money.

This battle is unlikely to be the last. The ogres and ogresses who live on the blood of Englishmen seem to have suffered only a pantomime death. They are still feasting, and the supply of blood seems unlikely to run out for a while at least, since the victims flock so willingly towards the giants' various castles, which are by no means all English.

In our children's books and in the tales of many lands the ways of evil have been displayed for us in the clearest possible manner if only we had eyes to see. As the Gospel describes and defines it, evil is many-headed; all the heads are human heads, but somehow drained inwardly of humanness so that, in their veins, a fine secretion of evil can flow and work. The malice of the weak whose desire is for vengeance, the greed and cruelty of the powerful (in knowledge or political or financial rule), the blind, insatiable appetite of the corporate ogres, all these are not only against us as enemies but are within us as traitors. In so far as we are weak we dream of a reversal of the *status quo* which would give us power to inflict, or at least witness, suffering in those who are now 'on top'. In so far as we have power we want to keep it and feel we are right to do so—parental power, class power, power of money or intelligence. This power is ours, and we have the right to it, to increase it, and to defend it by any available means. And as for the ogres, we live on their estates and therefore by their laws. We sacrifice our children to their appetite for 'qualified' servants and meekly pay them whatever tribute of honour, beauty or justice they demand.

It is easy to recognize the end of wicked witches and cruel emperors and greedy ogres. If we can also recognize the way the Gospel teaching is aware of them we can begin to recognize their presence in and around us. That is the first step. Until we see them for what they are we are helpless before their spells. These spells have worked their way into every aspect of our lives, and if their power is to be broken only very drastic remedies will do. The remedy has already been pointed out to us in the Gospel commandment which I quoted as the spell against witches, for this is our only protection against the spirits of wickedness in high places, whatever form they take.

Dietrich Bonhoeffer was faced with a particularly blatant manifestation of evil, for the Nazi phenomenon combined most horribly the witch's revenge for past humiliation, the emperor's arrogation of divine power and wisdom, and the idiot giant's simple lust for blood. Looking at all this, the Lutheran pastor knew that there was only one possible way for a follower of Jesus to react, and that was by utter obedience to the Lord's commands. He knew what was needed if true fellowship was to continue, and carry on the message. In 1937 he wrote in *The Cost of Discipleship*:

'When a Christian meets with injustice he no longer clings to his rights and defends them at all costs. He is absolutely free from possessions and bound to Christ alone. Again, his witness to this exclusive adherence to Jesus creates the only workable basis for fellowship, and leaves the aggressor for him to deal with. The only way to overcome evil is to let it run itself to a standstill because it does not find the resistance it is looking for. Resistance merely creates further evil and adds fuel to the flames. But when evil meets no opposition and encounters no obstacle, but only patient endurance, its sting is drawn, and at last it meets an opponent which is more than its match. Of course, this can only happen when the last ounce of resistance is abandoned, and the renunciation of revenge is complete. Then evil cannot find its mark, it can breed no further evil, and is left barren.'

We are reminded of the tales in which the wicked witch or ruler ordains his or her own punishment, not knowing that the fate they are suggesting is to be their own, for they do not recognize themselves as the criminal. Often, too, the giant is killed by walking into his own trap. This happens to the ogre in the Puss-in-Boots story; his power is his undoing. But it is easy to think about opposing evil when it is in a fairy-tale, or a history book. Bonhoeffer is not talking about a distant, symbolic evil that some heroic martyr–champion must overcome. We are all to be witnesses, martyrs of Jesus, and that does not mean letting the witches and ogres assume that their values are the proper ones:

'We are concerned not with evil in the abstract, but with the evil *person*. Jesus bluntly calls the evil person evil. If I am assailed, I am not to condone or justify aggression. *Patient endurance of evil does not mean recognition of its rights*. That is sheer sentimentality [the wizened little witches and pathetically stupid giants always try to make us feel sentimental towards them] and Jesus will have nothing to do with it. The shameful assault, the act of exploitation and the deed of violence [the deeds of the witch, the emperor, and the ogre, in order of appearance] are still evil.' (My italics, since that point is basic.)

What do we do about it? What does obedience require? It requires that we not only suffer evil without retaliation, but that we *love* our enemies. The command is so well known that we scarcely realize the enormity of it. To the first disciples it seemed fantastic. And they could not (nor can we) remove 'the enemy' into a conveniently distant area where he could be 'loved' without their actually *doing* anything about it. 'The enemy was no mere abstraction for the disciples', Bonhoeffer points out, and goes on to indicate how immediate 'he' was to them, and likewise is to us. 'They came across him every day. There were those who cursed them for undermining the faith and transgressing the law. There were those who hated them for leaving all they had for Jesus' sake.' If we are not hated, perhaps we have not left all? 'There were those who persecuted them as prospective dangerous revolutionaries and sought to destroy them. Some of their enemies were numbered among the champions of popular religion, who resented the exclusive claim of Jesus.' They still do, even while claiming to serve him. 'And then there was the enemy which would immediately occur to every Jew, the political enemy in Rome.' For Rome, read also Whitehall, Washington, the Kremlin, Stormont, etc. 'Over and above all these, the disciples also had to contend with the hostility which invariably falls to the lot of those who refuse to follow the crowd, and which brought them daily mockery, derision and threats. These are not the daily lot of most of us. If not, why not? Whose disciples are we?

It is these enemies whom Jesus bids his disciples love. Evidently they have first to be recognized as enemies, and this recognition will so change our attitude to them that they will recognize *us* as *their* implacable enemy. Hence the persecution. As long as we remain under their spell and so see things their way, they are not enemies, we are harmless and safe. The command to love our enemies only becomes real when we – and they – have realized that enmity utter and absolute exists between us. It involves a total upsetting and rearranging of priorities. 'To the natural man [the one who lives under the spell and knows no better] the very notion of loving his enemies is an intolerable offence and quite beyond his capacity; it cuts right across his ideas of good and evil.' It does this because to this bewitched creature 'enemies' are people I hate, envy, resent, fear or want to devour . . . the moral code of the witch and her allies. To love these is simply nonsense. But the enemy of the Christian is the one who hates *him*, and does so simply and solely because he is the disciple of Jesus, and therefore an offence and a scandal.

'We are to serve our enemy in all things without hypocrisy and with utter sincerity. No sacrifice which a lover would make for his beloved is too great for us to make for our enemy. . . . We are not to imagine that this is to condone the evil; such a love proceeds from strength rather than weakness, from truth rather than from fear, and therefore it cannot be guilty of the hatred of another. And who is to be the object of such a love, if not those whose hearts are stifled with hatred?'

So the answer of Jesus to the problem of evil, actual, daily evil, in ourselves and in our neighbours, social and political evil in all its forms, is twofold. First, it must be recognized for what it is, and its real nature proclaimed, whatever disguises it may assume, and whatever favourable terms may be offered in return for convenient silence. But open recognition and denunciation lead to open war, and in this war the only proper Christian weapon is the sword of the spirit—that is, love. And love, in the face of the enemy, means persecution. 'The cross is the differential of the

Christian religion,' says Bonhoeffer, 'the power which enables the Christian to transcend the world and win the victory.' Bonhoeffer knew what that meant and carried it through to its end in his own death as a martyr. This love of enemies is not 'natural', it is peculiar and extraordinary, it is 'the light which shines before men', and by which they glorify the Father which is in heaven. And it is scandalous, not only to open enemies of Christ but to those who only want to be left alone. Yet these are the unwitting servants of the evil powers, and if they are saved it will be because of the ones who recognized the enemy and stood against him in perfect love. Even the perfect lover, however, until he is perfected in martyrdom, must live among men, with men. The enemy is without, but he is also within, and we are in constant danger of being betrayed by him. What is the necessarily 'worldly' Christian to do?

A balanced yet uncompromising Christian verdict on the evils that arise from the abuse of power, in whatever way, is expressed in *Taliessin through Logres*, quoted earlier. Here, the Archbishop looks further than the abuses of money, wealth and the rape of souls, the mindless tyranny, the judgement of everything by financial standards—

(*Q*. How much is a Velasquez portrait worth?

A. What an art dealer will pay to stop another art dealer getting it.)

He looks to the Gospel answer to all the misery and hate, and defines the way of life which belongs to the Holy City though it subsists in the City of this world. We have to live with the mechanisms of money and power and possession, to some extent, because total renunciation is possible only in death. Can we love *this* enemy, without surrendering to him? The Gospel answer in the curious parable of the unjust steward is 'yes', and Williams gives it a deeply satisfying gloss:

> The Archbishop answered the Lords; his words went
> up through a slope of calm air:
> 'Might may take symbols and folly make treasure,
> and greed bid God, who hides himself for man's pleasure
> by occasion, hide himself essentially. This abides—

that the everlasting house the soul discovers
is always another's: we must lose our own ends:
we must always live in the habitation of our lovers,
my friend's shelter for me, mine for him.
This is the way of this world in the day of that other's;
make yourselves friends by means of the riches of iniquity,
for the wealth of the self is the health of the self exchanged.
What saith Heracleitus?—and what is the City's breath?—
dying each other's life, living each other's death.
Money is a medium of exchange.

He that loses his life shall save it. Whatever you did to the least of my brethren you did to me. Thou shalt love they neighbour as thyself. And so on. This is the City's breath, the life of the Kingdom which is not of this world, and which overcomes the powers of evil, whether they are found in the arrogance of nations, the ruthlessness of big business, the cruel lunacy of humiliated sects, the rigid self-conceit of established churches, the malice of the envious poor or the bland brutality of accustomed wealth. Without or within, the enemy is to be overcome by that final unbearable scandal of a love that refuses to hate. Even money is a medium of that exchange. But beware of inflation.

Chapter 5

The Quest

'A great dread fell on him, as if he was awaiting the pronounce-
ment of some doom that he had long foreseen and vainly hoped
might after all never be spoken. An overwhelming longing to
rest and remain at peace by Bilbo's side in Rivendell filled all
his heart. At last with an effort he spoke and wondered to hear
his own words, as if some other will was using his small voice.
   "I will take the Ring," he said, "though I do not know the
way." '

In these words Tolkien tells how the easy-going Hobbit Frodo,
who has such unexpected reserves of courage and honesty,
finally undertakes a mission which he does not want and feels
quite inadequate to accomplish.

The fantastic popularity of Tolkien's curious fairy-tale is one of
the oddest symptoms of the spiritual condition of Western culture.
When it was published it was expected to appeal to a reasonable
number of intellectuals with a taste for fantasy. It now sells some
100,000 copies a year, and a whole Tolkien sub-culture has grown
up around it. It enthralled American campuses and became a
kind of Book of Revelation for the anti-materialist tendency of the
young. Students at peace rallies or sit-ins wore buttons proclaiming
'Frodo lives!', and the official American paperback edition of the
trilogy carried a testimonial from the author to the fact that this
was the only authorized one, for the vast popularity of the book
had led to the publication of a pirated edition from mush-
room publishers hoping to make some quick money. They must
have made quite a bit.

Professor Tolkien has persistently disclaimed any specific
allegorical intention in his tale, and indeed it is clearly not an
allegory in the proper sense. On the other hand there is an
allegorical, or more precisely a parable element in all great
literature, and in fairy-tales in particular, for the roles and events

have an application greater than their place in the unfolding of the particular story. It is because we are challenged in the heart of our contemporary experience, personal or cultural, that books about remote periods or places can be so important to us that they achieve the status of the 'classic'. There may be no more workhouses in England, but the plight of Oliver Twist stabs at the conscience of a society that still tries to deal with misery by hiding it away under a pile of statistics. Anna Karenina lived a life utterly removed in style from ours, but her tragedy is a perennial one and raises fundamental questions about the nature of marriage, of loyalty, and of love. There may be no hideously bewitched Beast stalking Wimbledon Common to waylay the commuting City merchant and demand his pretty daughter, but the plight of a person or group whom a society has cast for the role of Beast can still only be relieved by the love of someone who can see further than the persona imposed by the evil spells of guilt and fear.

Frodo, Tolkien's hero, belongs to the race of small, hairy-footed, cheerful people called Hobbits, who 'love peace and quiet and good tilled earth', are fond of simple jests and of six meals a day, and are also 'hospitable and delighted in parties and in presents'. It is this peace- and pleasure-loving Hobbit who sets out on a quest he has not asked for, suffers hardship and horror and very nearly dies, because he realizes that this is his job. Frodo is every human being who likes to enjoy life and does not want power or responsibility, but who knows, somehow, that more is demanded of him. He realizes that to cling to the good and innocent things is to see them grow corrupt and die, that he who saves his life will lose it, and he who loses it will save it. For a whole angry and bewildered generation, Frodo is an assertion that goodness, honesty and love will survive all the efforts of the witches and emperors and ogres to destroy them. He is a sign that the gentle and meek are the real victors, if only they will set out on their quest in faith and hope—however faint.

For a generation that had lost touch with the old fairy-tales, except as Disney-fodder and bedtime stories for children, *The Lord of the Rings* built a bridge. This bridge was not a way of escape, if (as Tolkien himself pointed out in his essay on fairy-tales) escape is regarded as a flight from a necessary battle. It was an escape in the sense of gaining freedom from unjust imprison-

ment. The bridge Tolkien built has one end in the City of this
World. It is never mentioned by Tolkien but its existence is
implicit in the need to write such a book and in its enormous
appeal. This City is what we have made of our heritage of civilization, of natural and man-made beauty, and the spiritual kind too.
Tolkien's story is happily only one of the bridges that lead out of
it, for this City is the reason for the peril, spiritual and physical,
in which mankind now finds itself.

This City is a Technocracy. In it, fantasy and vision are
offences punishable under the Suppression of Lunacy Acts,
though children under ten and the very old are allowed to disport
themselves in special enclosures marked 'Religion', 'Art', and
'Nature', in which appropriately trained keepers are employed to
see that these legally tolerated pastimes do not overflow their
boundaries and constitute a nuisance to the real Concerns of
Society. (In these enclosures such interesting survivals as poets,
saints and farmers may be observed in their natural surroundings,
carefully guarded, of course, for the sake of public safety.) But
the other end of the bridge is in fairyland, which is the place where
durable human wisdom lives and can be rediscovered in each
generation. Here the real values that men need in order to work
out their salvation can be clearly seen, not simply in the form of
precept and principles but as living people, acting and interacting in the pattern of redemption which they freely create.

When Tolkien's bridge was opened there were strong protests
from people who regarded a journey to fairyland as a childish
waste of valuable time, which is needed to work at the pressing
concerns of the City of this World. (They had already opposed
the opening of several other bridges, often successfully.) Some
felt even more strongly and were afraid that people who crossed
it might never come back, or might come back bewitched, and
unable to concentrate on the real business of living. The protests
were useless, and attempts to classify the entrance to the bridge
as a Special Enclosure for children and the Psychologically Unfit
were also frustrated. This was because it soon became apparent
that so many apparently Fit Citizens were taking surreptitious
trips across the bridge that to reclassify them under the Suppression of Lunacy Acts (which would mean depriving them of
political power or responsibility) would lead to the total collapse
of the State.

If Frodo hadn't existed it would have been necessary to invent him. Somebody did, thereby proving that he does in fact exist, for, as the buttons proclaim, 'Frodo lives' in the human spirit and refuses to die. And by existing he proves that the fairy-tales are about basic realities which matter to people in the nuclear age, people plagued by problems of population control, of advancing pollution of earth, air and water, and the abiding terror of a war that would indeed end war, by ending the human race. It is just because people now, especially young people who are confronted with all this mess as their future, are acutely aware of the contemporary predicament, that they are sensitive to the hope contained in the fairy-tale account of what life is all about. And what it is about is a quest.

The Gospel is also about a quest. The language of Jesus constantly makes use of words that express the goal of human living in terms of a journey which is a quest. Disciples of Jesus are told to travel light, both physically and spiritually. 'Provide yourselves with no gold or silver, not even a few coppers for your purses, with no haversack for the journey or spare tunic or footwear or a staff' (Matthew 10: 9–10). 'Do not store up treasure on earth', or gather goods into barns, for 'it is a narrow gate and a hard road that leads to life', and those who are burdened with this world's goods and anxieties cannot travel that way. 'Many will come from the east and west to take their places with Abraham and Isaac and Jacob' at the feast, and these patriarchs are those who went on God's quest (Matthew 8: 11).

The repeated pastoral metaphor shows the shepherd leading his flock to the pasture, and the hard commandment of sacrifice bids the disciple take up his cross and *follow* his Master to death and beyond. In the parable the merchant *searches* widely for fine pearls, until he finds the perfect pearl 'of great value'. The prodigal, who had looked for happiness in a far country, failed to find it because his quest was purely for selfish pleasure. Repentant, he must travel back to his father. Jesus' great example of brotherly love is set on a journey, during which the Samaritan shows compassion for his fellow traveller who has fallen among thieves.

Those who want to be disciples of Jesus are told that they are setting out on a quest that allows no compromises. The rich young man must 'sell all' and then 'follow'. The guests who are called to the wedding feast must leave all normal business and come. The would-be disciple is warned that the Son of Man has no settled home, 'nowhere to lay his head'. Another who wants to wait until his father dies is told that his first duty is 'to go and spread the news of the kingdom of God', for 'no one who looks back is fit for the kingdom of God'. But the end of the quest is certain: 'Search and you will find, knock, and the door will be opened to you.'

A new idea or word recently discovered has a way of turning up all over the place. Once attention has been drawn to a new concept it leaps to the eye where before it remained unnoticed. So it is with the idea of the quest as a Gospel theme. Once the realization of this more-than-metaphor has dawned it leaps from the pages of Scripture. For St Luke it was more than a theme, it was the actual structure of his book, for the greater part of his account of Jesus is shaped around the symbolic journey to Jerusalem. It is towards this goal that Jesus' thoughts and actions are directed, for at Jerusalem he will find what he has been sent to find—death and the world's salvation. If the followers of Jesus must set out on a journey it is because they are his fellow travellers, and all are going to the same place. But this place is reached only through hardship and humiliation and death.

The words of Scripture are so familiar to most Christians that they don't convey any very startling message. The nature of what Jesus asks of his followers is illuminated by Tolkien's story, which is a fairy-tale for grown-ups linked closely both to the traditional myth themes and also to the Gospel account of what people are for. The link is not conscious or deliberate. If the book were an allegory it would have no value as a real link. It is a fairy-tale, a more self-conscious one than some of the fables that have been worked over and decorated and polished by generations of tellers, but still a real fairy-tale. It belongs to that genre not only in intention but in themes and images and roles, in mood, shape and limitations. This is why Frodo's quest can illuminate the Christian quest as a deliberately shaped allegory could not. Bunyan in *The Pilgrim's Progress*, Dante in his *Divina Commedia* or Spenser in *The Faerie Queene* pick their images purposely in order to illuminate a predetermined doctrine about the nature of the Christian quest. This approach is tremendously effective, but it does not bring the kind of deep-down illumination that comes from the fairy-tale which, *of its nature*, without any twisting, writes itself into a comment on the Gospel understanding of man's journey (a fact which is the basis of this study of fairy-tales and the Gospel).

Tolkien's tale is valuable here because it has such a nature, the nature of the true fairy-tale. He writes out of a consciously Christian cultural background, so his tale naturally reveals the relationship of the traditional forms to the Gospel more clearly than most. But the relationship is not created by the author, it simply exists because that is the nature of fairy-tales. One of Tolkien's many adverse critics, Mark Roberts, expressed a familiar objection to its 'relevance' to human life when he said that the story 'does not issue from an understanding of reality which is not to be denied; it is not moulded by some controlling vision of things which is at the same time its *raison d'être*'. Such an objection highlights very precisely the nature of the service which Tolkien is rendering to this generation. We are divorced from the relationship to the human truth of ourselves from which fairy-tales were born and in which they were acceptable, to such an extent that many intelligent people cannot see what is the nature of the 'controlling vision' which moulded *The Lord of the Rings*. The fairy-tale 'understanding of reality' is consistent and recognizable, though elusive. It only works when it is taken seriously, which is why some of the eighteenth- and nineteenth-century fairy-tales (the *Cabinet des Fées*, and Andrew Lang's own efforts at writing rather than collecting them, for instance) do not always ring true, though the themes and roles are traditional. Tolkien took it seriously, though he injected into it some extra ideas of his own, some of which are good and important on their own merits, some of which sound a jarring note. But if this 'understanding of reality' is taken seriously it 'is not be be denied', and it is indeed the *raison d'être* of the book, but in a more fundamental sense that the normal novelist's vision, which is personal, and important *because* it is personal. The personal, idiosyncratic vision can suddenly illuminate attitudes that a society has taken for granted: Lawrence showed up the sexual hypocrisy of his generation, and Dickens the sanctimonious cruelty of his. But the fairy-tale vision is beyond the control of a single writer. He cannot create it, he can only become sensitized to it, to the point where he is able to use the form with a kind of 'instinctive' rightness in the telling of a story. But the nature of the story is to a great extent dictated by the vision itself, though there is room for sub-intentions and the author's own themes. One shudders to think what kind of 'controlling vision' might have moulded a novel of Tolkien's writing; it would probably have been full of rationalized and romanticized class-consciousness and sex-prejudice, and a warrior mystique worse than those which make C. S. Lewis's children's tales at moments so repulsive.

Luckily Tolkien did not write a novel, but 'luckily' is the wrong word. He is not a novelist, but an inspired story-teller soaked in the modes and insights and background of the medieval fairy-tales. His theme is the quest, the most persistent and clearly shaped of all fairy-tale themes. The story comes through to grown-up people now because no one can mistake it for a nursery tale; yet the older tales themselves bear witness that this is the real thing. And because fairy-tales are about the reality of human desires and needs, it is a Christian theme—man's quest for salvation as Christ shows up its sharp demands. Frodo's quest is the Christian quest, it is the quest of Jesus himself. It follows the traditional way from the time of 'conversion' and calling to the moment of martyrdom and the achievement of peace. It is the path that has been traced by all the great mystics, and which is symbolically verified in so many other fairy-tales.

So the quest begins with only a half-awareness. Frodo is the ordinary person of goodwill, content with his life and not anxious to change, yet sufficiently sensitive to be aware of a need for sacrifice when the message comes to him. It seems to be only a limited demand. It will require leaving loved and familiar ways, undertaking a hard journey, but it is one Frodo can face with reasonable confidence. He simply has to take the magic Ring to the house of Elrond at Rivendell, 'the last homely home', and there any further decision and action will no doubt be taken by wiser and more experienced and worthy people. When he learns of the nature and danger of the Ring from the wizard Gandalf, Frodo tells him: 'I hope it may find some other better keeper soon. But in the meanwhile it seems to me that I am a danger, a danger to all that live near me. I cannot keep the Ring and stay here. I ought to leave Bag End, leave the Shire, leave everything and go away . . . but I feel very small, and very uprooted, and well—desperate. The Enemy is so strong and terrible.'

This is a good expression of consciousness of the need for sacrifice in Christ's service, and the separation it involves from many beloved and lovely things. But it is Frodo's own idea, and although he is afraid he is reasonably clear about the nature and limits of what he should do, and of his ability to do it.

This is the position of many good Christians. They want to follow Christ, they learn to give and to love, to sacrifice their own wishes and to serve cheerfully and without self-pity. They really are the salt of the earth. But they don't, at least for a time, see any need to go further. What they do is hard but clearly worthwhile. They recognize their weakness and their constant need of support from others with the same ideals (as Frodo is immensely cheered when he finds that his friends have discovered his plan and intend to accompany him), from God in prayer, and from both in the Eucharist; but they are quietly confident that they are able to live in this way, as the Gospel demands.

They may not always be successful but they can keep trying, and avoid discouragement. Suffering and humiliation there may be but it is not intolerable. So Cinderella remains cheerful and willing in spite of the petty bullying of her step-sisters. The youngest son is content for a while to be kind and helpful and loving, to meet teasing with good humour and patience and carry out his ordinary duties. Frodo travels to Rivendell through many ordeals and hardships, but he has old friends around him, happy interludes of comfort and cheer, and new friends to help him. He is never without hope and he doesn't carry the final responsibility. That is for greater folk. Like every youngest son, he expects his 'elder brothers' to be the ones who will carry out the really difficult mission. Such undertakings are not for the likes of him.

This is real Christian commitment, the basis of all discipleship, but it is only the basis. People who live this way lay themselves open to the Spirit and are able to be aware of his more radical demands when they are made.

To feel contempt for those who have not yet heard this further call of the Spirit is a far greater sin than the failures that grow from the weakness and comparatively uneducated conscience of the beginner. God is more realistic (which means more compassionate) than some of his servants, especially the enthusiastic ones. He makes the greater demand when people are ready for it, and how long the preparation may take is something only he can tell. For many people the final journey may begin on the threshold of death itself, for which their life has been a quiet an unassuming preparation. It is the quality of the response that matters, not the moment at which it is made. Jesus himself spent about twenty years of his adult life repairing people's houses and furniture, and at the end of that time he clearly had not made much impression on his neighbours, who regarded him as a nice helpful lad but could not see him as a Teacher, let alone a prophet. The great St Teresa was middle-aged before she was finally called out of the plain to climb the steeper slopes of the mountain of Carmel. Some great Christians seem to have set out for Jerusalem almost as soon as they could walk, but just as great a number needed what might be called a spiritual incubation period. A great achievement often requires a long period of preparation, but also there may be obstacles of temperament and situation which only a long time can overcome, and until that time is over the person is not ready to 'leave all things'.

It is easy to dismiss these 'incubating' disciples as lukewarm. When disciples have taken the next drastic step, but have not yet gone far on the further journey, there is a great temptation to be impatient and dismissive with the state one has left behind. One of the ways in which people just discovering Christ try to further their discovery is, for instance, the development of unusual and 'experimental' liturgies in which they explore the meaning of worship and try to understand better what Jesus is saying to them in their own immediate situation. The 'underground' liturgies and groups are part of a process of self-education for what Paul called 'babes in Christ'. The point of these is not their newness or 'relevance' but the fact that this is a 'natural' way for people new in Christ's service to find refreshment on their journey. There are occasions on which eccentric forms of worship and life are merely expressions of spiritual naivety or self-indulgence and they usually fade out quickly, but at their best these experimental liturgies and 'life-styles' draw on the real experience of the worshippers, and feed their enthusiasm, their comradeship, their pleasure in basic human exchanges and in the kind of basic human ritual which is as old as the mountains and as intimate as one's own skin.

This sort of thing develops real humanness and helps to prepare

Christians to respond to a call which will lead finally to the destruction of this humanness in order to release the fruit of transformed and completed humanity in the risen life. Such a liturgical experience is a transient part, but a proper part, of the early stages of the quest. It is strictly for 'babes' but none the less important, for these are 'babes in Christ', and they need the right nursery care if they are to be his pilgrims later. The immediacy of the experience, which is what people get enthusiastic about, is important at this stage. It is only when people cling to the satisfaction of the sense of fellowship, of exaltation, of 'relevance', and so on, that it ceases to be a necessary help on the journey and becomes an escape from commitment.

So, on the journey to Rivendell, Frodo and his friends are rescued from the evil power of the trees, the reign of the great dark forest which threatens to tangle and trap them. They have become drowsy with the magic of the place, and almost over-powered, when Tom Bombadil, the 'Master' of all natural things, saves them and takes them to his home. Here he and the Lady Goldberry (who is a mixture of earth-mother, fairy princess and Mrs Sowerby in *The Secret Garden*) offer them hospitality, which includes a meal whose Eucharistic symbolism is clear. The Scriptural echoes in the description of the food are unmistakable, and so is the ritual nature of the gestures used. But it is a 'natural' Eucharist, if I may use a contradictory phrase. It has the earth-born joy and warmth and comfort of an archetypal shared meal which can be (but has not yet been) formed into the sacrifice-meal of a Christian fellowship which is much more than a sort of sanctified camaraderie. As such it is right for these people at this stage.

The theological cliché that 'grace builds on nature' is not less true for being used too easily and thoughtlessly. Here, in Frodo's journey, and in the journey of all the people of many faiths who set out on the quest for salvation, is the necessary experience of the richness of 'nature', inexhaustibly beautiful and satisfying, and filled with a promise towards whose fulfilment it leads:

'A door opened and in came Tom Bombadil. He had now no hat and his thick brown hair was crowned with autumn leaves. He laughed, and going to Goldberry, took her hand. "Here's my pretty lady," he said, bowing to the hobbits. "Here's my

Goldberry clothed all in silver-green with flowers in her girdle. Is the table laden? I see yellow cream and honeycomb, and white bread and butter; milk, cheese and green herbs and ripe berries gathered. Is that enough for us? Is the supper ready?" '

The guests are then led away to prepare for the meal by washing.

'Before long, washed and refreshed, the hobbits were seated at the table, two on each side, while at either end sat Goldberry and the Master. It was a long and merry meal. Though the hobbits ate, as only famished hobbits can eat, there was no lack. The drink in their drinking bowls seemed to be clear cold water, yet it went to their heads like wine and set free their voices. The guests became suddenly aware that they were singing merrily, as if it were easier and more natural than talking.

At last Tom and Goldberry rose and cleared the table swiftly. The guests were commanded to sit quiet, and were sat in chairs, each with a footstool to his tired feet. There was a fire in the wide hearth before them, and it was burning with a sweet smell, as if it were built of apple wood. When everything was set in order, all the lights in the room were put out, except one lamp and a pair of candles at each end of the chimney shelf. Then Goldberry came and stood before them, holding a candle; and she wished them each a good night and deep sleep.

"Have peace now," she said, "until the morning." '

This is the end of the night office, the liturgical dismissal and the blessing. The appeal of the whole scene is mythic as well as homely, it draws on the nostalgia for childhood and home, but it points onwards; this is a meal and a rest for travellers. The associations with the stories of the Grail, the Water of Life, and various magic feasts assist the atmosphere. These are inexperienced and uncertain travellers, and they deeply need this refreshment of spirit.

Here is the real spring of the need so many have (and not just the young) for a liturgical experience less stark, less steeped in ages of hard theological experience, less dense in its complexity of many-levelled messages, than the traditional forms, or even the newer versions of them. The immediacy and availability of the 'new' liturgies can never be a substitute for the distilled peace of forms that have passed through the minds and hands of generations of disciples. They have changed and grown and shed, but kept a central 'hardness' which is the measure of the incommunicability of the deepest Christian experience. But the clumsy gestures of spiritual childhood are, nevertheless, the essential prelude to the assured movement of the one who lives with Christ. The apparently effortless grace of the ballerina grows from the sweat and effort of the adolescent student with dreams and wobbly ankles. But very great artists must be always learning, and to forget that is to fail as an artist. It is easy to despise one's own past in the persons of others.

In *The Lord of the Rings*, Boromir, that 'valiant man' whose courage is beyond doubt, cannot quite believe that people who do not share his single-minded devotion to his City can be worthy of his respect. He secretly begrudges the 'halfling' Frodo the Ring of Power which has been entrusted to him, and is confident that he, a mature warrior of undoubted honour, could carry out the mission as it should be carried out—which means the way *he* thinks it should be carried out. He is typical of the kind of valiant fighter for Christ who will sacrifice everything, but only on his own terms. He cannot help despising those who doubt their own wisdom or are simply not sure where (or even if) God wants them. 'These elves and half-elves and wizards, they would come to grief perhaps. Yet often I doubt if they are wise and not merely timid. . . . The fearless, the ruthless, these alone will achieve victory. What could not a warrior do in this hour, a great leader?' At the point in the story from which these words come, Boromir is already being corrupted by desire for the Ring. His real nature is chivalrous and generous, but it is because he relies on his own honour and courage that he can be corrupted.

The fear of the Lord is the beginning of wisdom. It is not Boromir on whom the mission of Ring-bearer is laid, because *he wants it*, and knows exactly what to do with it. The difference between what some mystics have called the 'first' and 'second' conversions is that the first one, however real and crucial, is a decision taken by oneself under God, whereas the second is a demand made by God to which the disciple responds in blind faith. Self-confidence here is not only misplaced but dangerous, for what is asked is impossible to human nature except that 'with God nothing is impossible'. It is because Frodo is the 'youngest son', obedient and unassuming, without pride as he is without self-interest, that he is chosen to be the Ring-bearer rather than Boromir, the seasoned warrior, or Aragorn, the king in disguise, or the wise and far-seeing Gandalf. 'I thank thee, Father, because thou hast hidden these things from the wise and prudent, and hast revealed them to little ones.' 'For God's foolishness is wiser than human wisdom, and God's weakness is stronger than human strength.'

So the great journey gets under way, and 'human' wisdom suggests crossing over the mountains which must be passed, difficult though this may be. But when the opposition of the enemy defeats the attempt on the mountain pass the Company of the Ring are obliged to go back and try to cross under the mountains, through the terrible dark of the Mines of Moria. And here they undergo the first of those periods of darkness which all the mystics have described. It is necessary to undergo this, it is part of the cleansing of the pilgrim from remaining self-interest or self-confidence and it often comes as the result of the failure of what seemed a right and admirable project. It is necessary to learn that what is undertaken in obedience to Christ is his work. As Bonhoeffer says:

'Obedience to the call of Jesus never lies within our own power. If, for instance, we give away all our possessions, that act is not in itself the obedience he demands. In fact such a step might be the precise opposite of obedience to Jesus, for we might be choosing a way of life for ourselves—some Christian ideal, or some ideal of Franciscan poverty. Indeed in the very act of giving away his goods a man can give allegiance to himself and to an ideal and not to the command of Jesus. He is not set free from his own self but still more enslaved to himself. The step into the situation where faith is possible is not an offer which we can make to Jesus, but always his gracious offer to us.'

This is the point of the darkness into which the traveller must go as he proceeds on his quest. It is not an arbitrary event, it is the psychological consequence of discovering that one's best efforts and resources are not enough. Such a reversal of all our normal standards of judgement (in a culture where self-help, independence and determination to succeed are primary virtues) is bound to produce drastic effects, and it does. It may lead to the classic 'dark night of the senses', especially in prayer, or to a pervasive sense of discouragement and futility, since all attempts to live as a Christian seem to be not only hard but ineffectual. Faults seem more embedded than ever, and the whole Christian set-up (traditional or radical) appears so heavily useless as to cast doubt on the worthwhileness of the Christian quest itself. It seems desirable and sensible to try to return to the comradely cheer and concrete achievement of a less demanding kind of commitment.

But to go back is not to return to the energetic hopefulness, valour and joy of spiritual beginnings, because the thing that makes the beginnings good and worthy of respect is hope, and to turn back is to abandon hope. As Gandalf says when the Company of the Ring have failed to cross over the mountains, and must face the unmapped and probably fatal journey through the Mines underneath them, 'To go back is to admit defeat, and face more defeat to come. If we go back now the Ring must remain there: we shall not be able to set out again. Then sooner or later Rivendell will be besieged, and after a brief and bitter time it will be destroyed.'

For Rivendell is that place of tremendous joy and beauty that people reach who have fully and entirely committed themselves to the Gospel, have struggled and suffered and won through. But it is only a resting-place, the place from which the real journey begins. To stay there, once the call to go forward has come, is to abandon the quest. John Tauler, fourteenth-century Dominican mystic, was very clear both about the rightness of this place of refreshment, and of the need to leave it behind. He compares the labouring soul to a garden that requires a great deal of heavy and uncongenial work in the spring:

'. . . but soon all is changed. The Divine sun begins to do its heavenly work in the well-prepared garden of the soul. When, therefore, the genial sun of God's grace begins to shine brightly upon this well-cultivated garden . . . then indeed the sweet flowers of May begin to bloom, and all the welcome gifts of summertime. The eternal God causes the soul to blossom forth and to produce good fruit of virtue; and the joy in that soul no tongue can tell. For the Holy Ghost now is there, and his brightness shines directly upon the soul . . . one drop of this Divine comfort is worth more than all the joys of created things put together . . . a man . . . would gladly sink down into its depths and rest and slumber in it for ever. . . . And all the souls who actually do so, remain stationary in their career. They amount to nothing unless they rise up and go forward.'

And going forward means going, sooner or later, into the darkness of discouragement and tedium, the sense that one is getting nowhere, either in becoming personally more conformed to Christ, or in effectively spreading the Gospel. But this need for reassurance of concrete results is precisely what has to be stripped away if the disciple is to be the kind of other Christ who alone can carry out God's will. 'One finds few such men', says Meister Eckhart firmly. 'Whether they know it or not, most men would like to prosper . . . but this is nothing but selfishness. You shall yield to God altogether and with all that you have, and you shall not ask what he does with that which is his own.'

This is a very unpleasant process, and the journey of the Company of the Ring through the Mines makes a fair image of what it feels like. It is a venture into the unknown places of one's own self, and echoes from deeper down, from depths of primitive evil below our deepest thoughts, make themselves heard also, to trouble even more an already wearying and frightening experience. For this is an opening up of the human spirit, calling out responses of patience and courage that nobody knew were there, in preparation for the difficulties ahead.

This particular generation of Christians is up against one consequence of discipleship which Christians living in a society regarding itself as Christian did not have to encounter nearly so frequently. This is a kind of isolation in which the disciple's conscience obliges him to actions which are not only difficult in themselves but which his contemporaries regard at best as stupid and at worst as positively mischievous or even criminal. There are bound to be examples of this kind of choice in any society, but when Christianity is given at least lip-service as a proper pattern of ordinary living then certain kinds of Christian 'eccentricity' are regarded as respectable, if unusual, types of behaviour.

In the Middle Ages very few people wanted to be hermits, but if someone did take up the eremitical life he or she was likely to attract a rather fascinated admiration from ordinary people, even if they themselves found the idea of such a life repulsive. Those who were pacifists could be acceptably anti-war in a monastery, and voluntary poverty was a recognized form of Christian vocation, though not everyone's cup of tea. St Francis's unkempt and haphazard way of life was regarded with suspicion by the clerical Establishment which (rightly) suspected an implicit criticism of its wealth and power-seeking, but nobody tried Francis for political subversion.

The Victorian scene has become almost synonymous with religious hypocrisy, but hypocrisy is 'the tribute vice pays to virtue', which means that, at least superficially, even the odder kinds of virtue have to be accepted. The white administrators of British colonies did not exactly welcome missionaries who insisted on treating the natives as people (especially as many missionaries did not) but they were not inclined to suspect such men of God of revolutionary plots, nor were the missionaries normally imprisoned or deported if they defended the human rights of their converts. They were undoubtedly an infernal nuisance to the Empire Builders, but they usually had to be tolerated for fear of what the sanctimonious press of the Mother Country might say if the underlying rapacity and racialism of the Empire system were revealed too clearly. The British public still needed to believe in the purity of its motives and in the Christian character of its relations with subjugated peoples.

At home, people laughed at the Salvation Army lassies and their tambourines and tears. They laughed even louder at middle-class women whose efforts to identify with the poor in the name of Christ led to dowdiness of dress, and to a clumsy, tactless approach to the real social problems of the time which endeared them neither to those they tried to help nor to the class from which they came. The 'converted' working-class man or woman was also a legitimate butt for humour. But even if people laughed they could not actually condemn such behaviour unless they themselves openly rejected the Christian principles which motivated it. The best they could do was complain that those who 'exaggerated' in such ways were mistaken in their methods. Nobody tried to explain it all away as the result of hormonal imbalance or repressed sexuality.

It is evidently always hard to choose a way that separates one from the familiar paths of one's friends and relations and colleagues, especially when these are reasonably like-minded people. It is that much harder in times like ours, when the behaviour demanded of the Christian disciple may well be not only 'more so' than the 'ordinary' Christianity of other people, but utterly alien to the values and goals of a society that has left Christ behind. For a culture like that of the modern West infiltrates the minds of all its members, Christian or not. Then it happens that the disciple who is taken in hand by the Spirit may find himself living in ways and by values that even sincere and fervent Christians find unacceptable. Close friends—good, generous, compassionate people, seem suddenly to switch off their previous sympathy when the Spirit demands of a Christian a kind of dedication that simply cannot be dovetailed into even the most Christian end of the range of socially acceptable behaviour. 'His enemies shall be those of his own household.'

When Philip Berrigan planned to pour blood on draft files as a protest against his country's bloody and immoral war in Vietnam, he shocked many friends and admirers, and one of them recalled how he tried to persuade Philip to choose a form of protest less calculated to alienate people. 'Phil, after all, is one of the four or five most valuable priests in the country,' he said later. 'I pleaded with him for hours at a time to use a more Gandhian tactic, to pick out an action which a larger segment of society could appreciate.' But there is a point for the disciple when this kind of argument becomes meaningless, because the only thing that matters is obedience to Christ, who has made his presence and authority unmistakably felt. Nobody can judge his action but his own conscience, and there lies the danger of self-delusion; yet there is no other way. Thomas More knew the danger and pushed his conscience as far as it would go in his fear of being misled. He was no natural protestor, but when the final decision came he could not accept even his beloved daughter's arguments in favour of saving his life by doing what so many good and sincere Christians found it possible to do. In the same way even the anguished pleading of Perpetua's father could not turn her from martyrdom, much as she loved him; nor was the pull of her yearning for her baby stronger than her purpose.

The great temptation of the Christian who really means business is to feel that, in the last resort, something that alienates others and threatens to undo good work *cannot* be the will of God. It seems so much more Christian to work for good in the existing situation, exploiting all the opportunities that occur. And this temptation is especially insidious because it is true, as Bonhoeffer pointed out, that great and obvious sacrifice is not necessarily service for Christ, it can be just a form of self-gratification. And for many people, most of the time, the energetic exploitation of existing opportunities in God's service (or the creation of new opportunities as the possibility occurs) is what Christians are supposed to be doing. Yet there comes a moment when this is no longer possible, when to continue in this way is to serve not Christ but the enemy.

A recent example that is right in the political picture of our time is the spiritual development of a South African minister of the Dutch Reformed Church, the Reverend Beyers-Naude, an Afrikaner and a former member of the ultra-racialist and right-wing 'Broederbond' secret society which dominates South African politics. He sincerely believed in the racial policies of his nation, and tried to live as a Christian in this setting. But his Christianity was real, so that when he was sent to work among Africans in the Transvaal he was able to face up to the discovery that the racial doctrines on which he had been bred didn't square with the reality of actually living among 'Kaffirs'. Eventually, after working with some others to change the thinking of his Church, he realized that the government had no intention of allowing any deviation from the 'pure' racial doctrine of the Church, and discovered that the Broederbond were planning to take control of the *Kerk* organization for this purpose. He saw that 'there was no possibility of working for change from within' and resigned from the Broederbond. At the time of writing Mr Naude is still working in the 'Christian Institute' which he founded for 'refugees from the compromises of the institutional churches', but pressure on it from the government is increasing. His past protects him to some extent: he knows too much, and is besides unassailably 'one of us' in the Nationalists' eyes. But if a pretext occurs to silence him it will not be overlooked. He took his way into isolation from his heritage and his Church. There was a moment when he had to choose between using the opportunities his power and influence gave him in the *Kerk*, and protesting against it in a way which would make him powerless to influence it, and might well end in the destruction of all he had achieved. He made his decision as the Gospel demands.

This same moment comes for Frodo when he has to choose whether to go with the Ring to the rescue of the City of Minas Tirith, and thus give it its only chance of resisting the power of the Enemy, or whether to take the Ring into the land of Shadow and try to destroy it in the fires of Mount Doom from which it came, as the Council had ordered. At this point Frodo knows he has to choose alone, and cannot turn for guidance to the companions who have supported him so far. It is here also that Boromir, as we have seen, does his best to persuade him to use the power of the Ring to help the forces of good, and even tries to get the Ring himself when Frodo shows signs of refusing, for he is terribly aware of the need for just such 'charismatic' power in the endless battle against evil. This is the classic Christian dilemma. Frodo knows that Boromir's advice makes sense, but 'something' makes him feel it isn't right—for him.

> ' "It would seem like wisdom but for the warning of my heart," he tells Boromir.
> "Warning? Warning against what?" said Boromir sharply.
> "Against delay. Against the way that seems easier. Against refusal of the burden that is laid on me. Against—well, if it must be said, against trust in the strength and truth of Men." '

'The language of the cross may be illogical to those who are not on the way to salvation,' wrote Paul to the Corinthians, and how right he was. It may be illogical even to those who *are* on the way to salvation, at the moments when the wisdom of this world comes up against the foolishness of the message of Jesus, and the harassed disciple has to decide which to back. One way out is to lay the responsibility on someone else, and there are always plenty of people to tell the hesitating disciple what he really must do if he has any sense. Any authoritarian type of Christianity can even demand the right to take over, just as Boromir tries to snatch the Ring. But there is no way out. 'Not to decide is to decide.' Then Frodo suffers his crucial struggle. He puts on the Ring, in order to be invisible to Boromir, and so becomes able to see a kind of vision of the struggle between Light and Darkness which is shaking his world wherever he looks. By wearing the Ring instead of merely carrying it he comes under the eye of the Enemy who desires it, and is drawn towards surrender to him. He knows by a kind of inner Voice that he must take off the Ring, if he is to be free of this pull towards the power of evil, yet the fact of wearing it binds him to that power. The agony of such moments reveals how close the way of the willed surrender to Christ is to a willing surrender to evil, for evil comes very near the surface in times of spiritual crisis. 'And I saw that there was a way to Hell even at the gates of Heaven,' says Bunyan.

But there is a real choice.

'The two powers strove in him. For a moment, perfectly balanced between their piercing points, he writhed, tormented. Suddenly he was aware of himself again. Frodo, neither the Voice nor the Eye; free to choose, and with one remaining instant in which to do so. He took the Ring off his finger . . . a great weariness was on him, but his will was firm and his heart lighter. He spoke aloud to himself. "I will do now what I must," he said.'

So he leaves the Company secretly, not wishing to involve them in his own decision. In the event, Sam refuses to be left behind and goes with him all the way, but Frodo's decision was taken alone, to go alone. It must always be so.

'If I had ten children,' wrote Franz Jagerstteter in reply to persuasions to abandon for his family's sake his refusal to serve in the army under the Nazis, 'the greatest demand upon me would still be the one I must make of myself'. His wife, mother, relations, village, pastor and bishop all advised him to accept the induction, and to try to live as a Christian in the army, where, they thought, such a man could do a great deal of good. Like so many before him and after him, he could not take that way, though he knew and admired excellent people who did so. He had put his hand to the plough and could not look back. He made his decision quite alone, and carried it out alone, purposely going to another town to refuse induction, so as to spare his family.

Fortunately, or unfortunately, according to one's point of view, not all Christians have to make this kind of choice. The greater number will do nothing obviously drastic, yet the attitude that relegates them to a kind of second-class citizenship of the kingdom of heaven is as unChristian in its way as the one which cannot allow for the extremes to which the Spirit may drive the disciple. There are choices as radical to be made without catastrophic outward change, though never without any change. But also there are – there must be – those of whom this kind of choice has not yet been demanded and who have other essential things to do. One such essential thing is keeping going some kind of organization which will ensure that the Gospel message is still available to the next generation, and to those who have not yet heard it in this one. There is also the need to make something of the secular world in so far as it is not yet corrupted. These are not trivial or escapist jobs, though they can be used as an escape. But so can martyrdom. 'The last temptation is the greatest treason,' Eliot makes the martyr Becket say, 'to do the right thing for the wrong reason.'

In *The Lord of the Rings* the huge tapestry of the fairy-tale depicts much more than Frodo's solitary journey into the Shadow. All kinds of other things are going on, above all the epic defence of Minas Tirith against apparently hopeless odds. To this task the rest of the Company, after the death of Boromir, are dedicated, and the story of the defence and all that contributes to it – the coming of the Riders of Rohan, the ride of the Dead behind Aragorn, the vengeance of the Forest on the Orc hordes and the defeat of Saruman – takes up more than half of the last two books. It is clear that unless Frodo's mission had succeeded, all the valour and cunning of the defenders would have been useless in the long run, but it is also clear that without the courage and endurance of the men of Gondor and their allies Frodo's mission could easily have failed.

It is in this part of the story that a character appears who is of a type very familiar to us, and is more recognizable in Tolkien's presentation of his character than in older fairy-tales. Denethor, Steward of Gondor, descendant of the long line of stewards who have ruled it in place of the long absent kings, is recognizable as a fairy-tale king, with touches of giant and witch, but he is more immediately identifiable as the gangster–hero of so many modern folk-myths. There is a certain glamour about the self-sufficient, clever, ruthless and successful criminal which has endured from Robin Hood to Jesse James and the Australian Ned Kelly. The breed shows no signs of dying out—one has only to think of the popularity of films like *Butch Cassidy and the Sundance Kid*; while in Northern Ireland, the I.R.A. gunman whom nobody has ever heard of before steps into the role of outlaw–hero almost as soon as the news of his death by an Army bullet hits the head-lines. Denethor is a legitimate ruler, or at least he thinks he is, not knowing that the real king is on his way to his City. But he is a gangster, an 'outlaw', at heart. He has no intention of surrender-ing his power to any king, should one turn up, any more than the film gangster will surrender to the representatives of the law. Yet he is not amoral; gangsters, even the Mafia, have an elaborate and consistent moral code of their own, within which they and their followers operate. (It is worth remembering that missionaries used to regard some 'savage' tribes as wicked and immoral when their tribal code was different from the 'usual' one.)

What is it about the gangster–hero that appeals to our kind of culture so much that the gangster film has become an established, scarcely varying, form? He becomes a tragic hero, though the original may have been a criminal thug, and he occurs in many cultural contexts, doomed like Orestes by a fate he cannot control, yet refusing to surrender his integrity as he sees it. But the gangster is an *illegal* tragic hero. Not the Furies, but the Law (the codified framework of everyday life) pursues and finally overcomes him. Is it because the State and the Law so often feel (and often *are*) like ogres to us that we welcome a champion against them? Nowadays, we love Robin Hood, and pirates who were ruthless murderers turn into splendid heroes in time. Denethor inspires homage and love and respect, and his servants are so bound to him that they feel they must obey him even when his doom is driving him mad. He is a hero, and the great gangsters and outlaws can become myth–heroes even in their lifetime. Men follow them with total devotion, blind to their crimes.

At first glance the gangster seems to be a type of 'youngest son', the subversive hero who emerges from obscurity and succeeds where the legitimate rulers fail. This is partly his appeal: the triumph of the one the great big ogre of Society has despised. Yet a closer look shows that he is the negative of this picture. The youngest son succeeds because he obeys. The gangster succeeds because his motto is that of Lucifer: 'I will not serve.' He is literally a law unto himself, and others follow him as king because he can convince them, and himself, that he is absolute,

Lord and God in his own Kingdom. Those who follow him feel that he has access to a power beyond that of ordinary mortals, one which makes him indestructible and beyond the morality of other men. Denethor has the Palantir, one of the Seven Seeing Stones whose power is similar to, though far less than, that of the Ring, and in it he can see far off, and read men's hearts. This is the symbol of the self-assumed superhuman status of the successful gangster. But Denethor does not know that Sauron, the Enemy, is feeding him false ideas through the Seeing Stone, and so using him for his own ends. 'He was too great to be subdued to the will of the Dark Power,' says Gandalf of him, 'he saw none the less only those things which that Power permitted him to see.' For the youngest son never rejects the law – the 'things that are' – he only challenges them by what he *is*, in faithfulness to his mission. His negative, the outlaw, asserts his own identity in the act of refusing service. 'I will not step down to be the dotard chamberlain of an upstart . . . I will not bow to such a one,' Denethor tells Gandalf when he learns, through the Seeing Stone, that the heir of the ancient kings is coming back to Gondor. His identity depends on his absolute power. 'If doom denies me this, I will have *naught*!' And naught, death by fire on the funeral pyre built at his orders, is what he chooses when hope seems gone. He will never surrender, either to force or to love.

Denethor's death is a pagan gesture, as Gandalf points out. The gangster becomes for many a tragic myth hero in the pagan style, and he is the kind of hero who naturally appeals to a culture which has lost the feel of the Christian type of myth, though it still keeps some of the Christian mythological trappings. He can even be a good sort of hero to have. He represents, for those who admire him, man's refusal to be dehumanized, arranged and legislated into nonentity, even when no clear reason can be found to justify refusal. A sort of divine obstinacy is articulated in words like honour and loyalty, and the doomed gangster–hero, the pagan warrior sailing into the sunset in the funeral pyre of his own flaming vessel, typifies this human refusal to surrender. The myth swallows up the historical reality. Brutal and ruthless criminals can touch the deep longing for a strong, liberating hero whom even death cannot cow. Only one thing can surpass the power of this kind of defiance, and that is the totally opposite heroism of the cross.

And it is only in the light of this, the patient and obedient suffering of the youngest son, that we can see that the courage of Denethor, the fairy-tale king who regards his own powers as ultimate, is a false courage, one misled by his own pride. The courage of the gangster–king needs success to maintain it. As the powers which it will not acknowledge press in, the ruthlessness that was used to achieve success is turned against even his own followers. Increasingly suspicious, in the end he can trust no one. In his isolation, unable to learn from anyone but himself, he grows mad with his own supremacy. The youngest son passes through failure and humiliation and death, to life. The outlaw passes through success and triumph and pride, to death. Yet something of this obstinacy sustains men and nations in their struggle against tyranny, when the deeper and final heroism of the cross looks too much like surrender. And perhaps it has its place, while it remains comparatively uncorrupted. For it was Denethor's determination to fight, and his refusal to consider that anyone but himself had the right and power to lead that fight, which drew the Enemy's Eye to the struggle at Minas Tirith, and so he did not notice Frodo's creeping progress towards Mount Doom.

But the success of Frodo's mission would have been futile without that other victory, which Denethor did not accomplish but to which his obstinacy contributed. Without the beauty and traditions of Gondor there would have been little left after the overthrow of Sauron except ruins and the graves of the valiant dead. The Christian quest is the lonely one of each pilgrim, but it is also the quest of the whole people, who have 'many gifts'. It is only in the setting of a consciously pilgrim Church that the individual quest makes sense. The solitary prophet or martyr prophesies and witnesses for the sake of all the people. The defenders and restorers have their work, without which the martyr's gesture is a word in a nonsense language, and in the psychological substructure of the Christian even the outlaw has his role, though he must be a warning of the deathliness of pride as well as a reminder of the divine toughness of the human spirit.

As several critics have noticed, the tale of the defence of Minas Tirith, and indeed all the 'royal' parts of the story, have a curious heraldic–romantic quality, the characters are more two-dimensional and the dialogue more archaic and formal than in the parts where the hobbits are downstage. The events and characters are more symbolic and less convincing, in spite of many moments of grandeur and terror and heroism. This area of the story is restricted to the heroic–romantic style of fairy-tale, which is a real fairy-tale but one fitted to a particular cultural view. And this is interesting, because it is in this area of Christian living – the necessary 'background' function of a Church which cannot and must not consist solely of martyrs and prophets – that Christianity *as a culture* has its place.

Christianity has to live within a culture, it cannot be purely a religious enclave even if it tries to be. But in its turn it modifies the culture which it uses. So most Christians, most of the time, live by a culturally coloured though perfectly genuine Christianity. The quasi-medieval style of Minas Tirith and the Norse-style of Rohan are probably quite unintentional symbols of the way something drastic in the way of personal purification is required in order to disentangle the total demand of the Gospel (as Frodo feels it) from the true but culturally 'screened' version which is all that most of us can be aware of. Frodo and Sam move beyond culture of any kind, and when they finally return to 'ordinary' life they each, in different ways, remain beyond its limitations, though Sam happily accepts the setting his own culture provides. Frodo wants to accept it, for he values it, but finds in the end that he has gone too far. He no longer belongs, as Aragorn and the other heroes and heroines still do.

But before that Frodo and Sam have accomplished the quest. It would be interesting to look at details of the last stage of their journey, for there are many situations and sayings that make particularly clear the links between the fairy-tale and the Gospel, and thereby illuminate the Gospel message for us. It is intriguing, for instance, to wonder whether Gollum is, for all his malevolence, a kind of animal guide. It is the vestigial 'hobbitness' in him that provides the 'real' wisdom of his role as guide, yet it is his 'monstrousness' that creates the circumstances in which he can be an effective guide. He, too, is under a spell. If he is a guide, it is against his will, but there is another will at work, which also works in the more attractive animal guides. And the princess in this tale, quiet, wise, self-denying, practical and yet mysterious, is Galadriel, who appears only briefly but whose gift of the phial of light makes her power 'present' when it is most needed. Both are elements of the human character on its quest, as the Gospel shows them up. The Christ-like quality of Frodo has been noticed by some critics, and this reference seems to be a conscious one. But it is only really convincing because, although it is a personal insight of the author, his 'Christ-likeness', in precisely this degree, is the Christ-likeness of the youngest son who is already familiar in so many other tales. Tolkien's 'youngest son' makes the link more explicit, and also shows even more clearly the way in which the youngest son is not Christ, or 'Christian', but both, and also the Church.

These themes, and many others, can be traced through the story, and their kinship with the traditional tales and with the Gospel can be annotated. In these ways Tolkien's tale is only a more complex and extended type of fairy-tale, one among many. There is one respect, however, in which the quest theme of the trilogy is unusual, if not unique, and that is in the negative nature of the quest. It is, in fact, more of an anti-quest.

Frodo is not sent to find the water of life, or rescue a captive princess, or steal the bird of immortality. He does not go in order to achieve anything at all, but in order to *un*do something. His mission is to destroy the Ring of Power, even if he himself is destroyed in the process. In one sense he is nearly destroyed, and in another sense he actually is destroyed, for he can no longer live like other people, and his future journey to the Gray Havens is implicit in his behaviour from the time of the destruction of the Ring. An extra, and extraordinary, quality of anti-quest is given to the story by Frodo's final failure, when the purpose of his journey is accomplished in spite of him. It is Gollum's consuming greed for the Ring that finally brings it, and him, to destruction, for at the moment when he stands on the brink of the Crack of Doom, to which he and Sam have crept so agonizingly, Frodo has no strength left to will the destruction of the Ring, and its own evil power finally overcomes and possesses him. At the end he cannot bear to part with the thing that has been eating away his vitality and hope for so long, and he claims it for himself; or rather it claims him. But he is saved from the results of his failure by the results of his earlier compassion, for Gollum, catching up with him, bites off Ring and finger and, in the struggle, falls with the Ring into the abyss. If Frodo had not spared Gollum's life when he was at his mercy there would have been no one strong enough to challenge his possession of (or by?) the Ring. (There is a constant ambiguity here which is very revealing about the nature of evil as it operates in human behaviour.) Sam, just because he does not know the passion of lust for power which grows in the Ring-bearer, cannot challenge its hold on Frodo. Gollum can, because he is almost wholly eaten away by the power of the Ring, and has no ordinary fears or doubts left.

This 'anti-quest' quality of the trilogy is not really out of keeping with other fairy-tales. In many cases when the hero steals the bird, or ring, or kisses the princess, the evil spell is broken and things resume their proper shape and function, so that the quest achieves the destruction of the power of evil, as Frodo's does. And the almost accidental quality of Frodo's success against his (distorted) will is implicit in the quality of dependence and spiritual neediness which is typical of the youngest son. He does not succeed by his own cleverness or courage but because, as Gandalf says, 'you were meant to'. The traditional quest-hero does not fail as Frodo does, but Frodo's final weakness is only an illustration of the essential weakness of the youngest son whose whole mission is one of pure obedience, and obviously beyond his expected capacity.

But although the anti-quest element in *The Lord of the Rings* does not contradict the fairy-tale structure and themes it creates a difference which is not merely one of degree. It gives to the quest theme a degree of explicitness at the spiritual level which takes it, at this point, outside the limits of fairy-tale. Without contradicting its fairy-tale nature this gives weight and value to the exception. The point of the negative value of the quest is that man's search for happiness, or salvation, or life, or knowledge, or any of the other philosophical colourings given to the universal spiritual journey, cannot be achieved by any human means whatever. Any attempt by men to achieve the goal of human striving by short cuts of legislation or manipulation leads inevitably to tyranny. The temptations of Jesus spell out the kind of delusory short-cuts to salvation which the real quest must on no account take. But if these ways are ruled out it means in practice that the Christian must destroy in himself the power to make effective use of these forbidden means.

The symbolism of the Ring is very clear and psychologically realistic. Its nature is inescapably evil, because the power it gives binds men closer and closer to the source of that power, which is evil itself. Those who use it in ignorance of its nature, or with good intentions, are not exempt from its effects (to suppose that they are is the very understandable mistake of situation ethics). But the disinterested and compassionate are to some extent protected. At least its power takes much longer to get a grip, and it 'fades' the bearer rather than actually corrupting him. The greater the wisdom and influence of the user the more likely his corruption, which is why the wizard, and the king, are both unsuited to bear it. The temptation, for them, would be too great. When one has power and knowledge these can only continue to be used with wisdom and compassion if their use is subordinated to principles higher than one's own will.

The kind of evil which the Ring seems to embody is the most fundamental human evil, the one which Christ overcame in the only way possible, by his death; that is, by refusing to make use of himself in any way but that of obedience to the Father. But this is not at all a passive following out of directives from above. It requires all one's acquired knowledge and experience, and all one's innate qualities of mind and heart and spirit. It requires decisions in the face of uncertainty and involves the possibility of mistakes and failure. This free, fallible obedience simply deprives the Ring of its power for evil, though the danger remains that at any point the temptation to take a short cut may become too great. But as long as the bearer of the Ring – and every human being is born with this Ring round his neck – remains obedient, he is not corrupted. And the final obedience means total freedom. The risen Jesus no longer bears the Ring, it has been destroyed by his final renunciation of its use. Therefore he is totally free.

This total freedom is not attainable except in death, but there are a few living people whose freedom is nearly complete and only needs to be perfected by death. In a sense they have already 'died with Christ'. These are the ones we call saints. At a certain point the living of obedience seems to have become so much a part of themselves that it is unimaginable that they should become self-seeking. They are not beyond the possibility of failure, but in practice their direction of mind is so entirely unworldly that situations that might present an agonizing temptation to others never suggest to them any opportunity to choose wrongly.

Sometimes this final plateau of spiritual serenity is reached up a gentle slope, by the gradual stripping of selfish fear. Sometimes it comes through some interior crisis, on the pattern of Frodo's final struggle to reach Mount Doom. Either way it is painful, and nearly always it requires the support of some person, or community, which can almost literally 'carry' the pilgrim at times when he has no strength or hope left. This helpless dependence is part of the process of liberation from the power of the Ring, because it deprives the Christian of any lingering feeling that he can achieve salvation by his own virtues if only circumstances will stop interfering and spoiling things.

It is also part of the reason why the Christian quest cannot be a solitary venture, even though the decision to set out must be a lonely one. However alone the Christian is, the reason and structure of his quest are communal. He is not going merely to save himself; the salvation of all is at stake if he does not. If he goes on his own behalf he already puts himself in the power of the Ring, as Saruman does. His wizard's insight and power are used for good, at first, but according to his own judgement and without obedience. He becomes enslaved to the Dark Lord of the Ring, though still pretending to himself that he is doing everything for his own good and ultimate profit. Frodo's quest would have failed if he had not had Sam's strength and comparative detachment to lean on and to follow. And both Sam and Frodo would have failed if they had not had Bilbo's gift of the magic sword, the enchanted elven cloaks, and Galadriel's phial of light. The elf 'way-bread' kept them alive, and at the end it was the victory of Aragorn and the others at Minas Tirith which, as mentioned above, made possible not only the success of the quest but afterwards a rescue in the nick of time, the snatching up of the exhausted hobbits from the slopes of the erupting volcano. The same interdependence of the characters who take part in the quest is evident in all the fairy-tales. Solitary though the hero may be, he depends on others to succeed, and they in turn depend on his success. The hero needs the princess and his various guides if he is to succeed, but the princess needs him to rescue or reinstate her, and the animals or dwarfs need him to release them from enchantment or just to save their lives.

The characters in Tolkien's tale, as in other fairy-tales, show both the interaction between separate but complementary roles in the quest, and the interaction of aspects of the total human being, who is at once hero, fool, princess, and animal guide, as well as ogre or witch. It is this baffling and tantalizing ambivalence which makes the study of fairy-tales in relation to the Gospel so fascinating and so important. The quest is everyone's, to be human is to be a traveller, but some may refuse to start, or turn back, or settle down half-way, and fail at the end—or try to decide for themselves on the route and the goal, so that they go to the wrong place in pursuit of the wrong things.

Success depends on more than goodness of heart, for the idea of obedience, which is fundamental, involves someone or something to be obeyed. A good understanding of the nature of the quest is needed, and this is why, although it need not take overtly religious forms, the quest is a religious thing. It is religion which tells people what this journey is all about, what the dangers are and how to avoid them. But it also promises to make sense of their efforts even when they cannot understand what is going on, provided they are obedient to the overall design and use all their own resources in its service. The Old Testament is all about the quest of a people for salvation, their obedience and disobedience, their guides and their tempters. The New Testament opens out the theme to propose the quest to all men, and to show also the individual nature of the quest within the journey of a pilgrim people. Christian writing, and the scriptures of non-Christian religions, plot the human quest in their various ways.

It would be interesting to compose a kind of anthology from the literature of world religions on this theme alone. Such an anthology would merely indicate briefly the variety and range of human experience of life as the quest for—what? Christian scriptures call it 'eternal life', or just 'life', and this concept is the one on which I shall look for illumination through the fairy-tales in the final chapter of this book. As a bridge to this study, what follows is a very limited and necessarily arbitrarily chosen selection of passages from various sources which may help to orchestrate the quest theme which Tolkien used in *The Lord of the Rings*. (Tolkien, of course, drew on many sources before his own version of the theme achieved its final form.) These passages speak for themselves. Some of them refer to only a point in the quest, others are brief snatches because the whole account would be much too long. Some elements may seem to contradict each other; for instance the usual insistence is on perils and trials to be endured, while the

Bhagavadgītā insists that by the true way there are no dangers. The difference is only superficial; there are no dangers to the *spirit* this way, the real danger lies in turning aside from it, a danger which is presented in tales and allegory in terms of dragons and tempters. A selection like this is intended to whet the appetite, no more, and to make clear the need to consider, finally, the end of the quest.

The first is inevitable: Bunyan's introduction to *The Pilgrim's Progress*, the book that 'set' the quest theme for English-speaking Christians:

> This book it chalketh out before thine eyes
> The man that seeks the everlasting prize;
> It shows you whence he comes, whither he goes;
> What he leaves undone, also what he does;
> It also shows you how he runs and runs,
> Till he unto the gate of glory comes.
> This book will make a traveller of thee,
> If by its counsel thou wilt rulèd be.
> It will direct thee to the Holy Land,
> If thou wilt its directions understand.
>
> (The Author's Apology for his Book—
introduction to The Pilgrim's Progress.
John Bunyan)

The 'everlasting prize' has appeared in myth and tale in many guises, and *The Golden Fleece* is one of the most famous. Here are the beginning and end of the quest presented by a writer for children:

'Jason's eyes glowed as he listened; before his uncle had finished speaking he resolved to sail to Colchis and win the Golden Fleece. King Pelias laughed to himself at his nephew's eagerness; for he was sure that from such a perilous quest the young man would never return alive. Jason, however, thought far less of the dangers he would meet than of the honours he hoped to win. . . .'

'The Argo arrived safely back at Colchis, however, having passed many perils on the way, and King Pelias, when he saw Jason alive and well, bigger and stronger than when he had set out, and carrying in his arms the golden fleece, knew that he

145

could no longer keep him from the throne. So he gave Jason the crown, and called him King.'

(*The Realm of Gold*. George Baker)

The quest is not a purely European idea, and the way to freedom and perfection is a familiar form of Hindu instruction:

'As the Spirit of our mortal body wanders on in childhood, and youth and old age, the Spirit wanders on to a new body. . . .
From the world of the senses, Arjuna, comes heat and comes cold, and pleasure and pain. They come and they go; they are transient. Arise above them, strong soul.
Hear now the wisdom of Yoga, path of the Eternal and freedom from bondage. No step is lost on this path, and no dangers are found. And even a little progress is freedom from fear. The follower of this path has one thought, and this is the End of his determination.
. . . for the man who forsakes all desires and abandons all pride of possession and of self reaches the goal of peace supreme.'

(The *Bhagavadgītā*)

The fairy-tale, however, shows that the quest is not only for individual salvation, but is involved in the salvation of all. The quest seeks to save the world:

' "Petru, my dear boy," cried the emperor. . . . "I will let you into the secret. My right eye laughs when I look at my three sons, and see how strong and handsome you all are, and the other eye weeps because I fear that after I die you will not be able to keep the empire together, and to protect it from its enemies. But if you can bring me water from the spring of the Fairy of the Dawn, to bathe my eyes, then they will laugh for ever more; for I shall know that my sons are brave enough to overcome any foe." '

(Roumanian fairy-tale)

But over against the positive though obedient decision of the youngest son we need the reminder that the quest is made, not by ourselves, but by Christ in us:

'The infinity of space and time separates us from God. How are we to seek for him? How are we to go towards him? . . . We

146

cannot take a step towards the heavens. God crosses the universe and comes to us. . . . He comes at his own time. We have the power to consent to receive him, or to refuse. . . . If we consent, God puts a little seed in us and he goes away again . . . it is not as easy as it seems, for the growth of the seed in us is painful . . . we cannot avoid destroying whatever gets in the way . . . a day comes when the soul belongs to God . . . when truly and effectively it loves. Then in its turn it must cross the universe to go to God . . . we can only consent to allow free passage in our soul for this love. That is the meaning of denying oneself.'

(*Waiting on God*. Simone Weil)

The eastern mystics emphasize the same thing:

'But those who are devoted to the worship of the Self, by means of austerity, continence, faith and knowledge, go by the northern path and attain the world of the sun. The sun, the light, is indeed the source of all energy. It is immortal, beyond fear, it is the supreme goal. For him who goes to the sun there is no more birth nor death.'

(*Praśna Upanishad*)

A familiar tale adjusts the balance again by making it clear that this quest is for love alone. It takes two, the soul and God, who are yet one. Hardship and patience are involved, as Simone Weil indicated, and as this old tale shows:

'After the bull had left her, long she sat and long she wept, till she wearied. At last she rose and went away, she didn't know where. On she wandered, till she same to a great hill of glass. . . . Round the bottom of the hill she went, sobbing and seeking a way over, till at last she came to a smith's house; and the smith promised, if she would serve him for seven years, then he would make her iron shoes, and then she would be able to climb over the glassy hill. At seven years' end she got her iron shoes, and she climbed the glassy hill . . . to a place where lived another old witch washerwife. There she was told of a gallant young knight that had given in some clothes to wash that were all over blood, and whoever washed them clean would be his wife . . . but they couldn't bring out even one stain . . . and as soon as she began, all the stains came out pure and clean, but the old witch washer-wife made the knight believe it was her daughter had washed the clothes. So the knight and the witch's daughter were to be married.

Two nights the girl bribed the fake bride to let her stay by his bed, but he had been drugged and did not wake:

'The third night . . . the damsel began her watch and, as before, she began singing:

> "Seven long years I served for thee,
> The glassy hill I clomb for thee,
> Thy bloody clothes I wrang for thee;
> And wilt thou not waken and turn to me?"

This time the knight heard . . . and he told her how he had been enchanted unto the form of a bull, but having defeated the Old 'Un he had been given back his human shape. . . . The knight and the damsel were married and for aught I know, he and she are living happy to this day.'

(The Black Bull of Norroway)

And the medieval mystic puts the same thing in directly Christian terms:

> I yearn for you so greatly, Lord,
> And wait for you so faithfully.
> If you will suffer me, O Lord,
> I shall pursue and seek you long, in agony.
> For well I know, You, Lord, must be
> The first to feel a want of me.

(Mechtild of Magdeburg)

Drawing together many of these themes in one strange poem, the following extracts from one of Charles Williams's poems in *Taliessin through Logres* give a new twist to the quest theme, for here the quest is also a homecoming, and the hero is the arche-typical quest-hero, Galahad himself. It is a sea voyage and the ship—the Church—is at once the means of travel and the place to which the traveller is going. All the themes are present here, though these mangled extracts cannot do more than encourage the reader to turn to the whole work. Here is the unlikely hero, the

illegitimate child of betrayal, here is the princess, faithful to death.
For lack of space I have left out the parts where the Arthurian
witch–mother–queen, Morgause, briefly appears, but the animals
(doves) guide and accompany the holy infant as pledges of the
Spirit which drives him. There are layers upon layers of associations, pagan and Christian, as the ship speeds towards Jerusalem.

But the actual ship, the hollow of Jerusalem
beyond the shapes of empire, the capes of Carbonek,
over the topless waves of trenched Broceliande,
drenched by the everlasting spray of existence,
with no mind's sail reefed or set, no slaves at the motivated oars,
drove into and clove the wind from unseen shores. . . .
Fierce in the prow the alchemical Infant burned,
red by celerity now conceiving the white;
behind him the folded silver column of Percivale
hands on the royal shoulders, closed wings of flight,
inhaled the fine air of philosophical amazement.
Bors, mailed in black, completing the trine,
their action in Logres, kneeling on the deck to their right,
prayed still for the need and the bliss of his household.
By three ways of exchange the City sped to the City;
against the off-shore wind that blew from Sarras
the ship and the song flew.
An infinite flight of doves from the storming sky
of Logres – strangely sea-travellers when the land melts –
forming to overfeather and overwhelm the helm,
numerous as men in the empire, the empire riding
the skies of the ocean, guiding by modulated stresses
on each spoke of the helm the vessel from the realm of Arthur,
lifted oak and elm to a new-ghosted power.
The hosted wings trapped the Infant's song;
blown back, tossed down, thrown
along the keel, the song hastening the keel
along the curve of the sea-way, the helm fastening
the whole ship to the right balance of the stresses. . . .

Before the helm the ascending-descending sun
lay in quadrilateral covers of a saffron pall
over the bier and the pale body of Blanchefleur,

mother of the nature of lovers, creature of exchange;
drained there of blood by the thighed wound,
she died another's death, another lived her life.

Through the sea of omnipotent fact rushed the act of Galahad.
He glowed white; he leaned against the wind
down the curved road among the topless waters.
He sang *Judica te, Deus*; the wind,
driven by doves' wings along the arm-taut keel,
sang against itself *Judica te, Deus*.
Prayer and irony had said their say and ceased;
the sole speech was speed.
In the hollow of Jerusalem the quadrilateral of the sun
was done on the deck beyond Broceliande.
In the monstrum of triangular speed,
in a path of lineal necessity,
the necessity of being was communicated to the son of Lancelot.
The ship and the song drove on.

Chapter 6

Happy Ever After

In one of the versions of her story Deirdre of the sorrows was imprisoned in a lonely tower by her guardian King Conacher, who wished to marry her. ('Her hair was black as the raven's wing, her lips red as the raven's blood, her skin white as snow', says the story.) But her old nurse arranged that she should be seen by the three sons of Uisneach, who were visiting their cousin the king. The youngest, Naois, loved her, and she fled with him and his two brothers to Scotland. But the king lured the three brothers back with false promises, and they, sick for home, believed him. So the king murdered the three brothers, and in the Scottish version of the tale they were laid in one grave. Then Deirdre, mourning her husband, came to the grave and said, 'Let Naois of my love move to one side, and let Aillean press closer to Ardan. If the dead could only hear, you would make room for me.' And the dead heard and made room, and she laid herself down by her husband's side and died. But Conacher could not bear to see them united, even in death, so he ordered the body of Deirdre to be taken out, and buried on the other side of the stream that flowed nearby. Then there grew up a pine tree from each grave, and they leaned towards each other, and their trunks met and grew together across the stream, until there was only one tree.

This ending is echoed in many ballads and folk-songs as well as in certain tales where the lovers are united only in death. The clear meaning is that death is not the end of their love, for love is stronger than death.

> For love is strong as Death
> jealousy relentless as Sheol.
> The flash of it is a flash of fire,
> a flame of Yahweh himself.
> Love no flood can quench
> no torrents drown.

('Jealousy' here means exclusive devotion.)

The words of the Song of Songs sum up this theme. The book is both a series of human love songs and a celebration of the love of Yahweh for his bride, Israel. The bride of the song is not just an image of the people, she is a real bride and this is a real marriage song. One school of thought insists that the Song of Songs is, in intention, simply the collection of love songs and bridal songs which it appears to be, a celebration of human love which is holy because in God such love is holy. The uninhibited and lyrical praises of the physical beauty of bride and groom, the moving description of the lovers' hope, longing, passionate excitement, grief and anxiety in separation and joyous fulfilment in union, show a feeling for the complete integration of the physical and the spiritual in sexual love which seems hardly to have been rediscovered until the metaphysical poets, after which it was again lost. (Lawrence's enthusiasm attempted to express it, and he failed, except in a few poems, because he could not rid himself of a lingering sadistic puritanism.)

The celebration of sexual love in the Song of Songs is wholehearted and *whole*, and even if the original authors had nothing else but this in mind it is no distortion of their intention if later Jewish and Christian interpreters saw in it the love song of Yahweh and his people, of Christ and his Church. The Song of Songs is not an allegory of love, it is a series of songs *about* love. What is said of the varied and developing bond that unites the bride to the bridegroom who calls to her is said also of the bond that unites the called people to each other in the Lord who is their calling. And it is this bond, which is the bond of love or it is nothing, which is 'strong as Death'. 'Love no flood can quench', and the tree from the grave of Deidre reaches across the stream to become one with the tree from her husband's grave.

But most fairy-tales end happily. The wicked are punished, the hero marries the princess, all the virtuous are suitably rewarded and 'they live happily ever after', an ending which has come in for a great deal of smugly cynical comment from people who point out that 'life isn't like that'. The romantic dream can end in the divorce court, or in the long-drawn out destructiveness of estrangement and cynical boredom. The witch and the ogre frequently do very well for themselves, while the faithful nurse is sent to an old people's home, the brave old horse ends up in the knacker's yard and the fool of the family, far from marrying the princess, is consigned to the subnormality hospital.

But the desire to make savage fun of the fairy-tale happy ending is as short-sighted as all assumptions that cruelty and injustice are somehow more 'real' than love and loyalty. The truth which the fairy-tales embody is more fundamental than any kind of wilfully blinkered optimism about the rewards of virtue. Nor is the general tone of positive hopefulness by any means the superficial brain-washing kind of happy ending optimism favoured by magazine romances.

To identify the two kinds of happy ending is very tempting, because superficially they often tell the same kind of story. It goes something like this: good girl is rescued by good boy after having been (a) persecuted by fate/parents/bad complexion, or (b) pursued by bad boy/middle-aged roué/unsuitable though adoring youth; or good boy finally finds helpful and ideal girl after having been (a) misled by bad companions/ambitious parents/sultry seductress, or (b) oppressed by wicked boss/lack of self-confidence/past sorrow. The variations on these plots are endless and can turn into 'literature' (for example *Jane Eyre* and *Mansfield Park*) just as readily as into third-rate stories to read under the hair-drier.

But whether they take flesh as Brontë or bilge, these romantic themes are intended to be about every-day, down-the-street people. They do not belong to the world of 'faerie' and are not fairy-tales except in the pejorative sense which the word has come to have, meaning childish escapist fantasy. It is true that there is in all of us a desire to escape which is sheer 'escapism' rather than the necessary desire for a rightful spiritual freedom from which 'real' literature grows. As an occasional 'holiday' from daily routines and anxieties romantic escapism is no more to be frowned on than a well-deserved trip abroad; and it has provided the formula for some of the greatest literature. At that level of literature, however, it also touches on the borders of myth, and escapes being 'escapist' by this means. The borderline is ill defined, but it can be said that the 'happy ever after' romance that implies a *right* to bliss without personal dedication or creative use of suffering is on the 'escapist' side of the border. The 'happy ever after' of great literature grows out of the myth-structure which is present, however oddly, in all great writing, and here it shows cousinship to the fairy-tales. In both cases the romantic form is purged and made truthful when the final union and bliss are reached through many trials and often through terrible suffering, which can only be endured because of the underlying singleness of dedication, the tough but flexible obedience of true love.

It is clear that the romantic myth, here, is the myth of death and eternal life, not an archetype of ideal domesticity. At this level the romantic form is not escapist but liberating. It is, in fact, not a description but a promise, not an evocation of human experience but a theological interpretation of that experience. The difference could be expressed by saying that the romantic form and the 'realistic' form of literature (or drama, cinema, painting, even music for that matter) are both about what life is like, but the latter is concerned with what life is *like*, whereas the former tries to assert what *life* is like.

And the romantic assertion, in this form which is that of the myths of passion, is the fairy-tale ending and is the Christian belief. It is not a universal belief, and the suspicious reaction against it, in favour of realism and courage, rejecting optimistic pie-in-the-sky, is recurrent. The solid, honourable and fairly cheerful pessimism of the 'realistic' pagan view of after-life (either none, or posthumous earthly glory, or the shadowy half-life of Hades) fits many of the attitudes and qualities we admire. There is a no-nonsense, homely courage in accepting death in this way which inspires respect and promises achievement within its limits. We have *this* life to make something of, and as to the rest, it's all dark, in every sense. So let's make the most of what we have.

This 'earthy' attitude is traditionally the one of comedy. Comedy is about what life is *like*, it asks no deeper questions about the nature of life, let alone whether it extends beyond physical death. Comedy does not have to be funny, but it must not allow elements that challenge normal everyday assumptions about living. In comedy, therefore, death itself (which is life's most everyday challenger) is robbed of its unsettling and fearful associations because, traditionally, only the wicked, or the very old, die. These either deserve to die or are fitted to die, so it is quite comfortable, and death-bed scenes can even be funny. But if the sympathies of an audience are with the dying person then the comic style is undermined by considerations of what *life* is like, and this must not be. This was why John Gay could not allow his highwayman–hero to hang, richly though he deserved it, and although the dramatic shape of the plot of *The Beggar's Opera* demanded it. The comedy is retrieved by an unlikely and last-minute reprieve, and we are saved from the challenge of tragedy.

For tragedy is about what *life* is like, and is therefore much concerned with death, especially the death of the innocent and heroic. Classical tragedy's verdict was that man's life was controlled by the gods, and all his twisting and turning was futile. Classical comedy could show people plotting to change situations, and succeeding: Lysistrata and her friends resoundingly succeeded in getting their own way, for comedy was about life as people actually experienced it. But tragedy would have none of this, and exposed the self-confident arrangements of man as the splendid gestures of puppets whose roles are determined beforehand. The only dignified course was to accept fate with courage, and go down into the darkness without whimpering. The blinded Oedipus is cast out of his kingdom, though he is innocent of all intentional wrong. Yet in *Oedipus at Colonnus*, when he has accepted his fate, he goes to a transfigured and mysterious death with triumphant dignity. Admetus, on the other hand, is to be despised because he could not face death when Thanatos summoned him, but was not ashamed to let his young wife Alcestis die for him. Heracles fights with death and wins her back from the grave.

Here Euripides came near to actually questioning the tragic axiom. In the *Trojan Women* he made a savage attack on the war mystique (which was supported by the notion of honour through death in battle, with the gods deciding the issue), but in *Alcestis* he showed man (well, half-man) actually reversing the decree of the gods and bringing the doomed one back to life. She herself had fully accepted death for her husband's sake, and this is perhaps the point of intersection of the classical and Christian notions of tragedy, for Christian tragedy is self-chosen doom, not an imposed one, and heroic and virtuous death can be the gateway to triumph and union, not just to the dark appointed end.

Fairy-tales, even the pre- or non-Christian ones, use either the comic style or the Christian-type tragic one, when the wicked bring about their own doom. But the death of the good, though sad, is not always the end. They may be given immortality in the form of bird or tree. For the heroes and heroines, fairy-tale death is often Romantic death, a way to glory or at any rate to symbolic eternity, like Deirdre. The old peasants Baucis and Philemon who were inseparable in life are united for ever in death in the form of trees, by the will of kindly gods. But the pagan tale can do no more than hint. The myths offer no real hope. Orpheus fails after all to bring back Eurydice. Gilgamesh, frantically searching for means to restore his dead brother to life and find for himself the secret of life, has to give up in the end. 'You will never find what you are looking for,' he is told, 'because the gods decreed that darkness is the end of mortal life . . . take food and wine, be merry and rejoice!' So in the end Gilgamesh resigns himself. This was also the rooted and traditional Norse attitude, for Valhalla was not an equivalent to the Christian heaven, it was a very select beatitude for those fortunate enough to die honourably on the battlefield. The shadowy city ruled by the goddess Hel symbolized the undefined destiny of ordinary mortals.

The encounter between this 'classical' or pagan attitude to death, and the Christian one which asserts a 'happy ever after' transcending and transforming whatever we can achieve in this bit of life, is very sensitively expressed in Bede's account of the council concerning the new religion summoned by King Edwin of Northumbria in 627 (*History of the English Church*, II. 13). It shows this race of proud, self-respecting Norse seafarers and settlers questioning their traditional attitudes. Clearly, even when they had no reason to look for anything beyond death they could not help speculating about it, and feeling it worthwhile to follow up any indications that led to a more hopeful view of the meaning of life.

Bede's account is also slyly amusing, in the contrast shown between the attitude of the professional religious man, Coifi, and that of an ordinary intelligent warrior and chieftain whose way of life brought him up against the reality of death. Coifi, the high priest, thinks it a good idea to have a go at Christianity, and the reason for his approval is that his diligent service of the old gods has not brought him the great rewards received by others less pious than himself. Evidently, the old gods are not a good bet. But one of 'the king's chief men' is less positive and more sensitive. Dr. Ellis Davidson, a scholar who has specialized in Norse literature, believes that Bede has here 'caught the authentic voice of the heathen Northumbrian, faced with a cold and hostile world'.[1] But it is more than that, it is also the authentic voice of humanity, in any time when people can no longer hide their real uncertainties and fears under the structure of civilization. Now, as then, men are under the constant threat of violence and a return to chaos.

Out of this doubt and fear speaks Edwin's chief:

'Your majesty, when we compare the present life of man with that time of which we have no knowledge, it seems to me like the swift flight of a lone sparrow through the banqueting hall where you sit in the winter months to dine with your thanes and counsellors. Inside, there is a comforting fire to warm the room; outside, the wintry storms of snow and rain are raging. This sparrow flies swiftly in through one door of the hall, and out through another. While he is inside, he is safe from the winter storms; but after a few moments of comfort he vanishes from sight into the darkness whence he came. Similarly, man appears on the earth for a little while, but we know nothing of what went before this life, and what follows. Therefore if this new teaching can reveal any more certain knowledge, it seems only right that we should follow it.'

This is great poetry, and as such it cuts through the intervening centuries as if the years were cobwebs attacked by a cosmic spring-cleaning. The down-to-earth Norseman did not hesitate to proclaim his desire to know more. He was not afraid of being accused of escapism, he was simply stating a widespread feeling. He recognized that the existence of a great longing, among all kinds of people, is as much a fact as the limits of their existing knowledge. This man still impresses us as much more realistic and admirable than the high priest, whose attitude is decidedly commercial. Coifi was the real, perennial 'pie-in-the-sky' merchant, and we can guess that in a few years he would be running precisely the same kind of religion-market, but with a Christian type of currency. *He* was the escapist, not the chief who knew he didn't know, but was humble enough to believe that his ignorance was not the measure of all things.

What the Norsemen were looking for was not new myths about the after-life and the end of the world—they had those. Their

[1] E. Davidson, *Gods and Myths of Northern Europe* (Pelican, 1964) p. 221.

imagery of the destruction of the present age and the rising of the new world out of the sea is strikingly similar to that of the Christian Book of Revelation, and such images are also to be found in many other mythologies. What the Norsemen wanted was to find a meaning to their own life, and they found this not in promises of heaven (except for the Coifi types) but in the doctrine of the resurrection. They (and that means we) still do. For this is the meeting-point of comedy and tragedy, when Classical tragedy is transcended and Romantic tragedy interpreted.

Some comparisons may help to make the point, and I have selected an oddly assorted group of texts which make a kind of necklace. Each bead is different, all are somehow related, with a changing spectrum of colours from one end to the other. From these we may string together the linked beads of man's unbreakable hope:

'Do we wish for our beloved, among the living or among the dead, or is there aught else for which we long, yet, for all our longing, do not obtain ? Lo, all shall be ours if we but dive deep within, even to the lotus of the heart, where dwells the Lord. Yea, the object of every right desire is within our reach, though unseen, concealed by a veil of illusion. The self within the heart is like a boundary which divides the world from THAT. Day and night cross not that boundary, nor old age, nor death. . . . The Self, which is free from impurities, from old age and death, from grief, from hunger and thirst . . . obtains all the worlds and all desires.'

(*Chhāndogya Upanishads*)

And the sea gave up all the dead that were in it; Death and Hades were emptied. . . . I saw a new heaven and a new earth. I saw the holy city, the new Jerusalem, coming down from God out of heaven, as beautiful as a bride all dressed for her husband. Then I heard a loud voice call out from the throne, 'You see this city ? Here God lives among men . . . his name is God-with-them. He will wipe away all tears from their eyes, there will be no more death, and no more mourning or sadness.' . . . and the city did not need the sun or the moon for light, since it was lit by the radiant glory of God. . . . Nothing unclean may come into it. . . .'I am Alpha and Omega, the beginning and the end. Happy are those who have washed their robes clean, so that they will have the right to feed on the tree of life and can come through the gates into the city.'

(Revelation 20–22)

'In the morning the princess was up early, and took off the mourning dress which she had worn for five whole years, and put on gay and beautiful clothes. And she swept the house and cleaned it, and adorned it with garlands and nosegays of sweet flowers and ferns, and prepared it as though she were making ready for her wedding. And when night fell she lit up the woods and gardens with lanterns, and spread a table as for a feast, and lit in the house a thousand wax candles. Then she waited for her husband, not knowing in what shape he might appear. And at midnight there came striding from the river the prince, laughing, but with tears in his eyes; and she ran to meet him, and threw herself into his arms, crying and laughing too. So the prince came home . . . and the old king wept with joy to see them. And the bells, so long silent, were set a-ringing again . . . and there was fresh feasting and rejoicing. . . . And happy indeed were the prince and princess, who in due time became king and queen, and lived and ruled long and prosperously.'

(Indian fairy-tale. Andrew Lang collection)

Since you have been brought back to true life with Christ, you must look for the things that are in heaven, where Christ is. . . . But when Christ is revealed – and he is your life – you too will be revealed in all your glory with him . . . he loves you, and you should be clothed in sincere compassion, in kindness and humility, gentleness and patience.

(Colossians)

Your glory pours into my soul
Like sunlight against gold.
When may I rest within you, Lord?
My joys are manifold,
You robe yourself in my soul,
And my soul is clothed in you,
If you loved me more I could
Surely go from here, and be
Where through all eternity
I might love you as I would.

When I flow, you must be laved,
When you sigh
You draw my heart, God's heart, into yourself.
When you weep for me
I take you in my arms.
But when you love
We two shall be as one.

When we are one at last, then none
Can ever make us part again,
Unending, wish-less rapture
Shall dwell between us twain.

(Mechtild of Magdeburg)

' "No! No!" exclaimed the prince. "I will never part from you. You must come with me and be my wife. We have gone through many troubles together, and now we will share our joys."

The maiden resisted his words for some time, but at last she went with him.

In the forest they met a woodcutter, who told them that in the palace, as well as in all the land, there had been great sorrow over the loss of the prince . . . so, by the help of the magic ball the maiden contrived that he should put on the same clothes that he had been wearing at the time he had vanished. . . .

The prince wept bitterly when he heard [of his father's death] . . . and for three days he ate and drank nothing. But on the fourth day he stood in the presence of his people as their new king and, calling his councillors, he told them all the strange things that had befallen him, and how the maiden had borne him safe through all. And the councillors cried with one voice, "Let her be your wife, and our liege lady".'

And that is the end of the story.

('The Grateful Prince.' Esthonian
tale from the Andrew Lang collection)

'Bernadette had opened her eyes again. She understood all that was going on . . . the prayers for the dying were begun . . . the words in which the human soul greets its bridegroom: "I was asleep but my heart waked. It is the voice of my beloved that knocketh, saying, 'Open to me my sister, my love, my dove, my undefiled. . . .'"

Bernadette's eyes flashed strangely into the void. . . . suddenly a great thrill made her body quiver and a new strength lifted her up. Therewith came, long echoing from her breast . . . the cry of her confession: "J'aime—I love."

"J'aime." That confession of love did not fade from the consciousness of Marie Dominique Peyramale. He was still kneeling by the door without motion. The nuns . . . flitted softly about and clad the dead girl in habit and coif and fetched long thick candles and . . . lit them. . . . He could see sundry fruit trees of the cloister garden in blossom. . . . All things had changed. Silvery was the light of day, golden was the light of the tapers. And daylight and candlelight played over the eternally remote face of Bernadette. To his own surprise he heard himself whispering: "Your life begins, O Bernadette." '

(*The Song of Bernadette*. Franz Werfel)

'Little Kay was quite blue, nay, almost black with cold . . . his head was like a lump of ice. Gerda . . . entered the large, cold, empty hall. She saw Kay, she recognized him, she flew upon his neck, she held him fast. . . . But he sat still as before—cold, silent, motionless. Hot and bitter were the tears she shed, they fell upon his breast, they reached his heart, they thawed the ice and dissolved the tiny splinter of glass within it. Then Kay burst into tears . . . he knew his old companion and immediately exclaimed with joy, "Gerda, little Gerda, where hast thou been all this time? And where have I been?" . . . and he embraced Gerda while they laughed and wept by turns. And Gerda kissed his cheeks, whereupon they became fresh and glowing as ever; she kissed his eyes, and they sparkled like her own; she kissed his hands and feet, and he was once more healthy and merry. . . . They took each other by the hand and wandered forth out of the palace . . . and as they walked on the winds were hushed into calm, and the sun burst forth in splendour from among the dark storm clouds.

Kay and Gerda walked on hand in hand, and wherever they went it was spring, beautiful spring, with its bright flowers and green leaves.'

(*The Snow Queen*. Hans Andersen)

Meanwhile, Mary stayed outside near the tomb, weeping. . . . she turned round and saw Jesus standing there, though she did not recognize him. Jesus said, 'Woman, why are you weeping? Who are you looking for?' Supposing him to be the gardener, she said, 'Sir, if you have taken him away, tell me where you have put him and I will go and remove him.' Jesus said, 'Mary!' She knew him then and said to him in Hebrew, 'Rabbuni!' which means Master. Jesus said to her, 'Do not cling to me, because I have not yet ascended to the Father. But go and find my brothers and tell them: I am ascending to my Father and your Father, to my God and your God.' So Mary of Magdala went and told the disciples that she had seen the Lord. . . . In the evening of the same day, the first day of the week, the doors were closed in the room where the disciples were, for fear of the Jews. Jesus came and stood among them. He said to them, 'Peace be with you', and showed them his hands and his side. The disciples were filled with joy when they saw the Lord.

(John 20)

'But Colin had actually dropped back against his cushions, even though he gasped with delight, and had covered his eyes with his hands and held them there, shutting out everything until they were inside and the chair stopped as if by magic and the door was closed. Not till then did he take them away and look round and round as Dickon and Mary had done. And over walls and earth and trees and swinging sprays and tendrils the fair green veil of tender little leaves had crept, and in the grass under the trees and the gray urns in the alcoves and here and there and everywhere were touches of gold and purple and white and the trees were showing pink and snow above his head and there were fluttering of wings and faint sweet pipes and humming and scents and scents. And the sun fell warm upon his face like a hand with a lovely touch. And in wonder Mary and Dickon stood and stared at him. He looked so strange and different because a pink glow of colour had actually crept all over him— ivory face and neck and hands and all.

"I shall get well! I shall get well!" he cried out. "Mary! Dickon! I shall get well! And I shall live for ever and ever and ever!" '

(*The Secret Garden*. Frances Hodgson Burnett)

'His resurrection must then be understood not as a mere return to life as such, but as a conquest of the deadliness of death. . . . It is then understandable, further, that Jesus' resurrection was not seen as a private Easter for his private Good Friday, but as the beginning and source of the abolition of the universal Good Friday, of that God-forsakenness of the world which comes to light in the deadliness of the death of the cross . . . as the source of the risen life of all believers and as a confirmation of the promise which will be fulfilled in all and will show itself in the very deadliness of death to be irresistible. . . . "And as the power of the 'flesh' is manifested in the fact that it binds man to the transitory, to that which in reality is already past, to death, so the power of the Spirit is manifested in the fact that he gives the believer freedom, opens the way to the future, to the eternal, to life." For freedom is nothing else than being open to the genuine future, letting oneself be determined by the future.'

(*The Theology of Hope.* Jurgen Moltmann, also quoting Rudolph Bultmann, *Theology of the New Testament*)

This necklace of passages moves through a range of subjects beginning with the pursuit of oneness through contemplative prayer which draws towards eternity and draws with it those united with it in love. This is immediately linked to the bridal theme which expresses the loving oneness of man with God, where man is already caught up in the movement of redemption which leads to the final completeness of union. The familiar happy ending of the fairy-tales is linked to the bridal imagery of the mystic who looks forward to the same happy ending, but the final bliss is preceded by the trials and separations which seem to be an essential part of the quest for eternal life. The death of a saint brings its conviction of achievement and hope, and it is love that liberates Bernadette, as it liberates Kay from the power of the Snow Queen. In the most loved of the resurrection accounts there is also the promise of new life, the oneness of love which already exists, yet can only be finally achieved through separation and labour for its sake. And the beginning of health for the sick boy, Colin, holds an implicit promise of eternal life, also realized through the power of love. Finally, the contemporary theologian, quoting the master from the generation before, shows the same essential movement—the reaching out to the future which involves man in the risen Christ, and is by him involved in that future.

The real theme, then, in all these extracts, is that of eternal life achieved in, and through, love, which is both human and (at the same time) divine. These pieces have been chosen to represent a great number of others in the same categories, mystical and apocalyptic writing, fairy-tale, biography, theology, and of course the Gospel itself. It would be rash to draw conclusions from such a small collection, and they are not put together here in order to prove a point, because this book is addressed to Christians, for whom the point does not need proving. It does, however, need understanding; it needs to be seen, felt, smelt, as well as heard, if we are to begin to realize what it means to believe in Christ risen, here and now. The purpose of these passages therefore, is rather to try to evoke an atmosphere, an atmosphere of Christian hope, whether it be expressed by a Hindu mystic or a Roumanian storyteller or an English writer for children.

This atmosphere has some very noticeable ingredients, though all are not present in every passage. One is a sense of quietness. At a certain point it is as if the winds of life dropped, as the winds were hushed when Gerda rescued Kay. There is a timeless moment which is eternity, making itself felt even in the middle of the journey towards it. The lotus of the heart is the place of that sudden peace, which is, in fact, present all the time once it has been discovered. Jesus sends Mary away to carry his message, yet the moment of knowledge of love is not ended, merely hidden by the preoccupation of the rest of the journey. The two traditional fairy-tales place this moment at the very end when all the searching and danger and waiting come to their appointed fulfilment, 'and that is the end of the story', as it is also when it is perceived in the experience of death. But this is only true because implicit in such a death is the knowledge that 'there shall be no more death'. In my end is my beginning.

The experience of the eternal moment is never stale. It may continue to be recaptured, and to be known under its veils throughout life, as intoxicatingly fresh in every encounter as in the first revelation. The image of this is the perfect one of spring. Whatever the accurate accounts of the flora and climate of Palestine may tell us, the reader of the Gospels sees Mary of Magdala kneeling among the wild flowers of the spring he knows in his own land. The hush in that garden is the incomparable quiet of the countryside at dawn, on an April morning. It is natural and right that when Kay rises from his icy tomb of lovelessness, and walks hand in hand with Gerda, they should find that suddenly it is spring. And we are not surprised that Colin's first experience of a garden in spring, after years in a stuffy bedroom, should make him feel that he must live for ever. In one of the fairy-tales the princess who is waiting and hoping for the return of the prince decks the house with flowers and ferns, creating a kind of little spring of her own for her lover. This is combined with the putting on of festive robes, and both are signs of celebration—the celebration of the beginning of new life. Paul's letter to the Colossians promises that the present (in a sense hidden) garment of compassion, kindness, humility, gentleness and patience is, in fact, the wedding garment. Now it is concealed under what the Upanishads call the veils of illusion, but it will be revealed in all its glory when Christ also is revealed in his final triumph. The garment of mourning is put off, and festal robes take its place, whose significance is the same as the robe which the earth puts on in spring.

Marriage, festivity, new life, the passing of the winter of struggle and sorrow, love set free from its prison and setting out into the future: all these are the themes of the passages chosen here, and the Song of Songs, in the most famous of all its celebrations of love, brings them together:

> My beloved lifts up his voice,
> He says to me,
> 'Come then, my love,
> my lovely one, come.
> For see, winter is past,
> the rains are over and gone,
> The flowers appear on the earth,
> the season of glad songs is come,
> the cooing of the turtle-dove is heard in our land.
> The fig tree is forming its first figs
> and the blossoming vines give out their fragrance.
> Come then, my love,
> my lovely one, come.
> My dove, hiding in the clefts of the rock,
> in the coverts of the cliff,

> show me your face,
> let me hear your voice,
> for your voice is sweet
> and your face is beautiful.'

Did Frances Hodgson Burnett hear the echo of those words when she described Colin's first sight of the 'secret garden' in spring? Perhaps, but not necessarily. This is a human symbol of salvation and hope which does not seem to require conscious models. The happy ending of the fairy-tales is this kind of happy ending. The Hebrew theologians set man's beginnings in a garden, where the first spring of all unfolded under the startled gaze of the newly created heavens. The first experience of the eternally new life of the risen Jesus is also set in a garden, at the very time of the brief Palestinian spring, while everyone is busy celebrating the paschal feast, which was originally a celebration of spring lambing. Deirdre's tree grows from her grave, the grateful prince will not be separated from the girl who saved him and all men celebrate their glory; the Hebrew bride is called out of seclusion into the spring fields. The fairy-tale ending is a wedding, and a royal wedding at that. It is celebrated with festive robes and music, as the earth also celebrates her wedding with the sun. The mystics long for the final union which the Apocalypse describes in terms of a traditional fairy-tale wedding, with all the good people made happy, and no possibility of future decline from this blessed condition.

So the fairy-tale happy ending is about man's hope of resurrection. This is the conclusion which is possible when the signs are read in the light of the resurrection of Jesus. The earthy and unwavering realism of the fairy-tale assessment of man's real nature and needs leads to this: he will not be satisfied with less than the perfection of happiness, which must, therefore, be eternal. And this ending is always expressed as a bridal, and is a triumph over deathliness. Sometimes the union-through-death theme is made more explicit, as in the story of Deirdre, or that of lovers turned into birds to save them from destruction, but even when the ending itself is the natural joy of a wedding it always follows grief and danger, for these are expressions of the deathliness which is opposed to the victory of life. Often this grief takes the form of a symbolic burial by enchantment in some animal form, from which love brings release. This is the case in the Indian tale whose ending is quoted here, and in many others of the *Black Bull of Norroway* type. And in all such endings there is – because it is about a wedding – a fusion of the concepts of an arrested moment of blissful achievement (the 'peace' of the Gospel, the 'eternal now' of the mystics) and of that movement into the future which the notion of bridal celebration implies. This is a specially Christian atmosphere, it is the air of the new time which belongs to the risen Jesus, walking with real feet through the wet grass of a garden in spring.

So what do we do about it? We cannot leave it to Fra Angelico, though there are always painters and poets and musicians who find themselves obliged to pass on this same message, even without meaning to do so. But if they do, it is because the message is in the air. We tend to keep our windows shut and exist in a fug of spiritually exhausted ideas, because we do not realize how much the fresh air matters—until someone tells us that spring has come. Then we open the windows and 'draw in long breaths of it', and, like Colin, we feel that 'something quite new and delightful' is happening to us.

Which is a way of saying that the recovery of spiritual vitality means the recovery of faith in the resurrection as an experienced fact. That, finally, is what this book has been about. The fairy-tales open up our understanding of what the Gospels tell us about human life, its meaning and destiny. We follow their themes and characters, and recognize their counterparts and echoes in every type of account of human experience, poetical, historical, mystical, and at last we come to this central assertion, which makes sense of all the rest, that man is destined to be united with Christ in the life of the resurrection. This is one assertion that only Christians can make and of course only those who are able to make this assertion can make this kind of sense of what fairy-tales tell us. The theology of the tales is not self-evident, and we cannot use it as any convincing argument to support or induce belief. But when faith is struggling to realize itself, and to see where to go, the stories provide a much needed renaissance of Christian language in which faith may understand its nature.

We need to live the life of the resurrection now, in order to share it 'hereafter'. This is scarcely a new idea. St Paul repeated it tirelessly, under various images and with much detailing of exactly what it meant in terms of behaviour. There are two peculiarities about the Christian assertion concerning the relation between man present and man future. One is that the transition from one to the other is also the revelation of the identity of the one with the other. Yet there is a real transition which cannot be dismissed as illusion, except in the special sense of the word illusion which belongs to Eastern mysticism. The other peculiarity is that this process of transition belongs fully to the individual and also fully to the whole community. Each person has to make his own journey, yet it is only possible for him to undertake it because it is the journey of the whole race. It is his human nature, caught up in Christ's human nature, which makes the journey possible and necessary. But it isn't possible to get there by being shuffled along with the crowd without personal commitment. (The guest who didn't choose to put on his wedding garment but relied on getting in with the rest was turned out.) On the other hand there is only one way to go, whatever the varieties of experience.

This curious series of paradoxes, fitting together like some kind of psychedelic jigsaw, is traditionally expressed in the concept of the Christian community as Christ's body. All belong to it, yet without loss of identity or personal responsibility. And Christ is both already risen and – by his bridal union with his as yet unperfected people – still on the way to the happy ending. The urgent reality of this interlocking of individual and community in openness to the future Christ (who is already present in order to make this openness possible) has motivated the study of the political nature of Christianity, which must now be considered.

If the Christian revelation about man's future is 'for real' it cannot be relegated to the remaining areas of domestic privacy, leaving the world of gainful work, of government and of technological decision in a limbo of spiritual irrelevance. It used to be fashionable among Protestants, and some *avant-garde* Catholics, to express contempt for the monastic ideal because it represented a flight from the Christian duty to deal with reality. This view is less often heard now, when it has become common for people to 'drop out' literally or psychologically, because they have lost hope of effectively changing a political and social set-up which appears past redemption. But there is still a sense in which a withdrawal from the world is inadmissible for the Christian. The resurrection faith forbids us to regard any human situation as past redemption, since a situation is made up of people. Their ways of relating (or not relating) may be hopelessly destructive but the people themselves are not beyond hope of recognizing other ways. In reacting to such a situation on any scale, the Christian person and the Christian community may not drop out, but may—indeed must—take the monastic way, in some sense or other.

This is the key to the political involvement of Christians in their world, for the real monastic gesture is one of hope. This is a hope which is a present experience, but which requires a certain kind of withdrawal in order to have room to make its statement with sufficient coherence and force. In this sense the Christian community is always apart, even when its members are most closely involved in direct political action, or in the perennial Christian work of practical alleviation of suffering, directly or indirectly, in the public or the private sphere, officially or unofficially. At a time when Christians often regard their efforts to help people in need as the most urgent and obvious Christian work, this monastic quality ('monastic' seems a better word in this context than 'religious') is even more important. Many people ask Christians, and Christians ask themselves, 'Isn't Christianity nowadays simply an ethical system, which humanists can accept and practise just as well, without the backing of an archaic religious system?' And there is (or soon will be) no answer but an affirmative one unless the Christian community can express its self-awareness as the community of the risen Christ. It can only do this by its firm decision to set its sights on him and judge the world by the standard of the resurrection hope towards which all creation is drawn.

There are many ways of doing it, but not all the ways in which Christians actually do try to live their baptism have, in practice, this clear relation to the resurrection hope. How can we judge which of our efforts, personal and communal, are part of the authentic work of the resurrection community?

The fairy-tales can help us to understand the proper nature of a Christian work that really does have the 'monastic' character of orientation to the right kind of happy-ever-after—not Utopian but according to the real potentialities of human nature transformed in Christ. A great number of fairy-tales, especially those of the 'quest' type, have particular characteristics which open up ideas here. One is the fact that the main characters in the tales are royal, more often than not. They belong to a ruling minority whose actions have therefore public relevance. Some of the eighteenth- and nineteenth-century fairy-tales preserve the royalty because it is traditional, but show no interest in this public dimension of the lives of the heroes and heroines whose fortunes are treated as important only to themselves. But the occurrence all over the world of tales whose main characters belong to a ruling caste makes it clear, as I suggested earlier in the book, that the story is about the whole people, whom the individual characters represent.

The mythology of 'blood' has partly disappeared from our culture, so that we no longer expect birth into a distinguished line automatically to confer spiritual and mental as well as social distinction. But belonging to an old and famous family does often bring out the very best in people, because it gives them a conviction of a kind of 'family vocation'. It can also give the confidence which is needed in order to try to measure up to the job, because 'our family always have'. Something of this kind is implicit in the almost universal ascription of royal blood to the girls who have the kind of task described in the chapter on the princess. When she is not actually royal by birth she has the same kind of qualities and ends up by *becoming* royal. The same applies to the various heroes. The idea that the Christian vocation is a 'royal' one has been used by preachers and prophets since St Paul, and it carries precisely the significance which it has in the fairy-tales. The Christian people, by their 'adoption as sons' have become a 'royal priesthood, a consecrated nation', the family of the King of Kings. This means that, whether they like it or not, a royal vocation is laid on them, and they are expected to strive to measure up to it with all their strength. Yet the ability to do so depends on something they cannot gain through any amount of effort, but which is 'in the blood', and this is the blood of Christ's body. This becomes more explicit when, as often happens, the reason the king sends his sons on a mission is to find a way of saving the kingdom from threats and danger, or to find out which one will make a good ruler and safeguard the future of the kingdom.

The king, by definition, is in charge of an institution, a definite form of human society with laws and customs and a history. He is responsible for it, and wants to ensure that it will have a peaceful and prosperous future. But often the king has the wrong ideas about what kind of ruler the kingdom really ought to have. Fairy-tale kingdoms and their rulers, like all human institutions, have an inevitable tendency to get stuck in the present, to lose momentum and concentrate on preserving the *status quo*—what St Paul calls 'the things that are'. This tendency arises from a lack of any standards by which to judge the situation other than those which are implicit in the situation itself. The human ability to make the best of a given situation, and get a lot out of life in spite of it (the 'comedy' style of life) helps to prevent any change. In our time the Churches have been insensibly pushed into a position where they are powerful forces against change, not on purpose, but because their spiritual resources enable people to get more out of those bits of their lives which are not conditioned by the demands of labour and the State. This makes them more content with their condition.

The fairy-tale king, if he is a good king, is very inclined to do this. The more genial and popular he is the less he is inclined to look for anything more for his people than a continuation of his own pleasantly opulent way of life, enlivening the lot of the populace with occasional festivals and dollops of largesse. And he is naturally inclined to value those counsellors who tell him that this is all he has to do, and to feel that those who call in question the value of the 'things that are' are traitors and rebels. The Cordelia motif, recurrent in many tales, is not concerned only with the rightness of the non-conforming child but, as Shakespeare spells out, with the destructive wrongness of a king apparently well-intentioned and unselfish.

The true successor's job, however, is to call in question the accepted values. Sometimes his royal father (or father-in-law, for winning the princess may be the appointed test of fitness for office) is looking for just such an ability to go for essentials and remain undeceived by the impressive facade of the *status quo*. More often the old king is angry at the challenge to accepted methods and either despises or actively persecutes the hero who will not toe the party line. But in the end his fitness to guide the kingdom into its future is proved by his determination to call in question all the accepted ways of doing things.

So the grateful prince will not accept the propriety of giving away a peasant's daughter in fulfilment of a promise that should have involved himself. Reasons of state simply wont wash, he insists on the priority of the basic human values of truthfulness and gratitude. And when, after a period of servitude and some hair-raising adventures, he escapes to freedom with the help of that peasant's daughter, he insists on marrying her, and she is acclaimed as 'liege lady' by the people. The boy whom the king had adopted, and who slapped the princess when she teased him to tell his long-kept secret, was imprisoned by her father in a tower and left to starve. He was punished because his action showed that he valued his promise of secrecy more than the respect and gratitude due to royalty as representing the rightful power of this world. And it was the princess herself who remorsefully fed him in his prison, and secured his release in time to prove himself the saviour of the kingdom.

In one strange tale the heir to the throne refuses to stay at home and learn to govern because he wants to discover the secret of immortality. After many adventures he comes to the City of Immortality and is saved in the nick of time by its queen, just as he is about to fall into the waters of death that flow under its walls. But he never goes back to his job as ruler. This story states more clearly than usual the dilemma of the Christian, whose natural loyalty is to his own place and people, and who loves what is good in their traditions and ways, but who is dedicated to the eternal coming kingdom, which inevitably calls in question the value of 'things that are'. It may be that an apparent betrayal of that first loyalty will better serve the real interests of the beloved people than the assumption of the expected old-style responsibility. The refusal to accept that responsibility as it is normally presented may be the one thing that can shake up the old ways and make it possible for them to grow towards the future. Even when, as usually happens, the hero's tribulations and rejection are resolved and the heir ascends the throne with his hard-won bride amid public rejoicings, he does so not as the errant son who has learnt by his mistake to accept the good old ways but as the one who challenged the old ways. By so doing he has proved his fitness to guide the people towards a happy-ever-after. And, as I showed in the first chapter, the one who proves to be the right kind of future ruler is the one who was disregarded, and despised; the foolish dreamer amongst the royal family of splendid, efficient types, or the boy of low birth who was befriended or adopted out of kindness, like the one who slapped the proud princess.

In a famous passage, Melancthon refers to Paul's words about the way God uses the weak and despised to confound the power of the devil, but his word for what is usually translated as 'weakness' is the Latin 'imbecillitate', which normally means physical weakness, or feebleness. But it was also used to qualify mind or spirit—that is, to indicate feeble-mindedness as well, and Melancthon was presumably not referring to the physical fitness or otherwise of Christians. Our common use of the word 'imbecile' translates his meaning better. This is revealing, for while many of us could put up with being described as 'weak', if this is understood as being powerless to cope with the sheer magnitude of evil that confronts us, few would relish being referred to as imbecile. But imbecility, or at least feeble-mindedness, is the kind of idea Paul put forward to suggest the normal estimate of those God uses, and what God does with them is precisely to oppose 'the confession of the saints' (that feeble-minded lot) to 'the kingdom of the devil'. The 'saints' challenge the power of evil over the community of man, by operating according to a standard which makes no sense to the world, which consequently regards them as feeble-minded. If they persist to the extent of becoming a real nuisance, the world is apt to take a Hitlerian view of what should be done with imbeciles.

But this designation of the 'saints' as weak or feeble-minded is a reminder of the wide gap that inevitably exists between the Christian and the worldly estimate of what matters and needs to be done. From one point of view the job of the resurrection community is to keep this gap wide enough, clearing the space between itself and the 'things that are', so that all can see precisely what the Gospel of the resurrection is about. The 'monastic' withdrawal is required to emphasize the 'imbecility' of the youngest son, the dreamer who dreams of eternal life, but the distance is only a spiritual distance, not a physical or emotional one. It separates the one on whom the responsibility of knowledge of the future kingdom has been laid from those who may obscurely hope for freedom and a future happy-ever-after, but who cannot see the way there 'unless some man show me'. This kind of royalty is a privilege, but it is primarily a dedication to a role which involves suffering, and is no guarantee in itself against abysms of irrelevance and silliness, and final lapse into treachery. For the elder sons are also sons.

So the youngest son is both royal and rejected, and it is this combination which enables him to make the decisions and undertake the ventures that call in question the way the existing institutions shape people. This is also the combination that justifies a direct Christian involvement in every kind of political, social, educational and domestic institution. For the youngest son is destined to rule, and that means being concerned with the shape of the institution which exists. Withdrawal into a private religious enclave is simply not possible for the resurrection community.

But his concern is always a calling in question, a breaking down of old patterns, not because they are evil but because what is good in them must have room to grow if it is not to stagnate, leaving only the evil as a living force. At present, the ways in which Christians are doing this are commonly experimental, and like all experiments some, perhaps most, will fail. This does not matter, because even the failure helps us to understand better what really needs to be done. The old ways of challenging the nature of worldly institutions – mainly religious communities of various kinds and in many different denominational forms – continue, but need to rediscover their purpose, which tends in time to accommodate itself to the things that are. New forms spring up, and new types of involvement in existing or newly created secular institutions. Some institutions can be shaped towards the coming Christ, others can only be called in question for their destruction, like the beam of an old house which, when it is exposed to the air, crumbles to dust.

One of the ways in which the resurrection community must keep on rediscovering the sense of direction in its quest is through its liturgical celebrations. These enable it to engage in the life of this world without becoming either identified with it, or relegated to a religious entertainment arcade. The celebration in the present of the bridal feast of the resurrection which is to come is the place where people can subject their everyday attitudes and priorities to the test of implicit comparison with the attitudes and priorities of the kingdom of God. The readings and preachings, the petitions and songs, aim at (or should aim at) calling in question all the various ways in which the community is acting as messenger of the risen Christ, with a view to correcting any loss of vision and renewing the determination to go on towards the future Christ.

But the eucharistic celebration itself is a complete judgement and renewal, since it is a prophecy of what is to come, and also a model of the institutional forms which really can help people to grow towards their future. The symbolism of the eucharist is complex, and in the context of this study it is linked to the bridal celebrations of the finally triumphant hero and heroine. It also calls up fairy-tale images of the comradeship of the journey, the help given to the weaker by the stronger, the advice of the wise and the reconciliation of those estranged by misfortune or mis-understanding. And all of this is there to help in the creation of a people who have the vision and the courage necessary to challenge the institutions of this world in love. They challenge them so that they may become, if possible, ways in which the past may open out towards the future, which is the life of resurrection.

It seems quite likely, to judge by the forecasts and suggestions being made by scientists of various kinds, that the resurrection community may have a chance to be a challenge not only in the sense of offering more human standards but of creating 'pilot projects' of a new human community for the post-technological age. One kind of Christian job is always to be where the trouble is, and try to help people there, but another, equally important, is 'monastic' in more than the 'distancing' sense of being single of eye and poor in spirit. It seems likely, in fact, that some new form of 'monastic' community life, one including families with their own degree of privacy yet with a sharing of resources, materials and means of life, will be of practical help to mankind at large as well as a means of living the Gospel. For it is one of the oddities of our time that the threats of the hell-fire preacher against the wicked city are coming true, and the sins of the fathers are visibly being visited on the children, unto the third and fourth generation (if there is one). And in response to this threat of doom the repentance required is where the sin lies, which is in attitudes to material things. So the task of at least some of the resurrection community may be to demonstrate a real and workable way of life (as the monasteries once did) in which things are cared for, not ex-ploited; in which the restriction of technical apparatus (scarce because of scarcity of raw materials) means a more human type of labour and more respect for the labourer; in which sharing and caring are obvious economic as well as spiritual good sense; and in which community self-sufficiency is not a smug isolationism but a contribution to the welfare of the nation and the earth.

Much more could be said, and is beginning to be said (though only in a whisper so far). In a book such as this the enormous implications for Christians of the *ethical* changes demanded by the ecological crisis can only be touched on. But they are incalculable, and full of hope. It may be that we have, now, an opportunity such as we have never had before.

If this calling-in-question is the job of the whole community of believers, it all depends on the individual within the community. To be baptized (and I do not mean getting the baby 'done', with cake and champagne to follow) means to be chosen to preach the resurrection. It means to be the youngest son, to have a built-in personal princess, and a whole range of wise animals to provide guidance in sticky situations. But it also means being sent on the usual arduous and unpredictable quest, all set about with witches and ogres. And it means going on to the end because there is a future, which is also a bridal, and a happy-ever-after, however unlikely that may seem at certain stages of the way there. The baptized do not commission themselves, the whole people does that, but once they have been chosen and sealed by the community, the progress of the people's journey towards the promised land depends on the way each one pursues his own quest.

This is where the fairy-tales make their final contributions to renewed understanding of the Gospel. The way they do this is by ending with a wedding. Not all do, of course, and there are many kinds of fairy-tales that offer different themes and interpretations of life from those studied here. There is the flip tale of the princess who turns out to be not the 'real thing' and is shut out of the kingdom, for all her pride and royal birth, to the tune of a mocking little folk-song. There is the hero who decides all this royalty is not his cup of tea, and having vanquished the dragons goes back to his farm. There is the tale of ambition that ends, after experience of undeserved opulence, back on the rubbish tip or in the fisherman's hut. There is the tale which turns on the loyalty of friends, who will not desert each other and are finally saved by one of their number. All these tales, and others, make their comment on the nature of human life, and assert as primary the Gospel values which our civilization regards as a private luxury, to be enjoyed when the demands of money-making and power-seeking allow. But the wedding is the ending to most of the 'quest' tales, which predominate both in number and in the popular imagination. The 'fairy-tale ending' means, to most people, the wedding of the prince and his bride after all their adventures, and a future guaranteed 'happy-ever-after'. Another version of the quest tale relates the adventures of the faithful queen, or other wedded heroine, who seeks her lost husband, often in disguise, and the ending is not a wedding but a glorious reunion and celebration of vindicated fidelity.

Whether it be a wedding or a reunion the point made is the same one: the quest is undertaken for love, empowered by love which nothing can overcome, and ends in an eternal celebration of that triumphant fidelity. Love is the reason for all that happens, and the reward that crowns all the suffering which it entails.

But the journey to a happy ending is made in that atmosphere of mingled hope, peace, newness and celebration which was evoked by the passages I quoted. It is not just any human love story, however satisfactorily it turns out; it has the paschal quality which distinguishes it from a fictional or biographical tale. This paschal quality is peculiar to the fairy tales (it is not found, for instance, in most romantic novels, even the very good ones), and once it is recognized it can make us turn over the pages of the Gospel with fresh understanding, for the fairy-tales are the distillation of vintage human wisdom. These shrewd, crude, often humorous statements of life's real values and purposes bring us back, finally, to those chapters of the Gospel of John which make explicit the truth that is acted out in the bridal motif of so many tales.

In these chapters (14–17) John expresses the paschal relationship of Jesus with his people. It is a bridal relationship which is made possible by the hard journey of the Passion, and sealed in the risen life which is both his and theirs. But the spirit of Jesus, expressed in the long discourses after the Supper, is the spirit which he gives to his people. It is by this that each one is enabled to respond to the call of the Gospel, and make it come true in his particular human work. So there is a proper sense in which the words of Jesus, in this particular context, which is that of the paschal relationship, are also the words of the Christian to other Christians. This is the youngest son on his quest speaking to the princess, and the princess offering her lucid wisdom to bring them both through passion to joy.

This understanding is complementary to the other, and fundamental, meaning to this discourse, which is John's urgent presentation of the Lord's personal testament to his beloved. It is because it is primarily such a testament that it is also the self-understanding of the Christian as one called to be another Christ. To know it as this kind of self-understanding is to realize far more clearly what the love of Jesus really means, and how all his people are involved in the journey to his kingdom, which he has gone to prepare for them.

Only brief indications are possible here, for though a whole book (or several) could be used to develop the possibilities of this approach, what matters is that each person should bring his or her own experience and temperament to the task of understanding the will of God for himself or herself, discovering at the same time the place of the disciple in the whole exodus of the people of God on its way to the promised land. All the same, a few bits of thinking along these lines may help to show how the fairy-tales open the door by which a post-Christian civilization may come in to the house of many rooms.

The very first verses of John 14 tell of an imminent but brief parting, and it has a purpose. The prince who has been loved and befriended on his adventures is going ahead to arrange a royal reception for his faithful companion and beloved helper. So the Christian, charged with the work of preparing the kingdom, must often go ahead of those he is sent to love and to help, and who have loved and helped him, because he works according to values whose origin is buried with Christ and risen with him. Those he leaves for this reason may well feel forsaken, but the parting is necessary for them also. And even within the one Christian personality there are hopes and achievements and plans which are good, and which are necessary to the growing person, but which do not belong to the kingdom. The peasant girl who has helped the prince to safety and home must wait until she is summoned to court, and then she must shed the clothes of her old laborious usefulness and put on the bridal robes, which are now properly hers.

This is a bald statement of a type of Christian anxiety which is very common now. The fear that a religious dedication may remove us from 'the world' which the Christian in Christ is sent to save is a real and proper fear. The proud princesses who were so conscious of their rank that they would not accept an (apparently) low-born husband, however valiant, are numerous in the fairy-tales, and they are just what the 'real princess', the divine wisdom, must never be. Christians are rightly anxious not to make this fatal mistake, and so they fear to accept fully a calling which obviously sets them apart. But the calling of the 'real princess' is apparent whatever the circumstances—dripping wet on the doorstep, or born in a shepherd's cottage. 'No one can come to the Father except through Me': if we are to be 'other Christs' we have to accept, realistically and painfully, the fact that other people will look to Christians for recognizable signs of their calling. The Christian must enter into the paschal relationship of hope and love, which is that of the royal wedding leading to 'happy ever-after'. This, if it is fully lived, is bound to give him or her that quality of life which St Paul refers to as being 'clothed' in the virtues that belong to the risen life. The clothing is a wedding garment.

In the next chapter of St John occurs one of the 'vine' passages, in which Jesus makes use of the prophetic image of the vine, deeply embedded in Jewish culture and poetry. The vine is Israel, God's people, whom he has planted in the land which, for its sake, he cleared of foreign people. Now Christ, the final and perfect fruit of Israel, is himself the true vine, and the people of the new Covenant, sealed in his blood, are the branches that grow from that stem. Developing this image, the evangelist shows that the sap that gives life to the branches, and without which they wither and die, is the Father's love, the love in which Jesus lives, and by which his disciples live in him and in the Father.

And the fruit of this love is *joy*. This love and this joy are the way of life of the follower of Jesus, which means that it is through the love and joy of Christ discovered in his disciples that the world is to know him. So the disciple, also, must be able to say to others, 'I call you friends, because I have made known to you everything I have learnt from my Father.' The prince comes into his kingdom, and when he claims his inheritance he is able to share it. His wedding is a celebration of his union with his people, who are involved in the 'happy-ever-after' through him, for in them also dwells the eternal princess Sophia. (It is she, of course, who from time to time expresses herself in fairy-tales, for they are a way in which people tell one another of a world which is human, and yet curiously at odds with the ordinary human arrangements, of which it provides what the jargon calls a 'critique'.)

But this love and joy are, as all fairy-tale princes and princesses discover, won through suffering, and not simply the inevitable pain and labour of a long journey through strange territory: the greatest suffering is caused by the deliberate malice of enemies. 'If the world hates you, remember that it hated me before you', and it will hate, in their measure, all those who are drawn into the bridal celebration of the prince and princess. This is a psychological fact that lies behind many of the acute moral problems of Christians who respond to their calling in a society that is sick but will not admit it. The atmosphere evoked by the string of passages quoted earlier is utterly foreign to the kind of happiness which our kind of society regards as desirable, and which depends for its existence on the unhappiness of a great many other people. (But one is not supposed to mention this aspect of the matter.) When people discover the joy of the paschal relationship, and begin to operate by the fairy-tale values, not only are they themselves a scandal to the world whose standards they treat with obvious (though often tacit) contempt; all those who admire them, are helped by them, or even refuse to condemn them, are liable to share the hatred which is inevitably the world's reaction to such a damning judgement of all it holds dear.

The fact that Christians who really live by the Gospel cause trouble and unrest, and that others attempt to suppress or at least to discredit them, is not new. But nowadays we find it hard to take because we have got used to a vague idea that we live in an at least mildly 'Christian society'. We don't. I don't think anyone ever did, really, but we certainly don't now, and the notion that we once had such a thing is the measure of a loss of sensitivity to what the Gospel is really about. Fortunately we have the fairy-tales to fall back on. They show us that the ogres and witches will do all they can to prevent the prince and princess from coming into their kingdom, because that means the salvation not only of the prince and princess themselves but of the people. The people are the vocation of the prince and princess: the reason for their existence is to serve and preserve the people—but they also 'are' the people. They symbolize (which means more than being a symbol of) the health and well-being of the whole people. While the prince is still unsuccessful his people suffer also, from the obscuring of hope and the tyranny of those who see in 'the world' their chance of power and happiness, attained by the suppression of others. The prince's struggle and persecution involve the suffering of all his people, while they remain in any way attached to him, which means that anyone who really decides for Christ will involve a number of others – usually including the people he or she cares for most – in trouble and anxiety at the very least. They will find themselves the subject of unkind gossip, and petty misrepresentation and harassment, and will easily be classified, by some convenient label or other, as unsuitable for certain kinds of employment, or position, or benefit. In certain places and situations they will have a presumption of guilt attached to them in all kinds of encounters with the law, where a 'respectable' person would be presumed innocent.

An example of this kind of result, already cited, occurred in the United States, when the Jesuit Daniel Berrigan was convicted for his share in the destruction of files in one of the offices concerned with drafting young men to the Vietnam war. This 'crime' was a protest against an unjust war; Berrigan and his friends regarded it as fully justified, and the government that prosecuted him as criminal. He therefore jumped bail, and instead of giving himself up he simply disappeared, that is, he stayed with a series of friends. Finally he was caught, as he knew he would be, but as a sequel to this the friends with whom he was staying were then charged with 'concealing' a criminal. They had, in fact, done no more 'concealing' than anyone does who closes the front door when a visitor is inside it, but their sympathetic association with a man who had challenged the conscience of a nation already writhing with suppressed guilt made it natural for the representatives of the 'things that are' to assume their guilt. They still had to find a charge that could actually be put forward in court (I am informed this one of 'concealing' was not sufficient), but that came afterwards. The order is, first presume guilt, then find a crime of which people can be found guilty. This curious legal inversion is characteristic of 'the world's' approach to Jesus himself (the whole trail before Caiaphas is an example of it), to his followers, and to any known sympathizers with them. Further back in time the famous trial of Thomas More shows the same search for a crime to pin on a man already presumed guilty, and for loving him his family and friends suffered poverty, disgrace and exile. He would have spared them if he could but that was impossible: 'If they persecute me, they will persecute you too . . . but it will be on my account that they will do all this, because they do not know the One who sent me.' These are the words of Christ, and of the Christian in so far as he shares the life of the risen Lord, because the calling to save the people involves the people, whether it is carried out well or badly.

This is the meaning of the royal estate of the fairy-tale heroes and heroines. Its real sense only becomes apparent when it is understood in the light of the explicit Gospel statements, which in their turn are illuminated by this ancient concept of the unity of prince and people. The 'royal people' are royal for the sake of others, not for their own sake, and it is royalty that demands the uttermost sacrifice for the sake of the people. Yet the sacrifice itself makes no sense except in the context of a paschal bridal relationship already experienced. We have to keep remembering that special atmosphere which is incompatible with morbid addiction to suffering, delusions of singularity, hatred masquerading as crusading zeal, or a thirst for power. The 'real princess' or hero is obedient, single-minded and joyful.

The very essence of the paschal doctrine is expressed with great intensity in the second half of chapter 16 of St John, and in the priestly prayer of the following chapter. Here, most of all, the proper atmosphere is evident. Here, arising from the words in all their extraordinary power and depth, is the sense of true nature of the Christian life. 'This joy no one shall take from you.' The characteristic words recur—peace, joy, courage, unity, glory, love and eternal life. This discourse is set in the hours before the Passion, that is in the days of the quest and before the prince comes into his kingdom, but it makes quite clear what we have already realized: the quest can only be undertaken in the power of the life to which it leads. Eternal life is life *now;* the paschal air is the air that must be breathed by those who are called to share the journey to the cross and beyond. 'In the world you will have trouble, but be brave, I have conquered the world.' And that victory is in some sense appropriated by the Christian in advance. He is *already* royal, or he would not be asked to save the people. 'I have given them the glory You gave to me, that they may be one as we are one.'

So in the end it appears that the happy-ever-after has to have begun before the pursuit of it makes any sense. It has to have *really* begun, it must not be an escape fantasy or a kind of rough justice for the presently miserable. It must have begun as it means to go on, in joy and peace and courage and love, and in the sense of that mixture of expansiveness and ritual dignity and richness and let-your-hair-down that we sum up in the word 'glory'. And all this adds up to hope, because to breathe this kind of air is to be the kind of creature whose natural atmosphere this is. We breathe it as hope because we know that the scents it carries to our Gospel-trained noses come from the garden which belongs to all mankind, in which man is destined to 'live for ever and ever and ever'. Only most people don't know it.

So the absolutely basic message of that passage of St John (which simply echoes and makes explicit many other words of Jesus) is that the Christian hope is of eternal life, whose nature is love which is present now and is to be revealed, and that this life is a life of the whole human being, body and soul, individual and social. 'This Jesus whom you crucified', Peter announced to the Jews as raised. 'This Jesus' had died, had been a corpse, and was not a corpse any more but was alive with the bridal aliveness of the victorious prince. He had wedded the divine wisdom and absorbed into his triumph all the strange creatures which assisted his quest.

The special paschal atmosphere has to do with a human body, Christ's body and ours—our essentially bodily being, transformed not abandoned. The new life is a promise in the body, and the fairy-tales are all about bodies. Queer things happen to these bodies, but they are bodily happenings. It is here, perhaps, that the Gospel atmosphere and the fairy-tale atmosphere are most clearly related, not in incident or character but in their assumptions about what human beings are, for the Gospels also are about bodies. They are not about 'spiritual' states in the later sense of a spirit as the non-physical being of a human person.

On two occasions, the evangelist directly contradicts the notion of the disciples that when they saw Jesus they were seeing a ghost, or spirit. On the lake in Galilee, during the period of the public ministry, the fishermen in the boat thought they saw a ghost coming across the water. In the upper room on Easter Sunday these same men were frightened by what they took for a ghost. On both occasions they were unequivocally told that it was no ghost. 'It is I,' said Jesus to the men in the boat, and proceeded to get into it himself (Matthew 14: 24, 33; Mark 6: 45–52). 'Yes, it is I indeed,' he said to the eleven waiting behind locked doors. 'Touch me and see for yourselves. A ghost has no flesh and bones as you can see I have.' After which, says Luke, he ate some fish (Luke 24: 36–43). Even if many exegetes hesitate about the meaning of the resurrection accounts there is no doubt of the writer's intention. He meant that the risen Jesus was a human being in the fullest sense, a bodily sense, though clearly not an ordinary kind of body. He was no more a ghost after the resurrection than he was when he walked on the lake. The resurrection is a bodily event, it is about bodily people.

It follows that Christians, who are incorporated in Christ, are sharing in the bodily life of the risen Jesus. Their own wholeness is somehow changed, touched, livened by this union, which happens simply by that act of adhesion in love which we call faith. How it happens is odd and mysterious. I made some attempt to show 'how' in another book called *Act of Love*, but that discussion is out of place here, for what we are contemplating is simply the fact that it is so.

It is visibly so. It is a matter of degree, of course, but we can learn to recognize the small degree of transformation in the risen Jesus which comes to most sincere Christians by noticing the greater degree which is manifest in the few whose love of Christ swallows up and glorifies all other desires and emotions. It is a curious fact of history that the Christians of all denominations who have been 'canonized' (officially in the Catholic Church or by common consent of veneration and admiration in other Churches) have more often than not been people whose values contradicted not only those of their particular culture and society but also of their Church, as it happened at the time to be adapting itself to its surroundings. Some have even been persecuted by their fellow Christians for those very qualities that later attracted veneration for them as genuine examples of Christ's transforming power. They lived in Christ, and this changed them to such an extent that they, other Christs, became a scandal and a judgement to their generation, as well as objects of intense love and loyalty among those who had got the Gospel message themselves in some degree.

One of the things recorded of many of these saints is that they were changed *bodily* in some way. Their union with Christ was – is – one of the whole person, and the whole person began to show signs of this incorporation. There are many reports, some quite recent, that the faces of saints 'glowed' or 'shone' or other phrases which remind us of the descriptions of the risen Jesus. In a less spectacular way, a person's expression may be transformed so that those who see him are overcome with a kind of awe, as at a revelation. We are inclined to regard the physical phenomena of mysticism as suspect or merely funny (levitation, living without food or sleep, insensitivity to pain, incorruption of the body after death and so on), and they are certainly uncommon; nor are they in any way proofs of holiness. But there are too many (often well-documented) examples to be dismissed as mere inventions, and they do show that the human body is even more mysterious than we usually imagine, and subject to influences that we do not even begin to understand. In themselves, these phenomena are perhaps nothing important, but they are part of the evidence that phrases like 'the body of Christ', and Paul's worlds about dying and rising with Christ, are not merely images to describe a psychological identification with Jesus, but refer to an experienced fact, which is bodily because spiritual, because human beings are like that.

This fact is the explicit and practical experience of what the fairy-tales are talking about when the culmination of all the adventures is a royal wedding which is sealed to be 'happy-ever-after'. A marriage is a bodily union, and in the tale it is a union in love, with full knowledge, and as the appointed end and reward of obedient dedication to the quest. Marriage changes people, all through. It dedicates them to a new life, which is a shared life. It is a life which grows from the fact of a love 'stronger than death' of which Alcestis' return is a symbol. The 'happy-ever-after' is eternal because it is the fruit of sacrifice that burns away all that could spoil the union of love, and that sacrifice is death.

Nothing else can do the necessary work on human beings. A handful of people have seemed to shed so thoroughly all that is not proper to this wedding that they scarcely needed physical death to provide the bridal canopy. (Perhaps the doctrine of the bodily entrance into glory of the mother of Jesus has something to do with this.) It becomes, for them, almost a formality, a gesture whose real meaning is already manifest. But for most of us death is anything but a casual incident. It preoccupies us, frightens us, makes us invent all kinds of fantasies and evasions to help us cope with the unavoidable fact of it. But the old Christian tradition is that death is the wedding day of the saints, and those who are even not very outstandingly saintly know this. The joy of so many Christians in the face of death has nothing to do with stoic acceptance of the inevitable, or the peace of finishing an appointed task. It is a bridal joy, a sense of excitement, of anticipation and longing, a feeling of quiet, and spring, and hope.

This is the joy Jesus promised to his disciples before he himself died – and he went to death with a sense of urgency and longing stronger than his terrible fear. This is the joy that his disciples communicate to each other, that the Christian at the gate of death can bequeath to those who still wait. It is there in the fairy-tales, and the many other tales that grow from those roots, it is the call echoed in the Book of Revelation when 'the Spirit and the Bride say, "Come"'. It is a joy that nobody can take away because it thrives on the expectation of exactly what other people regard as the final kill-joy.

This is the assurance we need to cope with a world frightened, agonized, lost, and corrupted by its false ambitions and empty values. Nothing is stronger than the love which issues in this kind of joy, and no sorrow is great enough to quench it, if only we will let it grow.

It takes a lot of faith to do that. All that the fairy-tales can do is to bring us back to the Gospels. They do it very well, but once we have found ourselves in the real and explicit world of the Gospels the implicit human reality of the fairy-tales is eclipsed. We can never again despise the tales as fit only for children, but realize instead that children, as Jesus told us, have a nose for the atmosphere of his kingdom and detect its presence where older people don't. But it is the sharp air of the Gospel we need to breathe. 'Take deep breaths of it', as Mary said to Colin. And we shall live for ever and ever and ever, beginning from now.

Bibliography

Author's Note

The books mentioned below appear under two main headings: the tales themselves and the 'criticism'. The tales are mostly as told to children, with the exception of ancient texts such as the *Nibelungenlied*, and some are modern fairy-tales, or stories with a clear fairy-tale 'form'. There are many more of these than are mentioned here, and the whole selection is necessarily a personal one consisting of books I possess, or have come across and happen to like, or find interesting even if I don't like them. This applies to the 'critical' section also, for although the number of books specifically about fairy-tales is comparatively small the scope of the subject has no well-defined limits, and extends into the fields of literary criticism, anthropology, poetry, history, theology, 'spirituality' and psychology. This section includes some which contain so much of 'tales' that they might well have gone in the other section, but their purpose is information, not entertainment. Again, the selection is limited and may even appear perverse to the scholar with a specialist interest in one aspect of the subject. They are not all books I like or approve of, but all deal with some aspect of the subject matter of this book, though the connection may not be immediately apparent.

This book itself is not a work of scholarship, and the critical apparatus of scholarship is not appropriate to its purpose. The selection of books given here is mainly intended to open a few more doors to the interested reader, though a few indications for the scholar are included. (Some books are out of print, and a few only to be found in reference libraries, but most are easily available.)

THE TALES

Anderson, Hans	*Fairy Tales*, illustrated by Rex Whistler
Bernanos, George	*The Carmelites, Diary of a Country Priest*
Bolt, R.	*A Man for All Seasons*
Browne, Frances	*Granny's Wonderful Chair* (1857)
Bulfinch, Thomas	*The Age of Fable*
Burnett, Frances Hodgson	*Little Lord Fauntleroy, A Little Princess, The Secret Garden*
Carter, Lin (Ed.)	*Dragons, Elves and Heroes, The Young Magicians*
Dickens, Charles	*The Magic Fishbone*

Garner, Alan — *The Weirdstone of Brisingamen, The Moon of Gomrath, The Owl Service*

Gay, John — *The Beggar's Opera*
Graves, Robert — *The Greek Myths*
Kingsley, Charles — *The Water Babies*
Kipling, Rudyard — *Kim, The Jungle Books*
Lang, Andrew (Ed.) — *The Blue Fairy Book* (and 25 other 'colours')

Lewis, C. S. — *The Lion, the Witch and the Wardrobe* (and six other 'tales of Narnia')

Macdonald, George — *At the Back of the North Wind, The Princess and the Goblin, The Princess and Curdie*

Masefield, John — *The Midnight Folk, The Box of Delights*

Oxford 'Myths and Legends' Series (Indian, Welsh, Scandinavian, etc. etc.)

Potter, Beatrix — *The Tailor of Gloucester*
Rose, H. J. — *A Handbook of Greek Mythology*
Ruskin, John — *The King of the Golden River*
Sexton, Ann — *Transformations*
Shakespeare, William — The Plays
Thackeray, W. M. — *The Rose and the Ring*
Tolkien, J. R. R. — *The Hobbit, The Lord of the Rings, The Adventures of Tom Bombadil, The Tolkien Reader* (inc. the essay on 'Fairy Tales')

Walker, L. J. (Ed.) — *Red Indian Legends*
Williams, Charles — *Taliessin through Logres*

ANCIENT TEXTS

Penguin Classics

The *Nibelungenlied*
Tristan
Sir Gawain and the Green Knight
Dante's *Vita Nuova*
Bede's *Ecclesiastical History of the English People*
The *Bhagavadgītā*

Everyman Library
Chrétien de Troyes — *Arthurian Romances*
Layamon and Wace — *Arthurian Chronicles*

Malory, Sir Thomas — *Le Morte d'Arthur*
Gordon, R. K. (Ed.) — *Anglo-Saxon Poetry* (including *Beowulf*)
Jones, T. (Trans.) — The *Mabinogion*

CRITICISM, HISTORY, THEOLOGY, ETC., AND REFERENCE

Allsopp, Kenneth — *The Angry Decade*
Armstrong, E. A. — *The Folklore of Birds*
Arne-Thompson — *Folk-motif Index* (reference only, a huge encyclopedia)
Ashe, Geoffrey — *King Arthur's Avalon*
Berrigan, Daniel — *The Dark Night of Resistance; Consequences: Truth and...*
Bonhoeffer, Dietrich — *The Cost of Discipleship*
Briggs, K. M. — *The Personnel of Fairyland*
Carter, Lin — *Tolkien: A Look behind 'The Lord of the Rings'*
Cohn, Norman — *The Pursuit of the Millennium*
Dodd, C. H. — *The Founder of Christianity*
Eliade, Mircea — *Myth, Dreams and Mysteries*
Ellis Davidson, A. R. — *Gods and Myths of Northern Europe*
Frazer, James — *The Golden Bough* (shortened edn, 2 vols)
Garrigou, Lagrange R. — *Christian Perfection and Contemplation*
Green, Roger Lancelyn — *Tellers of Tales*
Hilton, Walter — *The Ladder of Perfection*
Isaacs and Zimbardo (Eds) — *Tolkien and 'The Lord of the Rings'*
John of the Cross — Complete works, ed. and trans. E. Allison Peers
Jung, Carl — *Modern Man in Search of a Soul, Integration of the Personality*, etc. etc.
Klostermaier, Klaus — *Hindu and Christian in Vrindaban*
Knowles, David — *The English Mystical Tradition*
Lewis, C. S. — *The Four Loves, Medieval and Renaissance Literature, The Discarded Image*
Laing, R. — *The Divided Self*
MacCulloch, J.A. — *Mythology of All Races* (reference only)
Macneice, Louis — *Varieties of Parable*
Martindale, C. C. — *The Queen's Daughters*

Merton, Thomas	*New Seeds of Contemplation, No Man is an Island, The Sign of Jonas, Thoughts in Solitude, Conjectures of a Guilty Bystander, etc. etc.*
Muir, Percy	*English Children's Books*
Raphael, Chaim	*A Feast of History (The Drama of Passover through the Ages)*
Rheinhold, H. A. (Ed.)	*The Spear of Gold, Revelations of the Mystics*
Rougemont, Denis de	*Passion and Society, The Myths of Love*
Shideler, M. McDermott	*The Theology of Romantic Love*
Storr, Anthony	*The Integrity of the Personality*
Treharne, R. F.	*The Glastonbury Legends*
Underhill, Evelyn	*Mysticism*
Vann, Gerald	*The Paradise Tree, The Water and the Fire*
Weil, Simone	*Waiting on God*
Weston, Jessie L.	*From Ritual to Romance*
White, Victor	*God and the Unconscious*
Wicker, Brian	*Culture and Liturgy*
Williams, Charles	*The Figure of Beatrice, The Image of the City and Other Essays (ed. Anne Ridler), Witchcraft*
Zaehner, R.C.	*Hindu and Muslim Mysticism*
Zahn, Gordon	*In Solitary Witness*
(Anonymous)	*Cloud of Unknowing*